Lilac Mills lives on a Welsh mountain with her very patient husband and incredibly sweet dog, where she grows veggies (if the slugs don't get them), bakes (badly) and loves making things out of glitter and glue (a mess, usually). She's been an avid reader ever since she got her hands on a copy of *Noddy Goes to Toytown* when she was five, and she once tried to read everything in her local library starting with A and working her way through the alphabet. She loves long, hot summer days and cold winter ones snuggled in front of the fire, but whatever the weather she's usually writing or thinking about writing, with heartwarming romance and happy-ever-afters always on her mind.

Also by Lilac Mills

A Very Lucky Christmas
Sunshine at Cherry Tree Farm
Summer on the Turquoise Coast
Love in the City by the Sea
The Cosy Travelling Christmas Shop

Tanglewood Village series

The Tanglewood Tea Shop
The Tanglewood Flower Shop
The Tanglewood Wedding Shop

Island Romance

Sunrise on the Coast
Holiday in the Hills
Sunset on the Square

Applewell Village

Waste Not, Want Not in Applewell
Make Do and Mend in Applewell
A Stitch in Time in Applewell

Foxmore

The Corner Shop on Foxmore Green
The Christmas Fayre on Holly Field
The Allotment on Willow Tree Lane

LILAC MILLS

The Allotment on Willow Tree Lane

CANELO

First published in the United Kingdom in 2024 by

Canelo
Unit 9, 5th Floor
Cargo Works, 1-2 Hatfields
London SE1 9PG
United Kingdom

A CIP catalogue record for this book is available from the British Library.

Print ISBN 978 1 80032 884 6
Ebook ISBN 978 1 80032 883 9

Cover design by Rose Cooper

Cover images © Shutterstock

Look for more great books at www.canelo.co

Printed and bound in Great Britain by Clays Ltd, Elcograf S.p.A.

1

MIX
Paper from
responsible sources
FSC
www.fsc.org
FSC® C018072

To my family, all my love, always…

Chapter 1

Black was the colour of the day, despite the sun shining out of a clear blue sky and the lush growth of late spring. The graveyard was alive with shades of green, and dotted with highlights of yellow, pink, red and orange from the tulips nodding between the headstones. Birds sang, and squirrels scampered along the branches. So much life amidst the presence of death was hard to take.

Damon Rogers briefly closed his eyes, grief swamping him.

'OK?' Luke asked.

Damon felt a hand on his shoulder and took a steadying breath. 'Yeah.'

They both knew it was a lie. Luke looked as devastated as he felt. His friend and bandmate usually had a tan, but Luke's face was ashen and there were lines around his eyes that hadn't been there last month. He was still a handsome guy, with his shoulder-length blond hair and chiselled features, but now he seemed older than his twenty-eight years. Damon's heart ached. Aiden would never age – he would remain twenty-nine forever.

'Oh, God.' Luke jerked his head towards the road as a hearse and two black limousines pulled up.

'I can't do this.' Damon wanted to be anywhere but here. He didn't want to say goodbye to one of his best friends. He wasn't ready.

'You *have* to. It needs six of us.' Luke was shaking, but his expression was resolute. Hard, even. There was anger beneath the devastating grief.

Damon hadn't reached that stage yet. He was still battling with disbelief. How could this have happened? Aiden was too young, too full of life and laughter to be lying in a coffin.

Swallowing hard, he straightened his shoulders. Luke was right. The last thing he could do for Aiden was to make sure his send-off went smoothly.

A glance towards the door of the church revealed that the mourners were now inside. Then he looked back at the hearse and saw Aiden's mum, dad and his sister, Sadie, climbing out of the first car.

'It's time,' Luke said, taking hold of Damon's elbow and propelling him towards the pavement and the waiting coffin.

Taking his position, the funeral director uttering muted instructions, Damon felt the coffin's weight settle on his shoulders. He met Luke's eye and nodded slowly. He could handle this. They both could.

Aiden's father was at the front, one arm linked around the shoulders of the man on his other side, the other holding the coffin. He looked broken but resolute, and Damon couldn't even begin to imagine what he must be going through. It was bad enough burying a friend… burying a son was unthinkable.

Aiden's mother, sister, and the rest of the immediate family followed behind, and Damon heard someone sobbing quietly. He wanted to sob himself, but he knew if he gave in to his grief, he might break down completely.

He remembered nothing of the long slow walk to the front of the church, as he concentrated on maintaining his composure and putting one foot in front of the other, but when he finally took his seat on the end of the pew, he bowed his head and allowed tears to trickle down his face.

The service passed in a blur of regret, deep abiding sadness and memories.

When the band's manager and agent, Frank, spoke of how much Aiden had meant to the two surviving members of Black Hyacinth, and how sorely he would be missed, Damon had to bite his lip to stem the flow, and with every word Frank uttered, Damon's heart broke anew.

It was too much. Clutching the back of the pew in front for support, he gasped as the memory of that fateful night cascaded through his mind, unannounced and uninvited.

Knowing from bitter experience that there was nothing for it but to ride it out, the church around him faded. Eyes tightly shut, Damon's breaths came in juddering gasps as he was forced to relive the last few minutes of his friend's life.

Damon hadn't been there – Aiden had phoned him from his mobile – but in his mind's eye, night had fallen and he imagined the headlights flashing past on the opposite carriageway. Music loud enough to burst eardrums, blasted through his head as the memory rose up to sweep him away.

'Damon, these roads are effing ace, man! No effing speed limit!' Aiden was shouting to be heard above the music. He rarely turned it down, preferring to yell to make himself heard.

'Where are you?'

'Autobahn 2.'

'How long will it take you to get to Calais?'

'What?'

Damon took a deep breath and repeated the question, louder this time, 'How long will it take to get to Calais?'

'Hang on.' Mercifully, Aiden lowered the volume. 'Say again?'

In a more normal voice, Damon repeated for the third time, 'How long until you are in Calais?'

'Eight, nine hours tops, but I'm going to stop when I get to Düsseldorf. Shit! Who the hell are you? Where—? Get off. You can't—'

'Aiden? Aiden! What's going on?'

Shuddering, Damon heard Aiden's voice, screaming 'Stop! No!'

Music — one of the band's own records; Aiden yelling; a girl's voice screaming; the shrieking of tortured metal; roaring, thudding... then silence. Dreadful, heart-stopping silence.

The girl had walked away with nothing more than a broken arm and a bruised face.

Aiden had died at the scene.

Damon didn't think he would ever get over it.

It took several seconds for the visions and the sounds to fade, and several more until he regained control of his heart rate and his breathing. He would be shaky for a while, but the worst of it was over.

Until the next time.

—

Ceri Morgan slapped her brother's hand away from his cravat. Huw had been fiddling with it for the past ten minutes and he was getting on her nerves.

Talking about nerves, her brother was a bag of them. She'd heard him get up in the night several times, and when she'd ventured downstairs at ten-past six this

4

morning, he had been sitting in the living room with a black coffee in his hand. She suspected he might have already consumed the recommended daily amount of caffeine, and she had been tempted to whisk his mug away and force him to drink a cup of camomile tea instead to calm him down.

She couldn't blame him though. She would probably be just as nervous if she were the one getting married today.

'Let me do it,' she instructed, and Huw's arms dropped to his sides.

Ceri squinted at the material, tugging and folding until she was happy that the cravat was sitting just right.

'There,' she said, standing back to admire her handiwork. Damn, Huw looked good in his morning suit. Like her, he had dark hair and was tall, but his hair had less of a kink than hers and tended to behave itself. He also carried his height better than she did. She had a habit of slouching if she wasn't careful.

'Do I look OK?' he asked.

'You look fab. Rowena is one lucky lady.'

'I think it's the other way around,' Huw said, his fingers creeping towards his neck again.

'Don't you dare!' Ceri warned, narrowing her eyes.

Huw subsided, but Ceri knew he was itching to mess with it and she vowed to keep an eye on him. She just needed to make sure he looked presentable when he got to the church. After that, their mum could take over nagging him – if Rowena, his bride, didn't beat her to it.

He stretched his neck and winced. 'It's too tight,' he complained.

'Do you want me to fetch Mum? I could, you know. She would like nothing better than to be here, fussing—'

'God, no!' Huw shuddered. 'Do you realise how much effort it took to persuade her *not* to come to the house this morning? It's bad enough *you* being here.'

'Thanks!'

'You know what I mean – you can be so bossy.'

'And you can be so annoying.' Ceri grinned at her brother and he grinned back. 'Seriously, Huw, I'm so pleased for you, and I know Mum and Dad are too.'

'They just want grandchildren,' Huw replied darkly.

Ceri laughed. 'It's not just that – they want to see you happy. And you are, aren't you?'

'Ecstatically.'

'There you go. Grandchildren would be an added bonus, but secretly I think they're thrilled with Nia. They get a ready-made granddaughter without the nappy stage. Aww, she's so cute. I can't wait to see her in her bridesmaid dress.'

'Speaking of bridesmaids, shouldn't you be wearing your dress?' Huw asked.

'It'll take me all of two minutes to slip it on,' Ceri said. 'I've already done my hair and makeup – thanks for noticing.'

'Are you wearing makeup?'

Ceri pulled a face. 'When you get to the church, you'd better tell Rowena she looks beautiful,' she cautioned.

'I will. And so do you.'

She waved a hand in the air as she headed for the stairs. 'Too little too late, bro, too little too late.'

She was laughing as she said it though, knowing full well that he had noticed the effort she had taken with her appearance this morning. He should, considering how long she had spent in the bathroom, waxing and buffing, plucking and moisturising. The focus was naturally going to be on Rowena, but Ceri didn't want to let the side down. Anyway, being maid of honour was the closest she was going to get to being a bride for a while. Having only just moved to Foxmore and with a new job to tackle, she wasn't planning on adding a boyfriend to her already overflowing plate. Nothing serious anyway, although the odd date with a handsome hunk might do wonders for her self-esteem. The trick was to find a handsome hunk in the first place, and she was looking forward to seeing what Foxmore had to offer.

Ceri slipped the column of champagne satin over her head and wriggled into it, loving the way it clung to her curves and showed them off to the best advantage. She didn't usually wear dresses, feeling more at home in sweatshirts and jeans, but this one was gorgeous. It had crossed her mind that Rowena might want her to wear something a little fussier, but all Rowena had said was, 'Wear what you like as long as it's a dress and the right colour'.

Plain and simple was what Ceri had gone for, and she was pleased with the result. She hoped her soon-to-be sister-in-law would be too, but she guessed Rowena would have far more important things on her mind today than how Ceri looked.

She checked her appearance in the bedroom mirror to make sure she hadn't messed up her hair or smeared her lipstick as she'd put the dress on, and when she saw that she hadn't, she took her shoes out of the box. In the same colour as the dress, they matched perfectly, and neither were they ridiculously high, which meant she should be able to wear them all day and into the evening without resorting to kicking them off. Or dashing back to the cottage halfway through the reception to swap them for a pair of daps.

Daps... she smiled to herself. She had only moved into her cottage three weeks ago, and already she could feel herself becoming more Welsh. She actually *was* Welsh, having been born and brought up in Cardiff, but the city was a fairly cosmopolitan one and she hadn't heard the word 'dap' for a long time, not until she had moved to Foxmore.

Ceri decided to take her trainers downstairs with her and leave them in the hall, in case she needed to nip home and change into them. They weren't *daps* as such – the word usually meant the black plimsolls that primary school kids wore for PE – but people in these parts often used it to describe any trainer-type footwear.

She eased her feet into the heels, adding two inches to her height, and wiggled her toes. There, she was as ready as she could be, but as she glanced around the room to make sure she hadn't forgotten anything, she paused.

It still seemed unreal to think she was living here in Foxmore, in this house. When Huw had moved to the village last year, she had been so envious; not just because Foxmore was such a cute village in a picturesque location, but because he had also managed to purchase this wonderful cottage. The first time she'd set eyes on it, she had offered to buy it off him, never once believing it might happen. But when Huw had asked Rowena to marry him, it made sense for him to move in with his fiancée because her house was larger. Which meant that he needed to sell his.

Ceri had leapt at the chance and had officially taken ownership less than a month ago, on the proviso that Huw could spend his last night as a single man under its roof.

She figured that ensuring her irritating older brother got to the church on time was a small price to pay.

She could actually see the ancient stone church, where Huw was about to be married, from her bedroom window. It sat in the middle of an old graveyard, with a vicarage to one side and a large field behind it, which currently sported the marquee where the reception would be held.

Ceri's house, Rosehip Cottage, was the middle one in a row of three pretty cottages on the opposite side of the road from the church overlooking the field, and she thought how lucky she was to live in such a lovely little village.

Foxmore was small, and people here had a tendency to know everyone else's business, but that was what she loved about it. That, and the ancient stone Celtic cross in the middle of the village green, plus the lovely assortment of artisan shops and the whitewashed old pub that had once been a staging post and was now adorned with colourful planters and hanging baskets.

Foxmore sat at the bottom of a U-shaped valley, surrounded by lush green farmland with a pretty river running through it, and when she looked out of her window she could see the forested slopes of the hillsides above, and the heather-covered mountain of Aran Fawddwy beyond. The range of high, rocky peaks that bordered the village on the north were, for the most part, wild and untamed, home to red kites and kestrels, skylarks and black grouse, and rare wild Welsh ponies and elusive feral goats. Huw had taken her hiking there once, and she had been moved by its wild beauty.

'You look stunning,' her brother said as she descended the steep narrow staircase. 'I never knew you could scrub up so well.'

Ceri gave him an arch look, her heels clacking on the stone-tiled floor as she went into the kitchen, Huw following. He was tugging at the sleeves of his suit and looking pained.

'What now?' she asked, opening the fridge and bringing out the bottle of bubbly she had placed in there to chill.

'I feel a right prat,' he said.

'You look it too, but no more than usual,' she shot back.

'Not funny, Ceri.'

Seeing how pale he was, she stopped teasing him. Popping the cork, she poured the fizzy golden liquid into a couple of glasses and handed one to him.

'What are you so nervous about?' she asked.

He gulped down a mouthful before answering. 'That she won't turn up. That I'll lose the ring. That I'll fluff my lines…'

'The last two don't matter, and as for the first, *of course* she'll turn up. I've no idea why, but the daft woman thinks the sun shines out of your—' She stopped and grinned at him. Huw's smile was rather sickly. 'Right,' she announced. 'I'd better be off if I don't want to be late fetching Nia. And don't *you* be late, either. You've got twenty minutes.'

'It's only a two-minute walk.' Huw was fiddling with his cravat again and checking it in the mirror.

Ceri rolled her eyes. 'I know how long it takes to get to the church. What I'm saying is, make sure you are on time. If anyone is going to be late, it should be Rowena.'

Huw turned a worried face to her. 'You don't think she will be late, do you?'

Ceri smiled. 'No, I don't. I think everything will go smoothly, and everyone will have a wonderful time. And in just over an hour, you will be married to the love of your life.' She took both his hands in hers and looked her brother in the eye. 'You are so lucky to have found each other,' she said, 'and I wish you all the happiness in the world. You deserve it.'

Then she gave him a quick peck on the cheek and hurriedly left, so he wouldn't see the tears gathering in her eyes.

Damn it! She vowed she wouldn't cry, but she had started already. What was it about weddings that made her turn on the waterworks?

She didn't really need to ask herself the question though, because she already knew the answer: wishful thinking.

–

Aiden's parents hadn't wanted a wake, so after the church service and the harrowing secondary service at the graveside to which only the immediate family, plus Damon and Luke, had been invited, Damon was heading back to the car when Sadie waylaid him.

Her pretty face crumpled, and he opened his arms.

She fell into them and he let her sob, her tears dampening the front of his shirt as he stared wordlessly over her head wondering how he could possibly comfort her when he was in dire need of comfort himself.

But nothing anyone could say or do could change the stark reality that Aiden was gone.

'I'm off,' Luke said, moving in to hug them both.

Sadie pulled away, her face streaked with tears, her eyes red and sore. Damon suspected he looked just as ravaged. They all did: no one who had known and loved Aiden could believe he was gone.

'Home?' Damon asked him. Luke lived in the West Midlands.

'India.'

Damon blinked. '*India?* Why?'

'I can't stay here, man. I've gotta, you know… get away for a bit. Try to clear my head.'

'I wish I could come with you,' Sadie muttered. Her chin wobbled and she bit her bottom lip.

Luke shrugged. 'You can if you want. You, too, Damon.'

Damon grimaced. 'I'm going back to Foxmore.' He could hopefully grieve in peace in his grandmother's house in the depths of rural north Wales, where he had spent much of his youth and where he had been the happiest when he was growing up. The little village of Foxmore – and Willow Tree House especially – had been his sanctuary, and instinctively, like a wounded animal, he had fled to the only place he called home. That had been a fortnight ago, and as long as he was careful and didn't flaunt his presence, no one should find him there.

'Luke, Damon…' Frank called. He was standing a respectful distance away and he beckoned them towards him.

'I swear to God if he wants to discuss the band right now, I'm going to deck him,' Luke growled.

'I'll beat you to it.' Damon scowled at Black Hyacinth's manager.

Frank was brilliant at what he did, but his focus was always on the bottom line, and it must be tearing him apart wondering what the two remaining band members were going to do once the dust had settled and they'd had time to take stock of the situation. But Damon didn't want to think about the band right now. All he wanted to do was to return to Foxmore and hide.

As they approached, Frank said, 'I thought I'd better warn you that there are a couple of photographers on the pavement.'

Luke's expression darkened. 'What the f—' but before he could do anything daft, Damon grabbed hold of his arm.

'Leave it,' he warned. The press would do what they were going to do, regardless of whether they were told to clear off or not. They'd hounded both him and Luke since Aiden's death, and they certainly weren't going to wind their necks in and show any respect today, not when they had the prospect of some juicy shots of the two remaining band members on the day of the funeral, and not when the circumstances surrounding Aiden's death made such a good story.

Luke shook off his hand, but Damon was relieved he didn't go storming over to confront them. Aiden's family had enough to contend with, without anyone adding to the drama.

'There's another exit around the back,' Frank was saying. 'You can leave through there. Aiden's parents, too, if they want. I've sent the cars round.' He hurried off to speak to them and Damon watched him go.

'That's that, then,' he said wearily. He was so tired, he didn't know what to do with himself.

'See you, mate.' Luke clapped him on the shoulder, and Sadie stood on tiptoe to give him a hug.

'Will you be OK?' she asked.

With a lump in his throat, he countered, 'Will *you*?' She shouldn't be thinking about him at a time like this, but he appreciated her asking.

Her smile was small, sad and heartbreaking. 'I'll have to be, won't I?'

But that's the problem, Damon thought as he walked around the back of the lovely old church. He didn't think he'd ever be OK again.

–

'Doesn't Rowena look beautiful?'

Ceri glanced up from where she was crouching on the floor, rubbing an imaginary speck of dirt off Nia's pristine white shoes, to see Betsan, the vicar's wife, standing next to her.

Betsan was gazing at the bride, who had entered the marquee on the arm of her new husband after having what seemed like several albums' worth of photos taken. The happy couple were beaming fit to burst, and Rowena was elegant and regal in her dress of ivory satin. Her honey-coloured hair was swept up, soft curls falling around her face, and she looked radiant.

'She does,' Ceri agreed, 'and so does this little munchkin.' She straightened up and tickled Rowena's daughter on the ribs. The five-year-old (who kept telling everyone that she was nearly six) squirmed in delight and giggled. She looked so cute in her dress, which was similar to her mother's but shorter and not as voluminous, and her dark, curly hair was in the same style. Only now it was starting to fall down, so Ceri unpinned it, and using her fingers and a borrowed bobble from Betsan, she raked it into a respectable ponytail.

'Thanks, Bethan,' Ceri said. 'What else have you got in your bag?' It was rather large.

'I've got three kids, remember? I carry the kitchen sink with me wherever I go.' Betsan was in her mid-forties, and despite the fifteen-year age gap, was Rowena's best friend.

'Can I go see my mammy now?' Nia asked, for the umpteenth time that day.

Ceri had done her best to keep Nia occupied both during the ceremony and afterwards, whilst the seemingly endless photos were being taken, and she was now exhausted even though Nia's grandparents had stepped in to help on numerous occasions.

As Rowena glanced around the marquee, Ceri managed to catch her eye and point to Nia. When Rowena spotted her daughter, she smiled and opened her arms, and the little girl flew into them.

Once again, Ceri had tears in her eyes as she looked on fondly. Huw, Rowena and Nia made a perfect family.

'If Rowena needs rescuing, I'll look after Nia for a bit,' Betsan offered. 'She's bound to get bored during the speeches.'

'Thank you,' Ceri replied gratefully. 'I didn't realise just how tiring children could be.'

'You wait until you've got some of your own, then you'll discover what tired really means,' Betsan joked. She lifted a glass of wine from a tray that one of the circulating waiters was holding aloft, and Ceri did the same.

'It will be a while yet,' Ceri said. 'I need to find a father for them first. Not that I'm looking,' she added hastily, lest Betsan got the wrong idea.

Ceri had met Betsan several times since Huw had relocated to Foxmore, but she didn't know her particularly well. She would like to, though. From what Rowena had told her, Betsan was a right laugh, and Ceri was eager to make new friends. Her old ones mostly lived in Cardiff, and with it being a six-hour round trip from Foxmore to the Welsh capital and back, it was a bit too far to pop in for a cup of tea.

Her new life was here, in this village, and Ceri intended to throw herself into it with total abandon – and that meant making friends.

'How are you settling in?' Betsan asked.

'Great, thanks. I've even managed to get a job.'

'I heard,' Betsan said with a smile.

Ceri wondered how she could have forgotten that everyone knew everyone else's business in a small place like this.

'When do you start?' Betsan wanted to know.

'After May half-term.'

'Horticulture, I believe?'

'That's right.'

Ceri hugged herself. She still couldn't believe she had landed a job as a teacher in an agricultural college and, if she was honest, it terrified her. Her last job had been in a garden centre on the outskirts of Cardiff, growing plants in their polytunnels for sale to the general public, which was a far cry from teaching.

Her move to Foxmore hadn't been dependent on getting a job because she had been willing to turn her hand to anything, so something would have come up eventually, but at least she would be working with plants at the college, and the money was good. Good enough to save a bit each month so that one day she might be able to open her own nursery.

'Ladies and gentlemen,' a man in a suit called out. 'If you would like to take your seats, the wedding breakfast is about to be served.'

As Ceri made her way to the high table where the bride and groom were already seated, she couldn't help wondering why a meal that was being eaten in the middle of the afternoon was called a breakfast.

Oh, who cared what it was called. The joy on her brother's face and that of his new wife was all that mattered.

Let the celebrations begin!

Chapter 2

It was dusk by the time the car that Frank had organised to take Damon back to Foxmore trundled down Willow Tree Lane, and some of his tension eased. He let his head rest on the back of the seat and breathed deeply, waiting for the house to come into view. He'd chosen to sit in the front seat, not the back, despite Winston, the driver, giving him an odd look. So when the man slowed the car to a crawl and Damon saw him wince as it scraped underneath the overhanging branches of the trees lining the lane, he realised he should have had them cut back. But considering this house was the only property on the lane and the road was effectively a dead end, he hadn't seen the point. However, he supposed he better had, if he was going to stay here for a while.

He had been living in the house for the past two weeks, having fled to Foxmore as soon as the post-mortem and police report had been released, only venturing back to London yesterday for the funeral. He'd spent last night in his flat in the city, not wanting to travel down this morning, and he didn't know when he would next return. Right now, he didn't care if he never saw it again, because everywhere he looked reminded him of Aiden.

Except Foxmore. Aiden had never visited him here.

Heck, in recent years Damon hadn't visited much, either; his life had simply been too busy. It was a major regret of his, that he hadn't seen as much of his gran as he should before she'd passed away. It was over eight years since she'd died and he'd only been back to Foxmore a handful of times.

Damon's attention was caught by activity in the field bordering Willow Tree House. A couple of days ago, he'd noticed a marquee being set up but hadn't paid it much attention. Now though, he could see that some sort of event was taking place, and guessed it might be a wedding. People were milling around outside, the men mostly in shirt sleeves and suit trousers, and the women resembling colourful butterflies in their finest dresses. Fairy lights twinkled around the entrance, and he noticed figures sitting in the grass. He even caught a glimpse of the interior and people dancing, and he craned his neck as the car drove past. Seeing the smiles on their faces and the drinks in their hands, he wondered how much longer the party would go on. The field was just behind his grand-mother's house – *his* house, now – and he felt aggrieved that the peace he so desperately craved might be disturbed.

'Better him than me,' Winston said, with a nod to the marquee and the old church beyond. 'Been there, done that, got the decree absolute to prove it.' He gave Damon a look. 'You're not married, are you?'

'Er... no.' He wondered why it always came as a shock to realise that his private life wasn't as private as he would like. He should be used to it by now.

'Ever come close?' Winston asked, gingerly pulling onto the weed-infested gravel drive at the front of the house.

'Not really.' Damon unclipped his seat belt and reached for the door handle, debating whether to ask the man in for a coffee and a comfort break before the return journey to London. The poor bloke had a long drive ahead of him.

Before he could offer, Winson said, 'Don't blame you, not with all those groupies. Why settle for one when you can have a different girl every night?'

Damon sucked in a sharp breath. It was one of those girls who had caused Aiden's accident.

Winston must have realised what he'd said, because he turned stricken eyes to Damon, and began to apologise. 'Sorry, I—'

Damon cut him off. 'No worries. Do you want to come in for a quick break before you go?'

'No thanks, I'll be on my way. Sorry,' he repeated, not meeting Damon's eyes.

'Don't sweat it. Have a safe journey.' He watched as the car reversed and drove off, and breathed a sigh of relief to be home.

This house in Foxmore had always been his home. While he was growing up, his address might technically have been the large house in Shropshire that his parents owned, but his heart had never resided there. Over the years he had spent more time at his grandmother's house in Foxmore than anywhere, except for the boarding school that he had been packed off to at eleven years old. Since then, he had bought a place of his own – the flat in London, a penthouse that he sometimes referred to as 'home' but which felt nothing like it. His true home was this house on Willow Tree Lane, and deep down it always had been, despite his gran no longer being here. The house held his happiest memories, and it was the place he felt safest. Within its peaceful and tranquil walls, he knew his aching heart would have time to heal.

But there would be no peace or tranquillity tonight, because as he walked towards the front door, Damon became aware he could hear music. It was coming from the marquee, drifting on the faint breeze.

He didn't mind, though; to him, music was everything. It was in his blood, and he could no more live without it than he could live without oxygen. But since Aiden's accident, he hadn't touched his guitar. He hadn't been able to bring himself to, and he was harbouring a secret fear that he might never play again.

Recognising the song as one of Aiden's favourites, as the familiar raw notes of "Love Conquers All" filled his mind, Damon closed his eyes and let the tears fall once more.

–

It was hot in the marquee, the air barely moving despite the slight breeze tugging at the fabric walls. The lights were dim, and couples swayed and shuffled on the dance floor to the slow music. The guests had thinned a little, but many still remained, and laughter swelled the music.

Ceri fanned herself with one of the place cards, but it did little good. For mid-May, the weather was unseasonably warm, but she was glad it had been such a glorious day. It wasn't just the weather that had been wonderful – everything had been perfect, apart from her aching feet. But she had remedied that several hours ago when the dancing had started and she had kicked off her shoes, not bothering to go home to collect her daps. Ceri had no idea where her posh shoes were now, and to be honest she didn't care if they never turned up at all. She was hardly likely to wear them again.

With an indulgent smile, she watched Huw and Rowena on the dancefloor. They were holding each other close, Rowena with her head on Huw's shoulder and Huw's face buried in his wife's hair. Both of them had their eyes closed and wore blissful expressions. Not for the first time, Ceri thought that they were made for each other, and envy gave her heart a quick squeeze. One day, she hoped to have what they had. But she wasn't in any hurry – there was so much going on in her life right now which was new and exciting that putting love and romance on the back burner for the time being wouldn't be a hardship. In fact, it was probably a good idea, especially since there was no hint of a suitable guy on the horizon.

Ceri let out a huge yawn, catching her unawares, and she wondered if it would be OK for the maid of honour to leave the reception before the bride.

Did she have any more duties to perform, or was she done for the day? Having never been a maid of honour (or even a bridesmaid) before, she had no idea if anything further was expected of her.

With Rowena enfolded in Huw's arms, Ceri hoped it would be safe to escape for a while, so, desperate for some fresh air and a few minutes alone, she slipped outside.

Several people were sitting on the grass, but she didn't feel like joining them, wanting a quiet moment to herself. Instead, she headed for the empty corners of the field and any solitude she could find. She could still feel the smile on her cheeks. It had been there all day and her face was aching, but in a good way – and her voice was hoarse from talking and laughing so much. It had been a bloody good party. One of the best she had ever been to, made even more special because it was celebrating her brother's marriage.

She had also enjoyed spending time with their parents, and for once the pressure had been off Ceri, as her mum had concentrated her yearning to be a grandmother on her gorgeous new granddaughter, Nia. Ceri knew she wasn't entirely off the hook, but maybe now that Huw was married, their mother would nag him instead. He was, after all, the better prospect, and Ceri knew that he and Rowena had discussed having more children at some point in the future.

The haunting melody of "Nights in White Satin" faded into "Visiting Hours", the music following Ceri as she headed towards the furthest corner of the field, but it didn't hide the rustling from the hedgerow or the tweet of a bird settling down for the night.

Dusk was rapidly descending, that strange transition between day and night when it was still light enough to see but deep shadows were beginning to form. Being outdoors in the dark didn't scare Ceri. She relished it.

The scent of warm grass filled her nose, and she breathed deeply, her bare toes digging into the rough stems as she walked further from the tent.

Even as twilight deepened, Ceri could still make out the carpet of buttercups, daisies and dandelions, with the orange-yellow flowers of the Welsh poppy dotted amongst them. As she peered owlishly at the hedge, she recognised the creamy white blossoms and scent of hawthorn, and spotted the familiar spiked forms of foxgloves, as well as the feathery leaves of the common yarrow, whose white blooms reminded her of florets of cauliflower. The unmistakable scent of honeysuckle hung in the air, and she breathed deeply, closing her eyes briefly in delight, letting the perfume swirl through her.

Opening them again, she took a few steps further, keen to discover what other secrets the field might hold, and she had only ventured a couple more steps when she saw something else that made her smile.

It was a small weathered gate, almost completely obscured by foliage, and she put out a hand to run her fingers along the wood. So quintessentially English cottage garden, it fitted into its surroundings perfectly and she wondered what lay beyond it. Maybe she would come back in daylight and take a look.

Aw, there was no *maybe* about it. She definitely would. Foxmore was her home now and she intended to get to know every centimetre of it, especially the parts that involved secret gardens and plants. And when she realised the song had changed again and the DJ was now playing Simon and Garfunkel's "Scarborough Fair", she began to dance, dipping and spinning, her arms outstretched as she softly sang along, with joy filling her heart.

–

Damon used his sleeve to wipe his damp face, then took his suit jacket off, hooked his finger through the loop of fabric at the back of the neck and slung it over his shoulder. He had already removed his tie, having taken it off the moment he had got in the car, and he checked that it was still in his pocket. He didn't know why he was concerned; he had bought it especially for the funeral and would never wear it again.

He was about to step onto the columned porch and unlock the front door, when he had second thoughts.

Although he was tired, he was too strung up to sleep (besides, it wasn't even ten thirty – far too early to think about going to bed), so he allowed the music to lure him around the side of the house and into the garden.

To his shame, even in the dark he could see how terribly overgrown it was. Gran must be turning in her grave. This garden used to be her pride and joy. He really should tidy it up at least. But his heart wasn't in it. He couldn't summon either the energy or the enthusiasm.

A tool shed loomed into view, partly obscured by a sprawling rhododendron, and a few more steps led him past the greenhouse. He hadn't ventured this far into the garden for years, and he was dismayed to see so many broken panes of glass. Guilt flooded him as he left the garden behind and walked through the neglected, over-grown orchard. Even this needed a significant amount of TLC and he vowed to take a proper look in the morning to assess the damage. But, for now, "Nights in White Satin" drew him onwards, and his feet moved closer to the source, almost without his consent.

He reached the hedge separating his grandmother's property from the field beyond. The hedge was also wildly overgrown, with hawthorn, hazel, rowan and dogwood encroaching into the orchard with eager branches. It was scary how fast nature reclaimed her own. Take the field on the other side of the hedge, for instance. When he was younger, it used to be an allotment. In daylight, when the sun was in the right position and there was no marquee to hide it, it was just possible to make out the outlines of the former beds. But it was now a meadow, the brambles and other fast-growing shrubbery probably only kept at bay by regular mowing. Last week, Damon had seen a chap, who he thought he recognised as the vicar, trawling up and down it on a sit-on mower.

His gran used to love working there, planning where the peas and the runner beans were to go, the best place to plant the onion sets, and which part of her plot would hold the tomatoes. And she hadn't been on her own. Many villagers also had plots, and Damon remembered the pride and the gentle competition to produce the straightest carrots and the biggest marrows.

He couldn't recall when exactly the old allotment had fallen into disrepair. It had been a gradual thing, but he had only truly noticed after his gran had passed away. It seemed his grandmother's death had also been the death knell for the allotment.

Damon paused by the little wooden gate, remembering his gran holding it open for him, her wheeling a small cart with the implements of her trade slung in the back – spade, rake, trowel, seedlings – and him carrying an empty trug, ready for all the produce she would harvest.

He rested a hand on the top, feeling the warmth of the day trapped in the wood as he gazed across the old allotment, intending to listen for a while as Ed Sheeran was replaced by the gentle notes of "Scarborough Fair".

A movement caught his eye and he jumped, his heart leaping into his throat when he saw a pale figure wafting through the grass. For a second, he imagined it was his gran, and that his reminiscing had brought her back to ghostly life. Then common sense kicked in and he realised the woman must be one of the wedding guests.

Damon had heard the term 'dance as though no one was watching', but he had never witnessed it before, and he gazed at her, entranced. Graceful and ethereal, the woman dipped and spun, her arms outstretched, her face raised to the heavens.

Even from here he could see how lovely she was. The dress she wore clung to her waist, sliding over her hips to flare a little at the knees, the hem of the skirt skimming through the grass and making her appear as though she was floating. Her hair, gathered loosely at the nape of her neck, was dark, and strands of it curled around her face. She had a beatific expression, her eyes partially closed, her generous mouth parted as she sang along with the chorus.

He opened the gate and slipped through it, careful not to make a noise, and all the while his gaze lingered on her... her carefree dancing and her silvery voice lifting his heart. This was what music should be about – not sales figures and the number of units shifted. *This* was why he wrote, to elicit reactions such as the one in front of him, and for the first time since Aiden's accident, his fingers itched to pick up his guitar.

Inching forward, Damon moved nearer, the fairy-like dancing drawing him in the way a mermaid's siren song drew unwitting sailors. Mesmerised, he couldn't drag his gaze away, and before he knew it he was almost close enough to touch her.

As the song faded into another, she fell silent and her movements slowed, and Damon sighed as the mood was broken.

Then she realised she wasn't alone, and as their eyes met she let out a startled gasp.

Something inside him lurched, and Damon had the strangest feeling that nothing would ever be the same again.

–

How long had that man been standing there, Ceri wondered, her heart hammering. It had scared the bejeezus out of her when she realised someone else was lurking in her corner of the field when she'd assumed she was alone.

She hoped he had enjoyed the impromptu dance show. At least he hadn't laughed, although there was still time for him to hold up a score card, she thought, giggling softly to herself.

Turning away to head back to the reception, his quiet 'Hi,' made her pause, and she looked over her shoulder.

'Hi.'

He took a step towards her, and she glanced at the marquee, estimating the distance, worry pricking at her with warning thorns. She was out here alone; she hadn't told anyone where she was going and although the other guests weren't far away, would anyone hear her if she screamed?

The man looked harmless enough, but she knew looks could be deceiving. Just because he wore a suit, the jacket slung casually over his right shoulder, it didn't mean she shouldn't be wary.

He must be a guest, though, because why else would he be standing in this field, at this time of night, wearing a suit?

Despite the hour being late, there was enough light from the marquee to make out his features, and she tried to recall seeing him at the wedding. He was rather striking – black curls tumbling to just past his shoulders, dark eyes that glittered, reflecting the tent's twinkling lights. He had a strong jaw, nice-shaped lips, and a tattoo that she couldn't quite make out on the side of his neck.

Surely she would have noticed him? But then again, she had taken her role as maid of honour seriously and her focus had been on Rowena and Nia, and her brother too, to a lesser extent.

She was noticing the guy now though, and she liked what she saw.

The face, the hair, and the tattoo were at odds with the suit, but he didn't look uncomfortable in it. On the contrary, he looked very much at ease, and she wondered whether he wore one on a regular basis. Because of his job, maybe? Which led her to ponder on what he might do for a living. And whether he had someone waiting for him in the marquee.

All this just from a 'hi'?

Ceri tried to count how many drinks she had downed, but she couldn't remember. It hadn't been that many, surely? But even if she had drunk more than usual, there had been a three-course meal and a buffet to soak up the alcohol.

'Good wedding?' he said.

Ah, so he *was* a guest.

'It was, wasn't it?' she enthused, feeling a trickle of relief that he wasn't some random bloke. She still couldn't remember seeing him at either the church or the wedding breakfast, but she knew that Huw and Rowena had invited more people to the evening celebrations, so that was probably why. He must be on Rowena's side, she assumed. Or maybe he was a friend of Huw's from work?

'The DJ is playing some sweet tunes,' he said.

'He is now,' Ceri replied. 'I take it you weren't here for the "Macarena"?'

The man laughed, a rumble that sent a shiver of lust through her. Good lord – she fancied him!

'Thankfully, no. I missed that treat.'

'Lucky you, I wish *I* had.' She pulled a face, eliciting another rumbling chuckle.

'Simon and Garfunkel, eh?' He raised an eyebrow.

'You saw that?'

'I did. You looked as though you were enjoying yourself.'

'I didn't realise anyone else was out here,' she said.

'Sorry, I didn't mean to intrude.'

'You're not. After being forced to do the "Macarena", I've got no shame left. Nothing can embarrass me ever again.'

Neither of them said anything for a moment, and Ceri fully expected him to make his excuses and return to the party. She wasn't quite ready to dive back into the fray yet, so she would wait for him to leave. She had been enjoying wandering around the meadow, the darkness heightening the feel of the grass under her feet and her sense of smell.

Then she became aware of a new scent in the air. It was coming from the stranger, and the woody aroma with undertones of musk made her tingle.

'What's your name?' she asked abruptly. She found she didn't want to think of him as 'the stranger'. She wanted a name to go with that handsome face and enticingly fit body.

He hesitated for so long that she thought he wasn't going to tell her. 'Damon.'

'I'm Ceri.'

'A good Welsh name. But you don't sound like you're from around here.'

'I'm not. Born and bred in Cardiff.' She was aware that her Welsh accent was milder than the more musical north

Wales lilt, tempered by the cosmopolitan feel of the city. 'What about you?'

'Shropshire, mostly.'

'Where else?' she asked curiously.

He lifted a shoulder. 'Boarding school in Worcester, then London. I've travelled a fair bit.'

Another brief silence followed. Ceri wasn't sure whether she wanted him to stay, or wished he would leave so she could be alone.

The track changed again, this time a powerful rock ballad, and Ceri recognised it instantly. It had been a hit by some band that she couldn't for the life of her remember the name of, but she did remember the lyrics, and she began to sing under her breath.

Damon was still and silent, seemingly unmoved by the music, and it occurred to her that maybe *he* was waiting for *her* to leave.

Embarrassed, she stopped singing and cleared her throat. 'Sorry. You don't need to hear me caterwauling. I just happen to like this one.'

'You weren't caterwauling. You've got a decent voice, and I've heard worse renditions of it.'

'Thanks.' Feeling mischievous all of a sudden, she said, 'What was better, my dancing or my singing?'

'I preferred the dancing.'

'I thought you might say that. You were just being polite about my singing.' She smiled to show she hadn't taken offence.

'Not at all. You just looked so...' He appeared to hunt for the right word. 'Carefree.' He sounded envious and his gaze drifted towards the marquee. 'You looked happy,' he added.

Ceri's gaze followed his, and she thought about the newly married couple and the joy and love on their faces as they'd recited their vows. She sensed a sadness in this stranger, and wondered whether it had anything to do with weddings.

'Fancy a drink?' she asked, impulsively. 'I don't want to go inside just yet, so how about I fetch a bottle and we can drink it out here?' She knew there were some stashed behind the table holding the wedding cake because she had put them there herself, in case of emergency.

'Er... I... All right, yeah.'

'It's a dry white, if that's OK?'

'Sounds good,' he replied.

'Wait here, I won't be long.' Ceri scampered off, suddenly eager for a nearly-midnight tryst with this total stranger.

But once she was inside the marquee, she had second thoughts, almost deciding not to go back. It was only the knowledge that if she didn't, he would probably return to the tent anyway, which would make it awkward as they were bound to bump into each other now that the party was winding down and there were fewer people.

She would have one glass with him, just to be friendly, and then she would make her excuses.

After all, she didn't know him from Adam, and the likelihood of ever meeting him again was small to non-existent.

Chapter 3

Damon was where she had left him. He had spread his suit jacket on the grass and was sitting on one of the sleeves.

He smiled and patted the body of his jacket, inviting her to sit down next to him, but Ceri hesitated. If she sat on it, they would be almost touching.

Oh, what the hell! She might have brought the wine but she had forgotten to bring any glasses, so they would have to swig directly from the bottle, and considering they would both have their lips on the same place, in Ceri's eyes that constituted getting pretty darned close. They may as well snog and be done with it!

As the thought popped into her head, her eyes widened and her imagination went into overdrive. He did look incredibly kissable. His shirt sleeves were rolled up revealing strong forearms with tattoos disappearing under the material, the top two buttons of his shirt were undone, and his long legs were stretched out in front of him.

'Forgot glasses,' she announced, tucking her feet underneath her as she sank down onto his jacket. A waft of his deliciously woody and manly scent drifted up her nose, and she tried not to inhale too deeply in case he noticed and thought she was weird.

'You go first,' she told him, handing him the bottle.

He took it, his expression quizzical, then he lifted it to his lips and she watched him take a mouthful, his throat working as he swallowed. He passed the wine back to her and she wondered whether she should wipe the rim.

She didn't bother and was conscious of his gaze as she drank.

'Ugh. That wasn't as nice as I hoped it was going to be,' she said with a grimace. 'Too dry.'

'You prefer the sweet stuff?'

'You say that like it's a bad thing.' She shoved the bottle at him. 'Are you a wine connoisseur?'

'Hardly. I wouldn't know good wine if it bit me on the backside.'

'What's your tipple of choice?' she asked, watching him take another swig.

He gave her back the bottle, his fingers brushing hers and a spark of desire ignited inside her at the touch. She eyed the wine warily, wondering if it was a good idea to drink any more if it was going to make her act this way.

'Promise you won't laugh?' he asked.

'I promise.' She took a gulp.

'Sherry.'

Ceri almost choked as the alcohol went down the wrong way, and when she had finished spluttering, he said accusingly, 'You promised not to laugh.'

'I wasn't laughing. I was drowning. The wine went down the wrong way.'

'Yeah, because you were laughing,' he shot back.

'OK, maybe a bit.' She snorted, a most unladylike sound. 'Honestly, though – *sherry*?'

'It reminds me of my gran,' he replied haughtily. 'She used to love a glass before dinner.'

Ceri noticed the past tense and thought it best not to tease him any further. 'I like Advocaat,' she admitted. 'It reminds me of Christmas. And port.'

'You do realise that port and sherry are kissing cousins?'

'I'll shut up then, shall I?' she laughed. 'I haven't got a leg to stand on.'

'You won't if you keep knocking back the wine.'

'You're not as funny as you think you are,' she retorted snootily. 'And for your information, I'm nowhere near legless.'

He held out his hand for the bottle. 'And the puns just keep coming,' he chuckled.

They sat in silence for a while. It wasn't an uncomfortable one, and Ceri didn't feel the need to hunt around for anything to say. She was quite content to sit in the meadow, listening to the music. Having a handsome man to sit there with her was a bonus.

A breeze caught the tendrils of hair around her face, and Ceri noticed that her up-do was gradually becoming a down-do. She'd woven flowers into her locks at the start of the day but they were now beginning to wilt. One thing she couldn't tolerate was dying flowers. It was a pity they hadn't lasted longer, because she loved the hippy chick look. Absently, she teased them out of her hair and laid them on the grass, and debated whether to replace them with the daisies that were dotted through the grass, then hesitated. They had closed up for the night, looking more like shuttlecocks than flowers, revealing the pink-daubed undersides of the petals, so she left them where they were, as something else caught her eye.

It wasn't easy to tell what it was in the dark, so she lowered herself down until she was lying on her side and stretched out a hand to stroke the flower.

A faint but unmistakable scent reached her. 'Evening primrose,' she muttered.

'Excuse me?'

'These flowers. Can you smell them? They're evening primrose. Pollinators love them.'

Damon lay down and shuffled over. 'I can smell something nice, but I thought it was your perfume.'

'It's these. And there's honeysuckle, too.' She twisted over to look at him and got a shock when she realised how near his face was to hers.

He inhaled deeply. 'My gran used to have honeysuckle in her garden.' Abruptly he flopped onto his back as though realising he was invading her personal space. 'I wonder if she's up there, watching us.'

Ceri lay back and looked at the stars. 'Would you like her to be?'

'It would be a comfort, although she'd probably tell me not to lie on the grass in case I got a chill. She loved her garden, did my gran.' He pointed towards the heavens. 'I can see Mars, I think. I wish they'd turn the marquee's lights out; it's too bright to see anything else.'

'Do you stargaze often?' she asked.

'Not often enough.'

'Me, neither.' She really should rectify that, she thought, especially now she no longer lived in a city. Nights in Foxmore were considerably darker than those in Cardiff, and more stars were usually visible. Foxmore was more peaceful too, she decided, as the last bars of something she didn't recognise faded and she realised that the wedding reception was drawing to a close.

She should say goodnight to the happy couple, but she couldn't bring herself to move. Damon also seemed content to remain where he was.

'Do you have to go?' she asked, deciding she ought to check. She didn't want him to feel obliged to keep her company.

36

'Do you want me to?' he countered.

'No...'

'Then I won't.'

Ceri propped herself up on her elbows, watching guests trickle through the gate and onto the lane. Laughter and voices carried on the air, and she marvelled at how far noise travelled at night.

Keeping her voice low, she said, 'Will anyone miss you?' not realising she was fishing for information on whether he had come to the party with someone until she had uttered the words.

'No. You?'

His reply didn't address the question she wanted an answer to, but she could hardly ask him outright if he had a wife or girlfriend.

'I doubt it,' she said, lying down again and closing her eyes. 'I think I've done my bit for today. It was fun and I had a blast, but I'm shattered now.'

'You can't sleep out here,' he warned.

'I wasn't planning to. I'm just resting my eyes.'

'I think you've had too much to drink.' He got to his feet and leant over her.

Ceri opened one eye. 'I most certainly have not. *You* drank most of that bottle.' She opened the other eye. 'You can go if you want. I'll be fine.'

'I'm not leaving you on your own in a field in the middle of the night,' he protested. 'Come on.' He held out a hand.

Reluctantly she grasped it and allowed him to pull her upright, but as she got to her feet she stumbled into him, her body coming up against his, and she put a hand against his chest.

The night abruptly grew darker and more intimate as she froze, every cell tingling at the unexpected contact.

His hand was still holding hers; his other arm had encircled her waist to steady her.

She could feel the heat of his chest through his shirt, and the tension thrumming through him. The same tension that held her rigid and unmoving.

Her breath caught in her throat.

Ceri had no idea how it happened, but suddenly they were kissing, his mouth urgent and demanding as he pulled her closer.

Her lips parted and his tongue found hers, and desire tore through her. Knees beginning to buckle with the force of her unexpected lust, she clung to him, the kiss frenzied and all-consuming as it swept her away on a tide of longing.

Ceri thought she might have been the one to end their passionate clinch, but equally, Damon might have been the first to pull away. She couldn't tell. All she knew was that it was over, leaving her breathless and wanting more, but too shocked to make any further move.

To be fair to Damon, he looked pretty dazed too, but whether it was from lust or the suddenness of the encounter, wasn't clear.

What had got into her?

She didn't normally kiss men less than an hour after meeting them. The intense emotion of the day must have affected her.

It had been nice, though.

Wonderful, actually, even if it had been totally unexpected.

Damon's breathing was as ragged as her own as he stared deeply into her eyes. Ceri tried to read his expression, but apart from his obvious arousal, he was giving nothing away. He might be seriously regretting it, for all she knew.

'I'd... um... better be off,' she stammered, stepping back to put some distance between them.

'Let me walk you—'

'No. It's OK. I'll be fine. Thanks, anyway.' She took another step, half of her praying that he wouldn't stop her, the other half hoping that he would. She turned on her heel, calling over her shoulder. 'It was nice meeting you, Damon.'

'Are you sure you—?'

'Bye!' She darted away, the grass swishing at her bare legs as she headed for home before she said or did something she would regret.

–

Mind-blowing. It wasn't a phrase Damon often used, but it was utterly apt for what had just happened, he thought, as he sauntered back to the house.

Actually, what *had* just happened?

He wasn't sure, but he knew he'd enjoyed it. Right up to the part where she'd bade him a breezy goodbye and had left him standing in the field watching her walk away into the night. He hadn't taken his eyes off her until she disappeared from view.

The urge to run after her was strong but held firmly in check by knowing he didn't need any more complications right now. Even if she was up for more than a kiss, he wasn't the type of man to hop into bed with a woman without it meaning something. That had been Aiden's forte. Luke had his fair share of one-night stands, too

– and those nights had sometimes stretched into a couple of days if the timing had been right and the band hadn't needed to dash off to the next gig.

Damon had been the more reserved of the three. Aiden had called him boring, but Damon hadn't risen to the friendly teasing. He'd tried casual sex a few times, but it had always left him dissatisfied and restless. He'd also tried having a steady girlfriend, but that hadn't worked out either. Unable to decide whether it was his lifestyle that was the cause, or whether it was he who had been to blame for his failed relationships, Damon had knocked romance on the head and concentrated on his music.

Then Aiden had been killed and Damon had the awful feeling that he would never be able to concentrate on anything ever again.

The loss hit him anew. For a while this evening, he'd managed to forget, and guilt coursed through him. All it had taken was for a beautiful woman to kiss him, and the funeral and everything that had gone before had flown out of his mind. From the moment he'd seen Ceri dancing in the meadow, he hadn't thought about Aiden once.

Disgusted with himself, he wondered how he could have allowed such a thing to happen. Then abruptly he understood…

For the first time in far too long, he had felt like a normal guy. Ceri clearly hadn't recognised him. She hadn't had any idea who he was, and he relished the anonymity.

Yet, less than twelve hours since Aiden had been laid to rest, Damon had kissed a woman. His reaction to her had taken him totally by surprise, and the only excuse he could find was that the heavy emotions of the day had clouded his sense of right and wrong.

But it *had* been right, a part of him argued. Some fleeting stolen moments with a beautiful stranger who appeared to want nothing from their brief encounter, had given him a modicum of peace for the short amount of time he'd been with her.

The kiss had taken him by surprise, but it had felt so good, so natural, and he believed she had enjoyed it as much as he had.

However, fresh guilt pricked at him. He had no right to enjoy himself when Aiden lay cold in the ground.

Taking his phone out of his pocket, he thumbed Luke's number, but it rang and rang, until it eventually cut off.

Sadie, then. She was the only other person who he could talk to about this, who might understand.

'It's Damon,' he announced when she answered.

'Where are you? Are you OK?'

'I'm at Gran's house in Foxmore.'

'Are you OK?' she repeated.

'Not really. You?'

'Not really.'

'I didn't think you were,' he replied softly. Despite her bravado earlier, he could tell how badly she was hurting.

'He was my hero, you know?' Her voice caught, and Damon pulled a face. Was he being selfish in wanting to unburden himself, when she had just buried her brother? 'I really looked up to him,' she added with a sob.

'We all did. He was one of the best bass guitar players in the business.'

'Better than me?'

'Yeah, but not as pretty.' The joke was a feeble one, but he heard her chuckle and guessed she was laughing and crying at the same time. 'Is Luke with you?' he asked.

'He's on a plane. Caught the first flight out of Heathrow he could. I thought about going with him, but Mum and Dad need me here.'

'How are they bearing up?'

'You know Dad – stoic to the last. Mum, though… As soon as we got home, she shut herself in Aiden's old room and hasn't come out since.'

'What about you?' he asked.

'I had to get out of the house, so I went to the cinema with a couple of friends.'

Damon was surprised. 'What film did you see?'

'No idea. I felt so guilty being there, that I ate a whole tub of toffee popcorn by myself and cried all the way through it.'

'I kissed someone tonight,' Damon blurted.

There was silence on the other end, then Sadie said, 'Gosh! Who?'

'I met her in a field. She was dancing, so I kissed her.'

'That's random.'

'It was wonderful, and now I feel guilty as hell.'

'Don't. Aiden would hate that.'

'Is that what you told yourself when you felt guilty about going to the cinema?' he countered gently.

'You've got me,' she said, then sighed. 'Look, Damon, don't beat yourself up over it. You kissed someone – so what? Aiden kissed more women than he could count.'

That's not me, Damon wanted to say. That side of rock and roll had never really been his scene. He'd had his moments – he was only human – but he had been too interested in making music. Nothing could compare to the thrill of composing a piece, then singing it to hundreds, sometimes thousands, of people. Not even sex.

42

But the woman in the meadow had stirred something in him, and he wasn't sure what.

What he did know, was that for the first time since that awful night, he felt like playing.

Reaching for his guitar, he began to pluck the strings…

–

As Ceri let herself into the cottage and dropped her bag on the armchair, she realised she hadn't stopped to think when she had fled the field – she had simply run, pausing only to collect her little pouch bag from where she had left it on a table in the marquee. There had only been a few guests remaining; those die-hards who were wringing the last drop of jollity out of the evening, as well as the last drop of alcohol out of their glasses. Huw and Rowena had long gone. They were spending their first night as a married couple in Rowena's house (Huw's house now, too) before jetting off on their honeymoon tomorrow. The lucky things!

Right now though, Ceri's thoughts weren't on white sand beaches and swaying palm trees: they were firmly fixed on the man she had kissed.

Her heart still pounded, her pulse continued to race, and she could taste him on her lips. His scent lingered in her nostrils, making her head spin, and she could still feel the solid muscles of his back as her fingers dug into him. The impression his body had left on hers would take a while to fade.

That had been some kiss. The kind of kiss she wouldn't forget in a hurry. The kind that made a woman go weak at the knees and left her wanting more… *begging* for more. Which was why she had beat a hasty retreat, before she did something silly, such as suggesting he came back to her house.

She didn't do one-night stands. It simply wasn't her style, despite Huw teasing her that she had a new boyfriend every other week. It was partially true. Admittedly, she'd had a few, but that was because she was picky. If, after a couple of dates, she didn't connect with them, or they didn't live up to her (possibly unrealistic) high standards, they were toast.

Huw kept warning her that she would end up an old maid if she kicked every potential boyfriend into the sidelines, but she had yet to find one who touched her heart.

Regretfully she knew there was little chance of seeing Damon again. She lived here in Foxmore and he lived in London, and she didn't even know his last name, although she could probably find out if she asked around.

But what was the point? Knowing his full name wouldn't make any difference if she was unlikely to set eyes on him again. She just had to accept that she had been thoroughly and expertly kissed by a total stranger, and as much as she had enjoyed the encounter, there wouldn't be a repeat performance. And in a way, it made their brief encounter all the more magical – drinking wine, gazing up at the stars, and kissing a handsome stranger...

Ceri should be tired, but she was oddly wide awake, as though the kiss had sparked her energy levels, so she decided to take a glass of water into the garden and sit for a while.

The area might be tiny, but it didn't feel that way, because not long after Huw had bought the cottage, he had enlisted Ceri's help in her professional capacity as a horticulturist to make the most of the outside space. She had filled it with carefully chosen plants to provide structure and form, then had added other planting to provide colour, interest and scent, and to attract plenty of bees and butterflies.

Tipping her head back, she gazed up at the night sky and wondered what Damon was doing now. She presumed he had returned to whatever hotel or guest house he was staying in, and she wondered whether he was at The Jolly Fox, where her parents had booked a room for a couple of nights. She was planning on joining them there tomorrow for Sunday lunch, before they travelled on towards the Llŷn Peninsula and the spa hotel where they were basing their exploration of that part of north Wales from.

Would she see him there or would he have left already?

In some way, she hoped she didn't bump into him again, because right now she was viewing their encounter as enchanted. If she met him tomorrow the lovely bubble would undoubtedly burst and instead of remembering him as a handsome prince, he would most likely turn into a slimy frog and the memory of this wonderful evening would be forever sullied.

It was better to leave things as they were.

She didn't think she would forget him for a very long time though, and deep down she prayed their paths would cross once more, because she had the unsettling feeling that, given the opportunity, Damon could mean a great deal more to her than she was willing to admit.

Chapter 4

Ceri peered out of her bedroom window on the first Monday after the half-term holiday and checked the weather, unable to believe this day had actually arrived. One minute she had been excitedly (although nervously) attending an interview for a job she didn't think she stood a chance in hell of getting, the next she was waking up to her very first day as a teacher.

Oh, God, she would be *teaching*!

She'd never taught anyone anything before, so what made her think she would be able to teach anyone now? What had possessed her to apply for the job in the first place? And what on earth had the college been thinking when they had offered it to her? Were they *daft*?

She couldn't do this.

Panic pinged along her veins and she flopped down on the bed, the mattress bouncing under her weight. Her legs were like jelly and she hadn't even got as far as having a shower yet. Goodness knows what state she'd be in when she had to stand in front of a class for the very first time.

Swallowing hard, she decided to give the college a call to tell them she had changed her mind, or she was ill, or leaving the country. Anything to prevent her from feeling like this.

If only she could speak to Huw, but it was the middle of the night in Trinidad and he was on his honeymoon.

The last thing he needed was his sister whingeing that she was too scared to turn up to her new job.

She knew what he would say; he would tell her to get a grip and stop being so pathetic.

But it was all right for him, he was used to giving presentations and speaking to groups of people. He had a responsible position, working for Co-op Cymru, helping communities set up businesses. Even though Ceri had a degree in horticulture, the only thing she was trained to do was to advise customers on how to care for their hardy geraniums. It was hardly a sound base for getting a bunch of sixteen- to eighteen-year-olds to pass their City & Guilds or BTEC qualifications, was it?

The mentor who had been assigned to her had brought her up to speed on where the students were at, and she had spent every day since moving to Foxmore (except for the day of Huw's wedding) preparing lessons and going through the scheme of work that the previous teacher had left. But she was still terrified of the task ahead of her.

She was under no illusion that it would be easy to step into someone else's shoes, but she would simply have to grin and get on with it, and pray that her years of hands-on experience would count for something.

Her phone rang just as she was trying to force a piece of toast down her throat, and she scrambled to answer it when she saw who was calling.

'Huw! Is everything all right?'

'It's bloody marvellous!' her brother cried. 'You'd love Trinidad – so many exotic plants for you to swoon over!'

'What time is it there?'

'Um… three a.m.'

'Are you sure everything's OK?'

'I'm sure. We're having a brilliant time. Long days on the beach, longer nights in—'

'Enough already! I know you're on your honeymoon, but you're my brother. I do not want to hear all the sordid details. Ew.'

'I was going to say, longer nights in the bar,' Huw replied. 'Get your mind out of the gutter, sis.'

Ceri wrinkled her nose. 'Why are you calling me?' She briefly considered sharing her fears with him, but she held back. He was clearly having a good time, and didn't need to be worrying about her. She'd just have to grow up and stop being such a wimp.

'To wish you good luck for today. It *is* today that you start your new job, isn't it?'

'It is,' she said, touched that he'd remembered, her stomach once again churning at the thought of where she would be spending her day and how she would be spending it.

'Are you nervous?'

'Petrified. What if I make a total fool of myself?' Oh, dear, so much for not letting her brother know how she was feeling. But he'd asked, so…

Huw chuckled. 'I highly doubt you'll do that. It's strange to think that not very long ago I was in the same position as you are now – just moved to Foxmore and about to start a new job. It's even stranger to think that you're living in the same cottage I was living in back then. It's like a weird form of déjà vu, but it's nice to see you following in your big brother's footsteps. You'll be finding yourself a fella and settling down next!'

'Hardly,' she retorted, but the memory of a man with dark curling hair and sensual lips flitted through her mind, and she shook her head to clear it. 'Thanks for thinking of me, Huw. But you could have just sent me a message, rather than get up so early.'

'What are you talking about? We haven't gone to bed yet. Well, not really, we—'

'La, la, la,' Ceri sang loudly, cutting him off. 'Bye, Huw. Enjoy the rest of your honeymoon.'

Her brother's laughter was still ringing in her ears as she ended the call. Then she grinned when she received a message from him immediately afterwards telling her to 'knock 'em dead'.

–

Knock 'em dead, indeed! The only thing that was knocking was her knees, and Ceri hoped her students wouldn't notice. She had arrived incredibly early and was sitting in the staffroom with a cup of coffee, trying to remember what it was she was supposed to be teaching this morning and struggling not to give in to the temptation to flee.

Alongside the City & Guilds and BTEC qualifications she was employed to deliver, she was also supposed to be taking over the running of several shorter courses aimed at the more mature learner, although they were open to anyone who cared to enrol, of course. And although she loved the idea of modules such as 'Planning a Wildlife Haven' and 'Creating an Edible Garden', she wasn't convinced she was the best person to teach them. She wasn't the best person to teach *anything*.

And when Mark, the Faculty Lead (aka her Head of Department), walked into the room and said, 'Morning, Ceri. I forgot to tell you, but just to make you aware, the college holds an event at the end of the academic year where students showcase their work, and things like plants and other items are sold to the general public, so you might want to start thinking about that,' Ceri thought she might have a meltdown there and then.

Mark popped a hand inside one of the pigeonholes near the door and pulled out some papers. 'You'd think people would just use email in this day and age,' he said, rifling through them. 'Flyers, mostly. Huh!' He dropped everything in the bin and walked over to the sink. Several mugs were sitting on the draining board, and he picked one up and studied it. 'I've been looking for this.' He held it up for her to see. It had his name on the side.

Ceri gave a little smile. It was the best she could do, considering she was fizzing with nerves and felt positively sick.

Mark raised his eyebrows. 'Any issues before we start the day? Anything you're not sure about?' He glanced at the clock. Fifteen minutes to go before the first lesson began.

'Everything,' she replied, willing her bottom lip not to tremble.

He studied her for a minute then plopped into the seat opposite. 'You'll be fine. I remember my first teaching post. It terrified the life out of me, and I'd actually *got* a teaching degree, so it wasn't my first time in the classroom. I appreciate how hard it must be for you, Ceri, but you wouldn't have been employed if we didn't think you were capable of doing the job.'

It was good to hear, but Ceri wasn't convinced. She still had the awful feeling she had blagged her way through the interview, without really knowing what she was doing.

'Thanks,' she said. 'I'm sure I'll get used to it. To be honest, I was surprised to be invited for an interview.'

'Oh, why's that?'

'No formal teaching qualification. I know the advert said that for practical courses like these, experience is more important than a teaching certificate, but...'

'It's true,' Mark said. 'For hands-on subjects, experience *is* more important. If you can't do it yourself, you can't show others how to. And you clearly know your stuff. For the courses you are teaching, the college wanted someone who is well-versed in horticulture, and you are that person.' He smiled warmly and Ceri couldn't help but smile back.

She'd met him at the interview, and although it had been such a blur that she hadn't been able to recall many of the details afterwards, she remembered Mark. He had an open, sunny face and a ready smile, and throughout the interview she recalled him sitting forward in his seat, his head cocked to the side, as though he was interested in what she had to say. It had given her a much-needed boost at the time, and here he was doing it again.

'Don't be too hard on yourself,' he advised. 'I've every confidence in you.'

Ceri wished she felt the same, and as she made her way to the polytunnel where her first ordeal (sorry, *lesson*) was about to take place, she once again wondered what had possessed her to apply for the job in the first place.

Hurriedly, she checked that everything was set up, then swallowed nervously as voices drifted through the opening, becoming louder every second. Plastering a smile on her face, she took a deep breath and told herself she could do this. If she just pretended that the students were customers who wanted to learn how to measure the acidity of their soil (in the past, she had run a couple of drop-in sessions on this very topic for the garden centre she'd worked for), she'd be fine.

First though, she needed to know everyone's name, so she had a roll of sticky labels and some marker pens at the ready.

The first few students to step inside the polytunnel seemed happy to oblige, but a couple of the tardier ones rolled their eyes. One girl especially acted as though it was a big deal to scribble her name on a label, and she huffed and tutted at having to perform such an onerous task.

Ceri made a point of reading her name – Portia Selway – and smiled encouragingly at her.

Portia rolled her eyes again and nudged the girl standing next to her, before shuffling off to the side of the polytunnel and getting her phone out.

Ceri held onto her smile with difficulty and concentrated on greeting the rest of the students.

'Hi everyone, my name is Ms Morgan, and I'll be your teacher for the rest of your course. You can call me Ceri,' she added, remembering that when Mark had shown her around before half term, he had informed her that colleges weren't like schools in that students usually referred to teachers, tutors and the rest of the staff by their first names.

'And you can call me *Ms Selway*,' Portia muttered sarcastically, loud enough for Ceri to hear.

Several students sniggered.

Panic flared in Ceri's chest. How was she supposed to respond to that? Call the girl out? Ignore her? Take her to the side after the session ended and have a quiet word in her ear?

Was this what was meant by the low-level disruption that she had read about when trying to gen up on what to expect as a teacher? Most of the stuff she'd read had been aimed at teachers in schools, and she'd assumed that it wouldn't be as relevant in the further education setting, considering this wasn't compulsory and the students had opted to be here. Maybe her assumption was wrong…

Deciding to take the middle road between confronting the girl and ignoring her, Ceri sent her a level stare instead, holding Portia's gaze until the teenager looked away.

Feeling that she now had a modicum of control, Ceri straightened her shoulders, scooped a handful of rich crumbly loam from the smaller of the containers on a potting bench behind her, and said, 'Who fancies eating dirt?'

The group of nineteen youngsters looked at each other, confused.

There, that got their attention, Ceri thought, and she consolidated her small victory by pinching some soil between her forefinger and thumb and popping it into her mouth.

'Ew!'

'That's disgusting!'

'Did she just eat *dirt*?'

Their reactions were exactly as she'd hoped, and she turned away to hide a smile. Chewing, she swallowed, took a gulp of water from a bottle she had placed on the bench earlier, then opened her mouth to show her students that it was empty.

Portia's expression was particularly disgusted, and the others were staring at her in disbelief.

'Before the invention of soil testing kits,' she began, 'some farmers used to tell whether a soil was acid or alkaline by its taste. If it was acidic, it tasted sour. If it was alkaline, it was said to taste sweet.'

'You ate dirt,' the girl standing next to Portia said.

53

Ceri squinted at her name: Eleanor Curtis. 'Would you like to have a taste, Eleanor? Tell me if it's acid or not?'

'No, thanks!'

'Would *anyone* like to give it a go?'

There was a great deal of shuffling and exchanging of glances, before one of them, a tall, gangly lad who wore an air of bravado like Superman wore a cape, shuffled to the front. 'I'll eat some.' He was grinning, his expression goofy as he glanced around at his mates.

Ceri gestured to the container.

Hesitantly, he grabbed a pinch and stared at it. With his classmates urging him on, he grimaced as he brought his fingers to his lips, swiftly opened his mouth and popped the soil inside.

The look on his face as the chocolate sponge exploded on his tongue made Ceri laugh – and when the others realised that the loam wasn't soil after all, they all scrambled for a taste.

All except Portia Selway.

Ceri had a feeling it would take more than a bit of sponge to win that young lady over.

–

Damon, shirtless, grimy and sweaty, leant on the handle of the shovel and uttered a deep sigh. He was so unused to manual labour that today's excess of it had been a bit of a shock to the system. He was no stranger to exercise and often went for a run or used the gym in the basement of his London flat: but digging, weeding and lopping off overhanging branches was a whole different bag of compost, so to speak.

He had been at it since ten o'clock this morning and it was now nearly half-past one. During that time, all he'd had was water, and he was now feeling hungry and thirsty alongside dirty and knackered.

Deciding to call it a day, he picked up the shovel and dropped it into the wheelbarrow, feeling disheartened when he saw how little he had achieved. He had been hacking away for hours and the area he had managed to subdue was hardly larger than a couple of square metres. Which, if he was truthful, looked worse now than before he'd started. Bare earth was visible where he had torn weeds up by their roots, and several bushes had been chopped to within an inch of their leafy lives. He seriously doubted whether they would recover from the onslaught. Ragged stems of unidentifiable plants poked through the devastation like accusing fingers, pointing at him. And the path, which had been just about passable earlier, now lay under a mound of discarded vegetation.

With a surly grunt, Damon tried to see the silver lining in his morning's work by telling himself that at least the compost bins would benefit, and that by this time next year most of those branches, leaves and stems would have rotted down nicely. Unfortunately, he had a feeling that the composting area – hidden deep in a far corner of the garden – would also be overgrown, and by the time he finished clearing the large garden he would have more compostable material than he could handle. Perhaps he should burn it, instead? Or maybe not; he didn't want to risk a stray spark setting fire to the house.

Putting the rest of the tools in the wheelbarrow, he hooked his shirt from where he had hung it on one of the branches of the overgrown willow tree for which the house, and subsequently the lane, had been named, and stowed the barrow back in the shed, making a note to add 'Replace broken panes of glass in greenhouse' to his ever-growing list of jobs. It wasn't urgent, seeing as he wasn't planning on growing anything in it, but it did look very sorry for itself.

The potting shed was in better shape, and he pushed the door open and went in, breathing in the familiar smell of his childhood: a mixture of soil, dust, and warm summer air.

Although Damon could feel Hyacinth's hand in the garden, it was in this shed that his grandmother's presence was most keenly felt. He sensed her in the tidy stacks of empty terracotta pots waiting to be filled, in the dibbers and trowels hanging from pegs on the wall, and in the shelves on which sat baskets, metal watering cans, an ancient radio, and several old biscuit tins.

He ran his fingers across a grubby kettle, wondering if it still worked, and picked up one of the mugs next to it. It was chipped and stained from hundreds of cups of strong tea, and had sprigs of lavender decorating the rim.

Curiously, he opened one of the biscuit tins and peered inside to see loads of packets of seeds. They were mainly wildflowers, and another tin held packets of root vegetables. All of them would no doubt be years past the recommended use-by date, and he wondered how many would germinate if he ever got around to sowing them.

Opening several more tins, he smiled as the contents of each one was revealed. There were more seeds here than in the Millennium Seed Bank at Kew Gardens!

But some tins didn't hold seeds. They held old photos of the garden, and as he sifted through them, he found something even more remarkable underneath: journals!

Spellbound, Damon opened first one, then another, scanning the pages swiftly, and as he did so he could feel his grandmother looking over his shoulder.

'Your journals,' he murmured. 'How wonderful.'

There was page after page of notes on everything and anything concerning the garden. What to plant in a shady corner; how the camellia had recovered after a harsh winter; when to divide the sedum... There was so much in here, that it would take Damon weeks to read them thoroughly. Each one – there were five in all – was crammed with Hyacinth's small spidery writing and appeared to span more than four decades. What history must lie between these pages, he mused... the history of a garden and the woman who had loved it and nurtured it.

Once or twice a non-gardening-related note would catch his eye. *V bought me a car. A brand new one. Too expensive. He has to take it back.* The note was dated over fifty years ago, and Damon wondered who *V* was. Another read, *When you are young, they don't tell you about bunions*, and he laughed out loud.

Finally, though, hunger overcame his desire to carry on reading, so he carefully replaced the journals in their tin, and popped it back on the shelf.

However, before he stepped inside the house, he paused. He didn't know whether that brief stint working in the garden had honed his powers of observation, but something in the overgrown border just outside the kitchen door caught his eye, and when he looked down his heart missed a beat.

Bell-shaped flowers, in shades of such deep purple that they were almost black, grew in clusters supported by sturdy stems surrounded by bright green leaves. The plants were past their best, but he recognised them instantly: hyacinths. *Black* hyacinths. And he would bet his last pound that this particular variety was called Dark Dimension.

Sadness washed over him and he sank to his knees, the delicate perfume bringing tears to his eyes. Spring was morphing into summer and by rights these plants should have lost their flowers, but the fact that they were here and still in full bloom made him want to cry.

The band was named after this very plant, and their first single, as well as the album it had spawned, was called *Dark Dimension*. The other band members had loved the title, believing it to be eminently suitable for the kind of music they were fast becoming known for. Little had they realised it had been a tribute to Damon's grandmother. The band's name, Black Hyacinth was also a tribute to her – hyacinths had been her favourite flowers, as well as her name. And considering how much she had loved her garden, the allotment and all growing things, the name Hyacinth was perfect for her. It had also made a bloody good name for a rock band.

'Sorry, Gran,' he muttered, aware of how badly he had let her down. She had bequeathed her beloved house to him, and it had lain unloved and empty since she'd died, because Damon had been too busy pursuing a dream she hadn't lived long enough to see him achieve.

Guilt pricked at him with thorny fingers, and he stared at the blooms with tears in his eyes.

He should have spent more time with her, and visited her more often. She had loved him and nurtured him when he'd needed it most, more than his own parents who, let's face it, hadn't had much to do with his formative years because they'd been too busy visiting far-flung places digging around in the dirt. Archaeologists tended to do that a lot. As had his gran. But where his parents had lifted fragments of bone, tools and pottery from the soil with no thought to their only child, his gran had lifted potatoes, carrots and onions from the allotment, with him at her side.

Damon had been envious of his parents' ability to travel where they wished and make their home wherever they happened to be, yet he had also been envious of his grandmother's ability to ground herself to this house and its garden. In his desire to achieve both, he had achieved neither. But as this was the only place he felt he truly belonged, maybe it was only to be expected that he would hide himself away in Willow Tree House when his life had fallen down around his ears.

Damon suddenly barked out a laugh; he could have sworn he heard his gran telling him to buck his ideas up, but he knew it was only the wind sighing through the stand of trees that provided a backdrop to the garden. He had yet to venture that deep into the grounds and he winced as he thought of the state that part of the garden must be in.

His gran had always maintained that Mother Nature was quick to reclaim what she thought of as rightly hers. But his grandmother had never been at war with her – instead, she had tried to persuade nature to do her bidding, to work with her rather than against her. Saying that though, Hyacinth had been known to indulge in a minor skirmish or two with nature as she tried to keep the weeds at bay.

Damon guiltily realised that he should have done more than simply employ a property service company to check on the place once a month and do any repairs necessary. The house hadn't suffered too badly from his lack of care, but the garden certainly had. An annual cutting back of the shrubs by the same company hadn't done much for the appearance or the health of the garden.

Damon clambered to his feet, his back in bits and his shoulders aching. Flexing his fingers and feeling the pop as the joints realigned themselves, he was relieved that he wasn't due to be in the studio or on stage anytime soon. His hands were so stiff, he felt as though he was wearing mittens.

An image of the last night that the band had been together, performing to an ecstatic crowd of German fans, slammed into him, catching him unawares, and he sucked in a sharp breath.

The three of them had been jubilant, on top of the world, exhausted yet ebullient. It was the end of a brilliant tour, their best yet. There had been no inkling of how fragile life was, or how swiftly it could be snatched away.

He could feel tendrils of darkness as the memory of Aiden's last few minutes crept into his head once more and he was consumed with dread: the tyres screeching on the tarmac, the music filling the car, Aiden's frantic voice—

'No...' Damon muttered.

Gritting his teeth, his jaw aching, he screwed his eyes shut and willed the memory away. It was no use. It swept over him in a torrent, and as it sucked him under, his heart pounded furiously and his breathing became shallow frantic gasps.

He didn't know how long it held him in its grip but when it finally spat him out, Damon found himself sitting on the ground, his arms wrapped around his legs, his knees touching his chest. He was shaking and a trickle of sweat ran down his back.

That was a bad one, the worst yet.

Drained, exhausted and scared, he clambered shakily to his feet, a feeling of wretchedness washing over him. How much longer could he carry on like this?

Chapter 5

'You look like I feel,' Betsan observed, as Ceri stepped through the door of Foxmore's zero waste shop.

Ceri grimaced. Her first week in her new job had been tough, but she had survived. All she wanted this evening was to have something nice to eat, a glass of wine, and to put her feet up. And she had been all set to do just that when she remembered she needed some supplies. She had been so busy these past few days, that she hadn't had time to do any shopping, so as soon as she'd reached Foxmore late on Friday afternoon, she had parked the car outside the cottage and had dashed to the shops before they closed for the day.

She was relieved to see that the zero waste shop was still open, so she could stock up on cereal, yoghurts and milk, but the bakery had already shut, so she would have to pay the convenience store a visit.

'How was it?' Betsan asked.

'Exhausting and terrifying. I'm not sure I can make it to the end of term.'

'You will. I've got every faith in you.'

'I wish I had faith in myself,' Ceri replied, as she wandered around the shop, filling her basket. 'I'm so far out of my comfort zone I might as well be on another planet.'

'Aw, my lovely, don't be so hard on yourself. You're bound to find it difficult at first.'

'I know, and I hate being so wimpy. It's not like me.'

Mrs Moxley, an elderly lady with a lavender perm and a face full of wrinkles, was standing near the door leading to the back of the shop. She had a box of bamboo toothbrushes in one hand, hemp exfoliating mitts in the other, and a handbag dangling on her arm.

She said, 'It's a big change, jacking in your job and your house to move to a new area. But you're not the first to do it – look at your Huw. It's turned out pretty darned good for him.' The old lady popped the items onto their respective shelves, then announced, 'I'm off. My next shift is Tuesday – have a good weekend.'

'Bye, love,' Betsan called after her, then turned to Ceri. 'She's got a heart of gold, that one. I don't know what we'd do without her.'

By 'we' Betsan was referring to herself and Rowena. Rowena had set up the zero waste shop (with Huw's help) and many of the villagers had shares in it, including Mrs Moxley, and took turns helping to run the business.

'Did you find everything you wanted?' Betsan asked as Ceri lifted her basket onto the counter.

'I need some bread, but I'll pick that up from the convenience store. Oh, and some sweet peppers. It's such a pity there isn't a proper grocer in Foxmore.'

'I know what you mean!' Betsan gave her a sideways look as she rang the purchases through the till. 'I thought you would grow your own.'

'There's only so much I could bring with me,' Ceri replied. Her house in Cardiff had been rented, and although she'd brought several pots with her and had taken loads of cuttings, she hadn't thought it right to dig up any of the shrubs she'd planted. 'Anyway, my garden here is tiny. I did put some plants in when Huw bought the cottage, but most of them aren't edible because they were mainly for colour and scent, not for eating. I've planted some tubs up with veggies, but it'll be a while before I can harvest anything. Although, I do have some cut-and-come-again lettuces on the go, which are ready now. I'll just have to be patient for the rest.'

'I assumed gardening *was* all about being patient,' Betsan laughed.

'It is. I'm usually very good at waiting, and I'd love to be self-sufficient when it comes to growing my own veg, but with the best will in the world that's never going to happen, not with the size of my garden.'

'I'd offer you some of ours, but Terry loves his lawn. Or should I say, he loves his sit-on lawn mower. He was only telling me yesterday over dinner that he can't wait to mow the field out the back. He did it a couple of weeks before the wedding, but the grass is already long again.'

Heat flooded into Ceri's cheeks at the unexpected mention of the field, as an image of her and Damon kissing passionately leapt into her mind. Picking up one of the flyers lying on the counter, she fanned her face with it, saying, 'Is it my imagination or is it warm in here?'

She hoped she wasn't going to react like this every time the field was mentioned. Not that she expected it to suddenly become a hot topic of conversation. She hadn't been aware it existed until Huw had announced that he and Rowena intended to hold their reception there, so Ceri didn't think the subject would come up much in the future once the post-wedding excitement had faded.

'It's your imagination,' Betsan replied. 'Either that or the thought of a sit-on mower is getting you all hot under the collar. You gardening types can be rather strange.'

'Thanks!' Ceri pulled a face at her.

'How big a garden do you need?' Betsan was looking thoughtful, and hope flared in Ceri's chest. The vicarage was directly opposite Rosehip Cottage – it would be a perfect location if Terry could be persuaded to give up some of his lawn in exchange for a regular supply of fresh vegetables.

'An allotment-sized plot would be great,' Ceri replied. It would be a start, although she was aiming for something much bigger eventually. 'In fact, I would love to have a plot on an actual allotment, but Foxmore doesn't appear to have one.' And even if the village did have one that she didn't know about, there was usually a waiting list and Ceri wanted to get started *now*, not in two, three, or four years' time.

'No, it doesn't,' Betsan agreed. 'It used to, but the old lady who ran it died, and it fell into disuse.'

'Could it be reinstated?' Ceri asked, wondering where it used to be. The meadow down by the river perhaps? Although she suspected the area might be prone to flooding after heavy rain.

'Maybe. I'll have to have a chat to Terry.'

'Why? Where—?' The penny dropped. 'It was on the field behind the church, wasn't it? The one we've just been talking about?'

'It was.' Betsan nodded. 'Since Hyacinth Rogers passed away it's not been used – except for Rowena's wedding and a circus which set up there a couple of years ago but hasn't been back since. The church doesn't use it for anything and neither does the village so, if you want, I can have a word with Terry. Better still, why don't you pop over tomorrow and speak to him yourself? I suggest you go take a proper look at it first though, as I suspect you've only seen it when it had a great big tent plonked in it. No one ever goes down that lane anymore: it's a dead end, you see. The only thing down there is the entrance to the field itself, and Willow Tree House, where Hyacinth used to live.'

'I'll take a look now,' Ceri declared, her heart pounding.

With any luck the former allotment on Willow Tree Lane might be just the place to make her dream of owning a nursery come true.

Damon would have thought that all the time he had spent working in the garden recently would have yielded better results. OK, he hadn't worked on it all day every day – he had done other stuff in between – but he had dedicated enough hours to it that he should have been able to see *some* difference by now. But the garden looked almost as bad as when he'd started, and by Friday evening he'd had enough. He wished he could just wave a wand and the garden would be magically transformed.

He could always employ the services of a local grounds maintenance team to come in and sort it out… but there were two issues with that idea. The first was his reluctance to have strangers on his property in case someone realised who he was. The second was that he believed employing someone to do the hard graft would be disloyal to his gran's memory. She had never felt the need to have anyone do her garden for her, so he shouldn't either. Right up until the end, when a devastating stroke had taken her, Gran had managed on her own, and if he, a six-foot, thirty-year-old, relatively fit guy wasn't able to cut back a few bushes and subdue some weeds, what did that say about him?

But enough was enough, and he didn't want to risk damaging his hands. He could already feel callouses developing on his palms, and the fingers on his left hand were stiffer than they should be, so he decided to knock the manual labour on the head for the weekend. He would give his shoulders, back and hands a rest, then start again on Monday.

As soon as he returned to the house, he had a quick shower, cracked open a beer, and, after opening the French doors in his grandmother's high-ceilinged sitting room which she used to call the parlour, to let the evening air blow through, he reached for his Gibson.

Resting the guitar on his knee, he tuned the strings, his mind drifting.

The itch of a new song was just out of scratching distance, the notes tripping through his mind in elusive bursts, the lyrics hovering on the edge of his consciousness. He knew better than to force it; it would come to him when it was ready.

For now, he would simply play.

He began with familiar tunes, to warm up both his voice and his fingers, and also because it didn't require any effort on his part. He played without thinking and sang without having to search for the words, but after a while he felt the urge to create, to pluck a song out of the air and make it real. It was strange how a melody would come to him without any conscious thought; it was as though it had already been sung by the gods and was floating in the ether, waiting for him to claim it and make it his own.

The lyrics would follow later, and they too often seemed to sneak into his head as though the melody and the words belonged together, and no others could possibly fit. It was those, or none.

And while he made music out of nothing, the image in his mind was that of the woman he had met in the field beyond the orchard. Her face had hijacked his thoughts so thoroughly that he didn't realise he had woven her into his song until the last few notes faded into the calm evening air.

Feeling more at peace than he had since the accident, his fingers strummed the chords of the band's signature track, "Dark Dimension", and as he allowed the music to fill his soul, he wished with all his heart that Aiden was playing it with him.

—

Without a 'great big tent plonked in it' (to quote the vicar's wife), the field on Willow Tree Lane looked bigger somehow.

As she walked through the metal gate, Ceri's eyes automatically went to where the hedgerow grew thickest, where she knew a small wooden gate was hidden, and near to it was the place where she had lain in the grass and gazed up at the stars with a handsome stranger. The place where he had kissed her so very thoroughly.

She wondered where he was now.

Maybe she would ask Rowena about him when she and Huw were back from their honeymoon, which should be tomorrow if their flight landed on time.

She'd give it a couple of days before she mentioned Damon though, see if she could work him into the conversation without it looking as though she was digging for information.

Then again, maybe she shouldn't ask at all. What good would knowing more about him do? She was hardly likely to go haring off to London. Sleeping dogs were best left unpoked. Or was that a wasp's nest? Whatever. The sentiment was the same. The encounter had been lovely, and the mystery of the man she'd kissed had undoubtedly added to it. If she met him again, he might be totally underwhelming, so why spoil the most romantic night of her life with disappointing reality? Although, she had to admit that she had been saddened not to have seen him at The Jolly Fox when she'd had lunch with her parents on the Sunday after the wedding. She had spent most of the meal surreptitiously watching the door, hoping he might walk through it, and she had been disappointed when there hadn't been any sign of him.

Ceri closed the gate with a clang, determined not to waste any more time thinking about him, but even so, her eyes were drawn to the place where they had lain in the grass and gazed up at the stars.

There was no trace of the encounter, and she hadn't expected there to be. If the grass that the marquee had been resting on had sprung back, then the small indentation their bodies had left would certainly have faded almost immediately.

Talking about indentations, now that she was looking for them she could just make out the signs that the field had once been cultivated. If she squinted, she was able to see the faint outlines of beds, crisscrossed by paths that had most likely been grassed rather than paved. It was possible to see the tumps where the soil of the vegetable beds had been higher than the paths, and if she looked closely she could see some familiar plants, ones she wouldn't have expected to find in a normal meadow. Rhubarb was one. Its leaves might have been decimated by Terry's sit-on mower, but the reddish-coloured stalks were still recognisable. As were the clumps of celery. And she was sure she had spotted the delicate fronds of carrot leaves, too.

Making her way to the centre of the meadow, Ceri was delighted with the number of bees and butterflies flitting around, and she vowed that if she was able to rent the field from the church, they would still have a home here. As would the wildflowers that had sprung up in the grass.

Coming to a standstill, Ceri slowly pivoted on the spot, her focus on the direction of the sun and the daily arc it took from rising to setting. Once she had established that, she turned her attention back to the land itself, and studied it again.

It would be a massive job for her to turn the meadow back into cultivated land and one she wasn't sure she could handle on her own – not with having to work as well. It would be years before it would pay its way, but she was determined not to be disheartened. Hard work had never bothered her, she would just have to work twice as hard to make her dream a reality.

At the halfway point, Ceri stopped and scanned the field again, examining it from a different perspective, trying to visualise where she would site a greenhouse, where would be the best place for a tool shed and a potting shed, and how many beds the land could be divided into if she didn't want to replicate the ones that had been there before.

She would like a polytunnel at some point in the future (she would probably have to get planning permission for that), which she needed to factor in, but right now her immediate concern was a standpipe, because without access to water, some things, such as watering plants in a greenhouse, for instance, would get difficult. Eventually water butts would hopefully supply her irrigation needs, but until she was able to collect enough rainwater from downpipes attached to sheds and greenhouses, she would have to rely on mains water.

Maybe she would come across a standpipe further along the hedge, she thought, so she carried on walking, trying to take everything in.

With all those plans and ideas whirling around in her head like so many bees around a hive, Ceri almost missed the little wooden gate set into the hedge. The wood had the kind of smoothness and sheen that was only achieved by the touch of many hands over many years, and was warm and solid. It had been here a while, she guessed, and she admired its craftsmanship. This was what a gate should look like. Once again she was tempted to slip through it, but thought she'd better not. Betsan had given her permission to go into the field, but Ceri wasn't sure whether the land beyond this little gate was also owned by the church, and she didn't want to trespass.

From what she could see, there was an orchard, and an abundant one at that. Apple trees appeared to be the most plentiful, but she could also see a pear tree and a plum, and were those cherries...?

It would be fabulous if the orchard was attached to the former allotment, because growing one from scratch was a commitment of many years. To be able to harvest fruit immediately made her heart sing and—

She was pulled out of her thoughts by an unexpected sound.

Was that music she could hear?

Ceri tilted her head to listen.

A tiled roof and part of the upper storey of a house were visible beyond the orchard, and the sound appeared to be coming from there.

The melody was haunting, the notes swelling and dipping, but she couldn't make out the words.

Ceri breathed deeply, memories of listening to music in this very field in almost the exact same spot, cascading through her, and she closed her eyes and imagined that the man who had kissed her so passionately was by her side.

An abrupt change of tempo and rhythm jerked her out of her reverie as the ethereal melody was replaced by something wilder and harsher.

She recognised it as being the same rock ballad that had been playing the night of the wedding. "Dark Dimension", that was the title, and she sang along under her breath, the lyrics bringing Damon's face to the forefront of her mind.

When the song faded, Ceri blinked hard and gave herself a mental shake.

If she intended to work this field, she needed to forget that man and his kiss, otherwise she would drive herself mad if he popped into her head every time she planted a row of peas or lifted some potatoes out of the ground.

She needed to stop thinking about him and instead concentrate on making her dream come true.

—

'What did you think of the field?' Betsan asked when Ceri knocked on the front door of the vicarage.

'It's perfect,' Ceri said. 'Thank you for letting me take a look. Do you think Terry will let me rent it?'

'Let's ask him, shall we? He's out the back, supposedly preparing the sermon for Sunday, but in reality he's having a nap in his deckchair.'

Sure enough, the vicar's eyes were closed and his head was resting on the back of the chair when Betsan led Ceri through the house and into the garden. A notepad and a pen were on the grass beside him, and as Ceri grew nearer he snored so loudly that he woke himself up.

Frantically he patted at his lap, until he realised the notepad must have fallen to the ground, then grinned sheepishly when he saw his wife.

'It's tiring doing God's work,' he said.

'You ought to try doing a woman's work,' Betsan muttered, but Ceri could tell she was teasing. 'Ceri is here about the field on Willow Tree Lane,' she told him. 'She wants to do something with it. Take a seat, Ceri. Would you like a glass of wine? I was just about to open a bottle of white that's been chilling in the fridge.'

'Yes, please, that would be lovely.'

Ceri waited until Betsan returned with three glasses and the wine, before telling Terry why she was interrupting his Friday evening. 'You know I'm a horticulturist?' she began.

He nodded. 'I do, indeed. I'm looking forward to picking your brains about my lawn.'

'Pick away,' she said. 'If I can help, I will. But in the meantime, I was wondering if the field behind the vicarage is going to be used for anything, and if not, could I rent it from you? By *you*, I mean the Church, of course.'

'It's been unused for years,' he said, 'and as far as I know, there aren't any plans for it. What do you want to do with it?'

'I had been hoping to put my name down for a plot on an allotment, but it seems that Foxmore doesn't have one, but when Betsan mentioned that your field used to be an allotment, I thought it could be the ideal solution – if we could come to some arrangement.' By 'arrangement' Ceri meant not costing her more than she could afford.

Terry scratched his chin. 'Is that what you want to do with it, turn it back into an allotment?'

'Not exactly. I'd like to own a nursery, but it will be years before I'll be able to afford to buy my own land, so I was hoping to start my nursery business there – if the rent's not too high.'

'I see.' Terry took a sip of his wine. 'I'm not sure I can sanction that, not if you intend to use it for business purposes.'

'Oh, right… OK.' Disappointment hit Ceri hard. The field would have been perfect, especially since she had located a standpipe. The tap had been hidden deep in the hedge near the main gate, and she had only spotted it because the edge of an old enamel bath had been peeking out of the undergrowth.

'I tell you what, though,' Terry continued. 'I'd be more than happy for it to become an allotment again. I'm sure people will be queuing up to get their hands on a plot. It's Church land that isn't being used, and considering it was once used for that purpose, I don't think there would be any objection to it being used as an allotment again.' He paused. 'The Church probably isn't even aware that it has fallen into disuse, so turning it back into an allotment would merely be restoring it to its original state. There won't be any rent to pay, either,' he added. 'I want this to be a community space for everyone to use, but it'll have to be run properly,' he warned. 'However, I'll leave that up to you. How does that sound?'

Ceri was still disappointed but at least she would have a plot and it would be directly opposite her cottage, so the location was perfect. 'Thank you so much.'

'Don't thank me yet,' he chuckled. 'It'll take a fair bit of graft.'

'I'm not afraid of hard work,' she said, beaming widely as the thought of having a little piece of land to work on sank in.

'I'll see what I can do to drum up some help. If it's for the village, it's only fair that any villagers who want a plot have a hand in setting it up.'

'That's brilliant,' she said, thinking furiously. 'But can you keep it just between us for the time being? Because I want to work out what needs to be done and in what order, rather than going at it like a bull in a china shop. I would like to mark out the plots first and go from there, if that's OK?'

'Fine by me,' Terry said. 'Just one more thing. As the field stands at present, it's a magnet for bees and butterflies. Can you promise me that you'll keep some part of it for wildlife?'

'You and I are on the same page. I was thinking the exact same thing myself. I would hate to lose all those wonderful pollinators, because they're essential for the health of an allotment and for a good harvest. I'd much prefer to work with nature than against it.'

'Marvellous! You obviously know what you're doing, so I can leave everything up to you.'

'By the way,' she said, as she finished her wine and prepared to take her leave. 'Does the Church own the orchard on the other side of the field, or does that belong to the house at the end of Willow Tree Lane?'

'I'm fairly sure it belongs to Willow Tree House,' he said. 'But I'm not a hundred percent certain.'

'That's OK, I'll pop along there tomorrow and ask.'

'You won't get any joy – the house has been empty for years. It was owned by the same old lady who ran the allotment, but I'm not sure who owns it now. She did have a son, although she hardly ever saw him. She saw more of the grandson when he was a kid, but I haven't clapped eyes on either the son or the grandson since her funeral.'

Ceri's eyes narrowed. 'I don't think it *is* empty,' she said slowly. 'I could have sworn I heard music coming from there when I was in the field earlier.'

'Are you sure?'

She wasn't – it might have been coming from somewhere else entirely – but she was determined to find out. Because if someone was living there, they would hopefully know who owned that gorgeously wild and unloved orchard.

Chapter 6

Fragments of the song he had begun composing earlier that evening were still playing in Damon's head when the phone rang.

'Frank,' Damon said warily, as he carefully placed the guitar back on its stand.

'How are you?' his manager asked.

'Fine.' He wasn't, not quite, but he was getting there. He hoped.

Frank said, 'I've got some brilliant news! "Dark Dimension" is rocketing up the charts and has been since...' He trailed off and Damon pursed his lips. He *had* noticed, but he had been trying to ignore it. "Dark Dimension" was the band's bestselling track, but Damon thought it rather distasteful that the reason it was having a renewed surge in sales was because of Aiden's death.

'Anyway, that's not why I called,' Frank continued hastily. 'I've just got off the phone with Emmett. He was sounding me out about releasing those unfinished tracks.'

'But that's the problem,' Damon pointed out. 'They are *unfinished.*' Emmett, being a key player in the band's record company, should know better. How the hell were they going to finish them without their bass guitarist?

'He believes it won't take a great deal of work to knock them into shape. The basics are there; they'll need a bit of digital work, and you and Luke may have to re-record some bits, but I've been having a listen and they're not half bad. There's enough material for an album.'

Damon wasn't so sure. It felt wrong to even be thinking about releasing material that Aiden had worked on but wasn't alive to finish.

'We should strike while the iron's hot,' Frank carried on. 'With "Dark Dimension" getting so much attention, a new album will fly. And think about the royalties.'

'I don't care about the royalties.' For Damon, it had never been about the money.

'Aiden's family might,' Frank pointed out quietly.

Damon's jaw tensed. That was underhand, and he was about to tell Frank where to go, when he had second thoughts. Maybe Aiden's parents *would* like to see Aiden's final album finished, and he had no idea about their financial situation. Aiden had lived fast and furious, and hadn't been one for salting any money away for a rainy day, so maybe the additional royalties would help ease any financial burdens they might have.

'When?' Damon asked.

'The sooner the better.'

'Have you spoken to Luke?'

'Yeah. He's cool with it.'

'Is he back in the UK?'

'Not yet.'

'When is he planning on returning?'

'A couple of weeks,' Frank replied.

'Let me know when he does.' And with that, Damon abruptly ended the call.

He had to, because he couldn't breathe. Once again he was at the mercy of his hammering heart as the scream of tortured metal filled his head, and he sank to the floor.

When it was finally over after several long, long minutes, the episode left him shaken and wracked with guilt. Would the memory of that night ever leave him in peace? And if it didn't, what if it happened on stage?

Damon sighed wearily. *On stage...?* How could Black Hyacinth perform again when one of the band was missing?

Who would they find to replace him? The thought of actively seeking a third band member made him feel sick. It would have to be done at some point, but not yet. He simply couldn't face it. Putting his worries to one side, Damon reached for his guitar once more, fluttering his fingers across the strings. As he so often did, he played without conscious thought, the music flowing through him of its own accord. He was happy to allow his mind to drift, not consciously thinking about what he was playing, the music a mix of songs he had grown up with and ones he had composed, until he realised the chords that he was strumming were becoming overlain by a distinctive chorus, one he was playing over and over. It was lyrical and haunting, and bit by bit he built up the notes around it. As he played, the lyrics floated into his mind shimmering and ethereal until they solidified, melting into the music as though they were meant to be.

This is what he loved. *This!* The creation of something that was unique, yet was also a melding and a weaving of everything that had gone before.

It might be raw and unpolished, but it was good: he could feel it in his bones.

Hurriedly, he found a pencil and a blank sheet of music paper and hastily scribbled down the notes, printing the words underneath, terrified he would forget. Then he plugged the audio interface into his computer, connected a microphone and speakers and began to play.

Again and again, he sang and strummed, his fingers aching as he played and listened, tweaked and played again, repeating the process over and over until he was as happy as he could be, until his head ached from concentrating so hard and his limbs grew stiff.

Resisting the urge to play the song one more time – because he knew that if he did, he wouldn't be able to resist tweaking some more – Damon finally called it a day.

Elated, yet exhausted, he realised he was starving. Thirsty, too.

Opening a brown stubby bottle of beer, he gulped it down as he broke some eggs to make an omelette. His mind still full of the music he had just made, he didn't bother with the niceties of plates and garnishes, instead eating directly from the pan, wolfing his meal and washing it down with another beer.

Finally replete, he took his drink into the garden to watch the bats swoop and dive. But he soon discovered that he was too restless to settle. And when he remembered the hyacinths growing near the kitchen door, he knew what he needed to do.

–

Damon grabbed a trowel from the shed and set about digging up some flowers to replant next to his grand-mother's headstone.

The black hyacinths that he had found growing in the border by the back door was what he was after, but he took care to leave a few behind. It was fitting that they still grew in the garden she had loved so much.

Careful not to disturb the roots unduly, Damon lifted several plants and placed them in a plastic bag, then he grabbed a bottle of water and set off down the lane.

As he sauntered towards the graveyard, he heard the sharp 'twit' of a male owl, followed a few seconds later by the more melodious 'whoo' of the female bird, and somewhere down by the river a fox barked. The night was so quiet that he could hear the water gushing over the rapids, although the sound was faint and was only carried to his ears when the breeze was blowing in the right direction.

As he passed the main gate to the field, he glanced beyond it, his gaze drifting to where he had lain in the grass with Ceri, and he wondered what she might be doing now. Whatever it was, she had probably forgotten all about the stolen kiss they had shared. He sent a silent 'thank you' to her, nevertheless, because she had been the inspiration behind the two new songs he had just composed.

Late evening was the perfect time to visit Gran's grave. The encroaching night and the peace of the churchyard made him feel more connected to her. Also, there were fewer people around to witness him slipping through the lychgate, and no one at all in the graveyard. Only a daft idiot like him would want to hang around headstones after dark.

Damon made his way towards a far corner, stepping around snaggle-toothed headstones and careful not to walk over the graves they marked. He had no idea how old this church was, but he suspected it had been here for at least five hundred years, if not longer.

When he was a boy, he used to attend the Sunday service with his gran and whilst she chatted to friends and neighbours afterwards, he would explore the graveyard, tracing his fingers across the writing on the weathered stones, and try to imagine the lives that those people had lived.

Some of the graves dated back three hundred years, and some were older still, the names and the dates eaten away by rain and time. His gran was one of the last people to be laid to rest here, and when he reached her grave he sank to his knees.

The grass was warm and fragrant, dotted with poppies and cornflowers growing wild inside the churchyard walls. He could hear the rustle of a small mammal, possibly a mouse, and a hedgehog snuffled its way between the graves, ignoring him completely.

Sounds of human activity could still be heard, but they were faint, even though The Jolly Fox was only a few hundred yards away, and the rumble of an occasional vehicle passing along the main road through the village was also muted.

'Hi, Gran, it's me, Damon,' he began. 'I've brought your favourite, black hyacinths. I found them growing by the back door. Remember when you used to have pots of them on the kitchen table? Goodness knows why you loved them so much, but I'm glad you did.'

He had told her during a recent visit that the band had been named after both her and the flowers. He hoped she would have approved. It was such a pity she hadn't lived long enough to see his dream become a reality.

'I'm sorry it's taken so long, but I've finally made a start on your garden.' He uttered a soft laugh as he dug out a plug of turf ready to receive the plant. 'I'd forgotten how much hard work gardening is. Yeah, yeah,' he chuckled as though she had spoken, 'I know I've gotten soft.'

Even though he took care of himself physically and was a regular at the private gym located in the basement of his flat block, gardening used an entirely different set of muscles, and didn't he know it. He ached in places he hadn't ached before.

'I'm sorry I let it get in such a state,' he said, dropping a hyacinth in the small hole and firming it in.

After he had planted the rest and had given them a drink from the bottle of water, he crumpled the empty bag into his pocket, then leaned his shoulder on the headstone and rested his cheek against it. The marble was smooth, hard and unyielding, and he would have given anything to feel his grandmother's arms around him once more. She had been more of a mother to him than his own had ever been, and it was to Gran that he had turned whenever he needed comfort or advice.

He could sorely do with both right now.

Closing his eyes, he let the peace creep into his soul. He could see her now, leaning on a spade, her silvery hair in a bun, wearing baggy jeans and green wellies, and he wondered what advice she would give him. Huffing softly, he didn't need to wonder – he *knew*. She would tell him that he couldn't hide away in Foxmore forever like a modern-day hermit, that he needed to get his act together and—

What was that?

His eyes shot open, and he sat up, scanning the graveyard.

A shadow moved along the side of the church and he froze. How long had they been there? Had they heard him talking to himself?

It grew closer, and as it did so the streetlights from the road beyond brought it into focus.

83

It was a woman… one he recognised.

Ceri!

—

A figure was crouching beside one of the headstones and Ceri's stomach clenched in fear. Who was it, and what were they doing there?

Mind you, she thought, they might be asking the same questions about her.

The man (she was sure it was a man, despite the figure being little more than a shadow) didn't move, and she was tempted to turn on her heel and hurry off, but something made her take another step closer. And another.

Then the man moved, and she saw the pale disc of his face as he scrambled to his feet.

Her tummy clenched again, but this time it wasn't fear that caused it: it was recognition.

Ceri felt a sudden urge to sit down as her pulse leapt and a spike of desire caught her unawares. 'Damon?' Her voice was barely above a whisper, but he heard.

'Yesss…' He drew out the sound, the sibilance sending a shiver down her back and raising the tiny hairs on her arms.

What was he doing in a graveyard? And why at night? She might have imagined it, but she could have sworn he looked furtive when he saw her, and she wondered what he had been up to.

Ceri had to ask. 'What are you doing here?'

'I like graveyards.' He took a step away from the head-stone.

OK, now that was weird. 'Do you live nearby?' she asked.

'Not far.'

'I thought you lived in London.' He had definitely given her that impression.

He shrugged. 'I thought you lived in Cardiff.'

It was her turn to shrug.

'What are *you* doing here?' he countered, jerking his chin to indicate the graveyard.

'I was looking for sweet rocket.'

'In the dark?'

'The fragrance is more pronounced at night,' she explained, mildly surprised that he didn't ask her what sweet rocket was. She moved closer until she was standing next to the headstone he had been slowly inching away from. 'I want to dig some up to put in my garden.'

'Ah.'

Was that a judgemental 'ah'? 'I'll make sure not to take too much,' she assured him. 'But it does spread easily, so digging a bit up shouldn't affect it.'

'Good.' He backed away another step. 'I'll… er… leave you to it.'

'Oh, OK.' Should she say that it was nice seeing him again? Or that she would see him around?

But as she hunted for a witty retort, he turned and strode off. Then she heard the clang of the lychgate, and he was gone.

Ceri let out a slow breath. That had been awkward. She had gone from being wary of a strange figure lurking amongst the graves, to feeling an unexpected bolt of desire, and finally to wondering what she had done wrong.

Damon hadn't seemed at all pleased to see her, and she guessed she must have meant nothing to him but a quick snog with a total stranger; one who he had assumed he would never see again.

Ceri was about to resume her task of hunting down a clump of sweet rocket, when she remembered his strange behaviour. He had been sitting or crouching on a grave, and when she looked down, she noticed that he had left an empty water bottle next to it.

Shaking her head in annoyance (she hated litterbugs), she popped it into her basket. She would take it home with her and put it in the recycling bin. She had a good mind to go after him and tell him to dispose of his own litter, but her attention was caught by a cluster of plants at the base of the headstone.

They didn't look particularly well established, and the ground around them had been recently disturbed. It also looked damp.

Ceri bent down and touched the exposed soil. It had recently been watered. And those plants had not long been put in the ground, so she shone the flashlight on them.

Hyacinths, dark purple or black, by the look of them, although it was difficult to make out their exact shade. The colour was unusual for a graveside flower, but maybe it held special meaning for the person who had planted it, or for the person whose grave this was. She might be wrong, but she suspected Damon had just planted them himself.

Shining the light on the headstone, Ceri read the name of the person buried there, and realised the choice of flower made sense.

Here lies Hyacinth Rogers, aged eighty-six, sowing seeds in God's own garden.

Chapter 7

Although she lamented that the field on Willow Tree Lane wouldn't be hers to do with as she wished, Ceri was nevertheless grateful to Terry and eager to get started. Her original dream of owning a nursery would have to go on the backburner; right now, she had an allotment to create, a space where people could grow their own fruit, vegetables and flowers, a place where the villagers could swap produce, share tips and work together.

She even had a fledgling idea that any surplus could be sold through Sero. Rowena was forever complaining about the lack of a greengrocer in Foxmore, and where better to sell fresh local produce than the zero waste shop in the heart of the village? Ceri knew that even a small plot would provide more food than she could use herself, even if she did freeze, preserve or pickle as much of it as she could.

But she was getting ahead of herself. The ground had to be broken first, and the soil prepared. The infrastructure – such as sheds, water butts and compost heaps – should also ideally be in situ, before any serious planting took place. However, those things would be down to the individual plot owners, and the sooner she got started, the sooner she could plant something. Just a small patch of cleared ground could produce a surprising amount of food, even if the growing season was already well underway.

First though, she wanted to nip along to the house at the end of Willow Tree Lane to enquire about the orchard. It would be such a shame for all that lovely fruit to go to waste if it was, in fact, part of the old allotment.

With that in mind, Ceri hastily completed her Saturday morning chores, and when the last load of washing had been pegged on the line, she shoved her feet into her trainers and set off.

June was in full bloom and the hedgerows bordering the lane were alive with birds. Chattering, darting sparrows flitted from branch to branch in search of food, and at the top of a tall silver birch a blackbird perched, singing for all he was worth. Ceri stopped to listen for a moment, until the bird realised he was being watched and fell silent, eyeing her beadily. As soon as she moved away, he resumed his singing, and was joined by the distant call of a cuckoo and the nearby jackhammering of a woodpecker. She would have liked to have tried to spot them, but both birds could be elusive and she wanted to get on.

Having never ventured this far down Willow Tree Lane before, Ceri was curious about the house at the end of it, and as she drew closer she saw that it was a quite substantial property, old and rather beautiful. Set back off the lane in its own grounds, it was two storeys high – three, with those little windows in the eves – with a large open porch and an impressive front door.

The gravelled area at the front had space enough for several cars and was rather overgrown, the trees and bushes to either side unkempt and unruly. They could do with some attention, she thought, and she saw with dismay that bindweed was growing rampant, climbing up the tree trunks and clambering over the bushes. The owner would need to do something about that before it choked the life out of everything. And so many weeds were poking through the gravel that she didn't think the drive had seen any car action for a while.

In fact, there wasn't a vehicle in sight, which made her wonder if the house was empty, as Terry believed. Ceri could see why he thought that, despite her conviction that she had heard music coming from it. It looked unloved and appeared to be deserted, yet she had a sense it wasn't abandoned – the windows were clean, for one thing, and the porch was devoid of the dead leaves she would have expected to see if no one had stepped over the threshold for a while.

Hoping someone was home, she marched up to the front door and pressed the old-fashioned brass doorbell. From deep inside the house, she heard a jangle. It sounded like a proper bell, not a buzzer, and her eyes widened. How very Victorian upper class-ish.

After waiting several seconds without any response, she rang it again.

Still nothing, and she was about to walk away, beginning to think that Terry was right, when she heard a key turn in the lock. Hastily, she stepped back, not wanting to crowd whoever came to the door, and smiled broadly, hoping she would get the answer she wanted.

'Hi,' she began as the door swung open, then she stopped abruptly and her heart lurched. 'You!' she cried. The last person she had expected to see was *Damon*.

He appeared just as surprised to see her – surprised *and* annoyed. The scowl was a giveaway.

'What do you want?' His tone was equally as unwelcoming as his expression.

'I… er… just wanted to know—' she began.

'Are you stalking me?' he interrupted.

'What? *No!* I'd never— I didn't— I was told the house was empty.'

'So why are you here, if you thought it was empty?' He clearly didn't believe her.

Oh my God, did he think she was *casing it out*? That she was planning on breaking in, or something?

Ceri drew herself up and pressed her lips together before she answered. 'I heard music yesterday and—'

'Does that give you the right to knock on my door?'

'Actually, I rang the bell. I didn't knock.'

He stared at her.

Ceri stared back. Was this surly git the same man who she had lain next to under the stars? The same man who had kissed her so passionately? Or was this man his nasty twin?

Feeling uncomfortable under his stony gaze, Ceri broke the silence. 'Sorry to have bothered you.' She began to walk away, anger bubbling, but couldn't resist saying over her shoulder, 'By the way, you should sort that bindweed out before it's too late.'

'Excuse me?' His voice was cold enough to make a tender annual wilt.

'Bindweed.' She turned around, but kept walking, taking small backward steps. 'You've got a problem.' She pointed to a particularly vigorous patch of bright green foliage dotted with white trumpet-shaped flowers.

He followed her finger, his eyes narrowing, before returning his attention to her. 'What's it to you?'

'I wouldn't care, except it grows like billy-oh and spreads like wildfire. Once established it's a bugger to get rid of and I don't want any germinating in my garden, if it's all the same to you.'

'I know what bindweed is.' The icy tone hadn't thawed.

'Then you also know you should get rid of it,' she retorted sharply.

'Are you some kind of plant police?'

'No, I'm some kind of horticulturist.'

His scowl lifted. 'Is that why you are here, about the bindweed?'

Ceri stopped walking backwards. 'I'm here about the orchard, actually.'

'The orchard?' He moved onto the open porch and into the daylight, and Ceri noticed how grubby his T-shirt and jeans were.

He had either been gardening in them or rolling around in the grass; she recognised the green marks on the knees of his jeans. She should do, she'd collected enough grass stains of her own over the years.

'Do you know who it belongs to?' she asked.

'Yes. Me.'

That took the wind out of her sails. For some reason, even though he had answered the door and was acting like he owned the place, she hadn't really believed he did. The house was too... vintage? A better word than old-fashioned. This house and the garden (what she had seen of it) looked like a throwback to the 1930s and she fully expected a pinafored maid with her hair tied up in a scarf and a feather duster in her hand to appear at any second.

'Why?' he asked, as she gathered her wits.

She said, 'I was in the field yesterday and I spotted it through the gate. It's a bit overgrown.'

'So?'

'It's just a shame, that's all.' Ceri wasn't getting anywhere fast, and despite the attraction she felt for him, Damon was seriously irritating. He clearly didn't give two hoots about the orchard, so why should she? It was none of her business and not her problem. It would have been nice if it could have been incorporated into the allotment, but… She shrugged. People could always plant their own apple and pear trees, and some varieties grew fast enough to produce a decent crop in their third or fourth year.

'It is,' he agreed as she was about to walk away again. 'But I've got enough on my plate with the garden. The orchard will have to wait.'

She glanced around the drive. He was right – if he didn't want to risk the postman getting flattened by a falling tree or an unsafe branch, he *should* see to this first. He would need to employ the services of a tree surgeon to check that the larger trees were safe, though. It would also take a fair bit of digging to remove all the bindweed roots, but the rest was cosmetic. Boiling water on the weeds sprouting up through the gravel would sort them out (kinder to wildlife than weedkiller and less backbreaking than digging them out) and the bushes could easily be trimmed into shape. There would probably be room for a few perennials or bedding plants to liven it up and bring colour to the borders once all that was done.

'It won't take long to set it straight,' she said.

'I'm talking about the garden to the rear of the house,' he retorted. 'And yes, it will.' His face fell and he looked so defeated her heart went out to him.

When she found herself saying something she knew she would regret, she wished she wasn't such a soft touch.

'Would you like me to take a look? Gardening *is* my thing, after all.' An expression she could only describe as suspicion flirted across his face, and she swiftly added, 'You don't have to. It was only a suggestion.'

He wasn't going to take her up on her offer, she realised, and thank goodness for that. She had more than enough to be going on with, and she wanted to go home and begin planning out the allotment.

But he surprised her. 'I would like that, please. If it's not too much trouble.'

And suddenly she was very curious indeed to take a look at his garden. She would defy any serious gardener not to be.

Expecting to be led around the side of the house and through a wooden gate that was taller than her and in dire need of a coat of wood preserver, she was delighted when he gestured for her to go inside the house.

Oh, my, she was going to see the interior of this stately old building and she couldn't wait!

Trying not to let her interest seem too obvious, she stepped over the threshold and into a spacious hall. To her right was a door through which she could see a sofa and a wing-back chair. A guitar, propped on a stand seemed incongruous and at odds with the old-fashioned décor, but before she could get a proper look, she had to scuttle to catch up with Damon who was striding past an ornate staircase and through another door. This, she saw, led to the kitchen and she had no sooner entered it, catching a quick flash of pine cupboards and a wooden table, than he was opening another door which led outside.

Abruptly all thoughts of the house were swept away as she caught sight of the garden, and she sucked in a quick breath to let it out slowly in a low whistle.

She could tell that it had once been loved and tended to with great care, but right now it was more akin to a jungle than a garden. It had once been – and still was – a typical cottage garden, with a mix of small trees, shrubs, perennials and annuals, and flowers bloomed everywhere, jewel colours sparkling amongst the abundance of greenery.

There were pink, red, white, and yellow roses with their fragrant blooms giving the garden a romantic and nostalgic feel. Peonies were another cottage garden staple, and their tall showy blooms in shades of pink, white, and red grew in swathes throughout the overcrowded borders.

She could also see foxgloves, their pink, purple and (slightly less common) white spiky flowers adding height and texture to the planting. Their nectar-rich flowers were covered in bees and other pollinators, which were also buzzing and fluttering around the lavender, poppies, sweet peas and hollyhocks that spilled across the path, their scent filling the air with sweet perfume. All in all, the garden – what she could see of it – was a riotous, glorious mass of colour, and wonderfully whimsical and romantic. It was beautiful, wild and enchanting, and although she could appreciate the charm of it in its natural state, she knew how much more wonderful it would look if it was re-tamed.

After the first impression had sunk in, Ceri did another sweep, this time concentrating on the details. Beneath her feet, a crazy paved path, weed-infested and with moss growing between the cracks, disappeared around a corner and she wondered where it led.

Immediately beside the back door was a flower bed, and she could tell that someone had worked on it recently because it looked considerably neater than anything else in the garden. She also recognised the hyacinths growing in it as being the same variety as the ones that had been planted on Hyacinth Rogers's grave last night, confirming her suspicions that it was Damon who had put them there.

There were so many things vying for her attention that she didn't know where to look – a wooden archway with climbing roses tumbling all over it; a glimpse of a bench that would be a gorgeous place to sit if only you could get to it. A wheelbarrow sat a few feet away, filled with leaves, twigs and branches, and when she looked closer she could see the raw wounds of those plants who had lost bits of themselves to a wicked-looking pair of shears propped against the wheelbarrow. These poor plants hadn't been trimmed with care, but had been hacked and assaulted, and she guessed Damon was the perpetrator. She didn't blame him, because the easiest way to bring a garden like this back into line was to chop down everything that made getting around it difficult. But there were ways and means of doing it to ensure the plants weren't decimated and would recover well.

'I see you've made a start,' she said, shooting him a quick look.

A spot of colour appeared on his cheek. 'I have, but I don't think I've made a very good job of it. It's just too much, and I have no idea what I'm doing.'

'I can see why; it's a big job,' she commiserated. 'How long is it since the garden was tended to properly?'

He pulled a face. 'Probably not since my grandmother died, eight years ago.'

Ceri scrutinised it again. Eight years was a long time, and if that were true she would have expected it to be far more overgrown than it was.

He must have sensed her doubt, because he said, 'A maintenance company comes in to cut it back once a year.'

'It's going to take a fair bit of work to knock this into shape,' she warned.

'I know.' The tone of his voice implied that he wanted her to tell him something he *didn't* know.

'Will you be doing the work yourself?' She caught him looking at her out of the corner of his eye.

'Yes.' His reply was wary.

'What is your vision for it?'

'I want it to look like it did when my grandmother was alive.'

'Would her name be Hyacinth by any chance?'

His sudden tension and the way his jaw hardened, suggested he wasn't happy with this line of questioning. 'Who told you that?'

'You did, kind of. It was you who put those hyacinths on her grave, wasn't it?'

He hesitated, then reluctantly said, 'Yes.'

OK, she thought, filing the information away. 'You wouldn't happen to have any old photos of the garden, would you?'

He seemed to relax slightly. 'I do actually. I found loads in the potting shed.'

'Excellent! They will give you a vision to work towards. But I would suggest you do a bit at a time. If you try to tackle it all at once, you'll become demoralised. How big is this garden anyway?'

'Too big,' he sighed. 'Do you want to take a look at the rest of it?'

Did she ever! 'If you think it would help,' she replied mildly, resisting the urge to clap her hands in glee. What she wouldn't give to get her mitts on a garden like this!

Once again, she followed him, this time on a meandering path that passed underneath the rose-adorned archway and deeper into the garden. All the while her senses were overwhelmed by the colours of the flowers, the dappled light through the leaves, the scents of the blooms as she brushed past them, the low-level hum of bees and other pollinating insects, and the sounds of birds

– many, many birds. This garden was no sterile uninspiring stretch of lawn with a couple of shrubs to frame it. This was a living, breathing entity, and she felt honoured to be there.

'The trick is not to lose this,' she murmured, as her mind whirled with what needed to be done, what could be done, and what should never be done. The three lists were roughly equal in length.

'Pardon?'

'You should preserve as much of this as possible,' she advised. 'It's beautiful.'

'There's more,' he warned, pushing aside a large hydrangea to reveal what should be the beating heart of the garden but was sorely neglected: the greenhouse. 'And there's a potting shed behind that,' he added, pointing to a magnificent rhododendron. 'And a shed for tools.'

She could just make out the roof of a shed above the glossy dark green leaves. 'That's a great start.'

'There's also a compost heap – three in fact, although they're just piles of soil at the moment.'

'Brilliant! That'll save you from having to buy any. Can I see?'

'Be my guest.'

Ceri inched past, trying not to brush against him on the narrow path, and as she did so his cologne wafted up her nose. It was the same one he had worn the night they'd kissed, and she swallowed hard as the fragrance brought the memory into sharp focus.

Better not think of that right now, she warned, hurrying towards the greenhouse and conscious of his eyes on her as she peered through the glass. It was sad to see pots that had probably once held seedlings, with nothing in them now but dried-up compacted dirt. At this time of year, a greenhouse such as this should be full of plants, but the only things in this one were dust motes and cobwebs. It was lucky she didn't mind spiders.

The potting shed was no better, but it was tidy and had some interesting things in it, such as biscuits tins which Ceri suspected probably held seeds that were long past their sow-by date. She wanted to root through them, but thought she'd better not, so she fought her way to the tool shed instead.

When she opened the door she was met by an impressive array of implements, many of them decades old but still perfectly serviceable. Everything was very neat, and Ceri had an acute case of shed envy – mainly because she didn't have one. Her tiny garden didn't have room for even the smallest of sheds, and most of the tools she had collected over the years were currently safely stored in her parents' garage. A shed would be one of the first things she would need in the allotment, she thought, because without the appropriate tools at hand, she wouldn't make much headway.

The compost heaps, all three of them, were tucked away to the side of the shed, and they were brimming with lovely rich material. She dug her hands into it and breathed deeply as she turned some of it over. To her, it smelled just as wonderful as the most expensive perfume.

But not as wonderful as Damon, she mused, before pushing the thought away in irritation. He might have kissed her once, but he had shown no inclination of wanting to kiss her again, so she should stop thinking of him in that way. It wasn't easy, though – she had never been so attracted to a man in her life. All her previous boyfriends paled into insignificance by comparison.

She had no clue as to why that was. It might be because of the way they had met. A magical evening such as the one they'd shared was bound to leave a lasting impression. But she didn't think that was the sole reason. Damon was charismatic; there was something about him that made her think if he was in a room full of people, everyone's eyes would be drawn towards him.

Dear Lord, was she being fanciful or what? Damon was an average bloke, who probably did an average job. If she ever got to know him better, she would ask him what he did for a living – but she had to admit it would be a bit of a let-down if he was a boring desk-jockey. He didn't live in an average house, though, and his garden was very far from average. It was magnificent! At least she had met him first, before she had seen his garden, because she would seriously have doubted her motives for wanting to get to know him better if it had been the other way around. A garden such as Damon's was almost worth selling her soul for.

Chapter 8

'What's your verdict?' Damon asked when Ceri reluctantly dragged herself away from compost sniffing.

'You've got some good stuff,' she enthused. 'It's very rich and loamy, so you'll probably want to mix it with perlite to aerate it, otherwise it might be a bit dense. And if you're going to use it in any pots around the garden, I suggest adding vermiculite to hold moisture, else you might find yourself having to water your pots twice a day in high summer. Mind you, you might have to do that anyway,' she advised, 'depending on what you plant in them.' She stopped talking when she noticed an amused expression on his face.

'I meant the garden,' he said, 'but thank you for letting me know about the compost heap.'

Ceri felt the slow burn of a blush creeping into her cheeks. 'Sorry, I do tend to get a little carried away when I'm talking about gardening.'

'It's a good job you're a horticulturist,' he replied. 'Have you got any tips for the garden in general?'

'As I said, it's going to be a big task and one that would probably benefit from being broken up into bite-sized pieces. My first recommendation would be to make sure that the greenhouse, the potting shed and the tool shed are easily accessible; it's the wrong time of year to cut back the rhododendron and the hydrangea, but needs must. After that, I suggest you tidy up your paths, again to make it easier to get around the garden. The last thing you want to be doing is trying to ram a wheelbarrow through an overgrown bush.' She could see that he'd had a go at cutting back some of the shrubs. 'Butchered' was the word that came to mind.

'I've already found that out,' he said ruefully.

She gazed at him earnestly, whilst trying not to lose herself in the depths of those dark eyes. 'If you can afford it, my advice would be to bring in an experienced gardener.'

Those dark eyes turned flinty. 'Such as yourself?'

Ceri flinched at the accusation and her own eyes hardened. 'I'm not touting for business, if that's what you're thinking. I've already got a job, thank you.' In fact, she really should be sorting out her lesson plans for next week, not taking on more work. If she was honest, she was daft to even be considering restoring the allotment, because of the amount of work it would entail. She would be better off pouring her time and energy into settling into her new job. The last thing she wanted was to make a hash of it and for the college to sack her.

The thought of going to work on Monday made her stomach churn. Things hadn't got any easier in that respect over the course of the week, and she still wasn't convinced this job was right for her. But she needed the money and it paid a darned sight better than working in a garden centre.

Damon had the grace to look contrite. 'Sorry, it was wrong of me to assume.'

'Yes, it was.'

'Sorry,' he repeated. 'Would you like to have a look at the orchard?'

'Only if you want to show it to me.' She wasn't going to let him off that easily, even though she dearly wanted to see it.

As he ushered her back along the path, she noticed that he hadn't responded to her suggestion of employing a gardener. It would cost a pretty penny to restore this garden to its former glory and would take many weeks, if not months. It wouldn't be cheap, although it would be time-effective. But maybe he didn't have the funds, or perhaps he wanted to work on it himself? That would be Ceri's preferred option, if this garden belonged to her.

They were almost back at the house when Damon cut off to the right, following the little winding path she had noticed earlier, and she smiled as she realised her wish of wondering where it led would be granted.

This side of the garden bordered Willow Tree Field, she guessed, getting her bearings, and when she saw the little wooden gate set into the hedge and her allotment beyond it, she knew she was right. A shiver of desire travelled down her back as she realised Damon must have walked through it the night he had seen her dancing in the field.

Ceri swiftly stamped down on her libido, and tried to focus her attention on the first of the apple trees as it came into view.

It was a lovely old specimen, its thick gnarled trunk leading to spreading branches laden with small unripe fruit, and was in dire need of a good prune to open it up to the air. But even as part of her registered what needed to be done, most of her attention was on Damon.

He was gazing around the orchard as though he hadn't seen it before, and she wondered how long it was since he was here last. It was badly overgrown, with brambles clawing their way between the trees, and rosebay willowherb – a perennial self-seeding weed – growing abundantly. It seemed to be very happy here. But at least there was no sign of the bindweed she had seen at the front of the house, so that was one less thing for him to worry about.

'It's lovely,' she said.

'It's full of brambles. Oh, buggeration.'

'Buggeration?' Ceri bit her lip. 'Is that a technical term?'

'It was one of my grandmother's favourite swear words.'

She laughed. 'I think I'll adopt that for myself.' Then she became more serious. 'I agree the brambles are a problem, but if I were you I'd leave them for now. Look at all the flowers. You'll have a bumper crop of blackberries in a couple of months. Think of all the delicious things you could make with it.'

'The only thing I can think of is apple and blackberry tart.'

'Nice… but what about blackberry sorbet, blackberry ice cream, smoothies, muffins, crumble? You could add them to pavlovas, pancakes, cheesecakes…' She trailed off when she saw his expression. 'Or maybe not.' She thought some more. 'You could always sell them. I bet Sero would take them off your hands.'

His jaw clenched, and she guessed the idea didn't appeal to him. 'I might pick a punnet or two,' he conceded, but Ceri got the impression he was just saying that to shut her up. 'You're welcome to help yourself,' he added. 'And to the apples and pears. I believe there is a plum tree or two, and a cherry. There may even be a quince, if it hasn't died.'

'That's very kind of you. I might take you up on your offer.'

'Please do. I'd hate for all this fruit to go to waste.'

But not enough to pick it yourself, she thought, and her eyes dropped to his hands.

They were well-manicured with long fingers – what some might call a pianist's hands – and she imagined them cut and scratched after an encounter with a bramble, and decided he was probably wise. Brambles were vicious enough for Ceri to wonder if they were being deliberately spiteful. She'd had her fair share of shredded hands (arms and legs, too) and she would hate to think of his in such a state.

But it wasn't the state of his hands that flashed into her mind, it was what he might do with them, how he might caress her with them, how they might feel on her skin and— She pulled herself up. Best not to think of that, right now. Actually, it would be a good idea not to think about that at all. Nothing was going to happen, so there was little point in tormenting herself with such fanciful notions.

Ceri worried at her bottom lip as the silence stretched between them. Her awareness of him was so acute that every nerve ending fizzed, sending bolts of desire through her.

She should leave before she did or said something silly.

'Let me know if you need any advice,' she said. 'I live in Church Lane – Rosehip Cottage. Thanks for showing me the garden. It's lovely.'

'Thanks for taking a look. I appreciate it.'

Did he really? She narrowed her eyes at him.

'Honestly, I do appreciate it. And sorry for the...' He pulled a face.

'No problem.' She hovered for a moment. 'Is it OK to leave through the gate just there?' She pointed at the wooden gate leading to Willow Tree Field.

'Of course. I don't keep it locked,' he said, but a flicker in his eyes gave her the impression that he thought he should.

Maybe his offer to help herself to fruit had been made out of politeness and not because he meant it?

'Right, I'll, er, see you around,' she said. 'Good luck with the garden.' And with that, she dashed off, hurrying through the gate and across the field as fast as she could without actually breaking into a run.

She'd had enough of Damon for one day – her libido needed time to calm down!

–

Damon followed Ceri's progress as she skipped across the field, conflicting emotions tumbling through his mind. When he had first seen her on his doorstep, he had felt a flash of such acute pleasure that it had taken his breath away, swiftly followed by the suspicion that she knew who he was and had flushed him out. God, he had even been crass enough to accuse her of stalking him, and he cringed, remembering the look on her face. He cringed again when he recalled that he had then gone on to accuse her of trying to sell him her gardening services.

How to make a total prat of yourself 101. What must she think of him? That he was a weirdo, probably. First, he kisses her under the stars, then she discovers him lurking in a graveyard, and when she rings his doorbell to enquire about the orchard, he insults her, then invites her to look around his garden, before offering her all the fruit she can pick.

Could he have been any more strange? No wonder she'd made a run for it. And he was none the wiser as to why she wanted to know who the orchard belonged to. He would ask her next time he saw her – if there *was* a next time. He wouldn't blame her if she went out of her way to avoid him. Damon could picture her now, telling her friends all about the weird man who lived in Willow Tree House...

The one consolation was that at least his cover wasn't blown. She'd clearly not recognised him, even though this time she had seen him in daylight, and he hoped it would stay that way. Apart from Ceri, it had been a long time since he'd had any meaningful interaction with someone who didn't know who he was or what he did for a living. Black Hyacinth had a while to go before it reached the success of bands such as Thin Lizzy or Alter Bridge, but it was up there with the likes of Elbow or Wolf Alice, and the band had even played on the Pyramid Stage at Glastonbury, so they were getting there.

Had been getting there.

Damon had tried not to let the band's snowballing fame go to his head, but it had been hard not to be affected when everyone wanted a piece of you. At the risk of sounding conceited, it was a refreshing change to be thought of as a regular Joe Bloggs. Although, after his less-than-stellar performance just now, Ceri couldn't be blamed if she thought him a very surly and rather odd Mr Bloggs. And... he was back to watching her run away across the field, whilst she tried to pretend that she wasn't running at all.

Damon didn't make a move until she had clambered over the metal gate at the far end and disappeared from sight, painfully aware that she hadn't given him as much as a backward glance.

Dazed, feeling as though he'd just had an encounter with a force of nature, Damon dragged his attention back to the garden: the overgrown, bursting-with-life garden that seemed strangely empty without her. She had filled his senses so completely whilst she had been in it, that everything had faded into the background. There was a song in that, he thought, smiling ruefully – oh, yeah, some guy by the name of Denver had already sung it.

Humming the tune to himself, and occasionally breaking out into a smattering of lyrics, Damon decided to heed Ceri's advice and get to work on the rhododendron. After all, she was the expert.

A couple of hours later, he stepped back to admire his handiwork, and saw that the poor rhododendron looked as though it had been attacked by a madman with a machete. Actually, he had used a pair of still-sharp pruning shears and a saw, and now the bush (it had been more like a small tree) was looking decidedly sorry for itself, as well as being a third its original size.

Piles of sawn branches lay strewn around him, and as he clambered and picked his way over them to put his tools away, he realised he had made the problem of accessing the tool and potting sheds worse, not better. Hopefully that was only temporary until he cleared the path of the discarded vegetation.

This was where a shredder would come in handy, he mused, because he had no intention of breaking this lot up into small enough sections by hand to put on the compost heap. He would take a look online later and order one. It would come in handy for the rest of the garden, too.

Hoping the bush would recover – he didn't *think* he had killed it – Damon unscrewed the cap on a bottle of water and drank thirstily. When he wiped his mouth with the back of his hand and saw the dirt streaked across his knuckles, he sniggered – a rock-and-roll lifestyle this most definitely wasn't. If Frank could see him now, he would be horrified.

Luckily for Frank, the man had no idea that Damon had blisters on his hands and a mind full of shredders.

He blew out his cheeks as it occurred to him that if he did buy a shredder, he wouldn't have anywhere to dispose of the resultant chips of bark and wood. He had taken a look at the compost that Ceri had delved her fingers into and realised it would be criminal to dump fresh stuff on top. The compost in the three bins was ready to be used, but it was unlikely that he would pot anything and it needed using now, to free up the bins. Maybe he could move it and store it somewhere? Or maybe a certain horticulturist would like it...?

It wouldn't hurt to ask, and Ceri might be grateful. Or she might think him even stranger than she did already. Then again, wasn't that what most gardeners did – trade seeds, borrow tools, swap tips? He remembered seeing his gran in the field on the other side of the garden, when it used to be an allotment, leaning on her shovel, discussing the pros and cons of different varieties of brassicas. She had always been quick to offer advice or lend a hand. Just like Ceri.

Ceri reminded him of his gran in some respects – feisty, forthright, passionate about gardening – and he had a feeling the pair of them would have got on like a house on fire. Yeah, Gran would definitely have liked Ceri.

He liked her too...

Ceri practically danced along the pavement as she headed to Huw and Rowena's house. They were back from their honeymoon and had invited her for dinner this evening. She felt honoured to be the newlywed's first guest, and she also couldn't wait to see her brother. She had missed him, and wanted to hear all about their honeymoon. Ceri had her own news to share, too, and after her first week at work she was eager to kick back and relax with good food, good wine (she had bought a couple of bottles of decent plonk to take with her) and good company.

She was walking past the vicarage when she heard her name being called.

'I'm glad I caught you,' the vicar said. 'I wanted to let you know that I've put out a few feelers about the allotment, and I'm delighted to say that the response has been very positive. Everyone I've spoken to thinks it's a great idea, and many people have fond memories of working there. I didn't mention where it would be or who will be running it, but now I know the village is in favour, I can put the word out. I'm sure loads of people will be keen to put their names down for a plot.'

'Thanks, Terry, that's wonderful news. Do you mind delaying the announcement for a couple of weeks? I've been working on the layout – which will be very much the way it was originally – but I thought it might be a good exercise for my students to see the field in the raw, so to speak, and give them an assignment to design an allotment from scratch. It will be a good learning experience for them.'

'That's a terrific idea!' Terry exclaimed. 'I don't suppose a couple of weeks will make any difference. I have a favour to ask, too. Could I have one final mow?'

Ceri laughed. 'Betsan told me all about your sit-on mower. I'd be cross if you didn't. I was counting on you to cut the grass down to size, as it will make it easier to stake out the plots. As soon as that's done, the tenants can begin work on them. I can't wait to see it bursting with all that lovely veg.'

'Did you manage to find out who the orchard belongs to? I reckon it's part of Willow Tree House.'

'You're right,' she confirmed. 'I spoke to the owner myself.'

'So there *is* someone living there! Who is it, do you know? Did you get a name? Actually, I think I can guess. I bet any money that it's a relative of Hyacinth Rogers. Someone has been leaving flowers on her grave. I wonder if it's the son or the grandson?' The vicar gazed at her hopefully.

'It's her grandson.'

'Well, well, Damon has returned, eh? He used to spend all his school holidays with Hyacinth when he was a boy, but I suppose he grew too old to want to visit his grandma every five minutes. It will be nice for the old house to be lived in again. I don't like seeing it empty.'

After she said goodbye to the vicar, Ceri's thoughts continued to linger on the owner of Willow Tree House, and she had to give herself a mental shake to dispel his image from her mind when she reached her brother's house.

'Look at you!' she exclaimed, as Huw opened the door. She didn't think she had ever seen her brother looking so happy and relaxed. Married life suited him. He held his arms wide to give her a hug, and she clung to him.

'I missed you,' she said, inhaling his familiar scent. They might fight like cat and dog on occasion, but he was her brother and she loved him.

'I didn't miss you,' he retorted, with a laugh.

'I'd be worried if you had. I take it you had a good time?'

'The best!'

Rowena appeared in the hall, a huge smile on her face. She, too, was looking happy, and the light tan she had acquired from the Caribbean sun added to her glow. Love radiated from Huw when he smiled at his new wife, and Rowena basked in it. And, for her part, Rowena looked besotted with her man.

A pang of envy took Ceri by surprise when she realised she wanted what they had.

'Here, open one of these,' Ceri instructed, thrusting the bottles into Huw's hands.

She needed something to dilute their palpable bliss before it threatened to overwhelm her. Unbidden, Damon's face flitted across her inner eye, and she realised she would give anything to be in their shoes.

'Go on, tell me all about it,' she ordered, once the wine had been poured and she'd taken a seat at the table. A rich aroma of onions and tomatoes filled the kitchen, and her tummy rumbled. Lunch had been at least six hours ago, and her hastily eaten sandwich hadn't done a particularly good job of filling her up.

'Aunty Ceri?' a little voice called from upstairs.

'You'd better go and kiss Nia goodnight,' Rowena suggested. 'She'll refuse to go to sleep until you do.'

Ceri didn't need telling twice. She had been hoping Huw's new stepdaughter would still be awake.

As Ceri perched on the little girl's bed, Nia snuggled into her. 'Did you miss your mum and Huw?'

'Yes. I had to stay with Nanny and Grandad. They said honeymoons aren't for children, but Mammy said she'll take me to Cornwall in the summer holidays, if I'm good.'

'I'm sure you will be – you're always good. I bet you were spoilt rotten when you were with Nanny.'

Nia's expression became sly. 'I'm not supposed to tell anyone.'

'About how much you were spoilt?'

'Uh-huh.' Nia nodded. 'I got to stay up late and I had lots of sweets. Mammy doesn't let me have sweets.'

'Mammies aren't supposed to. It's against the law. But it's OK for nannies to give sweets,' Ceri told her, inhaling the scent of apple shampoo and freshly bathed child. God, she could eat her all up!

'I cried when Mammy came home,' Nia said, her bottom lip sticking out. 'I missed her this much!' She held her arms out as wide as they would go. 'I missed Huw, too. I don't want them to go on honeymoon again.'

Ceri bit her lip. 'I don't think they'll have another honeymoon,' she said, trying not to laugh.

'Will you have one?'

'I've got to get married first.'

'Can I be your bridesmaid? I liked being a bridesmaid.'

'That might be a long time yet.'

'Why?'

'I haven't found anyone I want to marry.'

'Why?'

'Would you like me to read you a bedtime story?' Ceri asked, eager to change the subject.

'Yes!! *Two* stories.'

Ceri would happily have read Nia six, if it meant she didn't have to answer any more questions about her lack of a love life.

After being persuaded to read three bedtime stories, Ceri was eventually allowed to go back downstairs.

'We thought you'd fallen asleep up there,' Huw teased, handing her the wine she had barely touched.

Ceri took a grateful sip and sank into a chair. It had been a long week and she was tired. She was also hungry, so when Rowena placed a bowl of steaming, fragrant pasta in front of her, she tucked in with enthusiasm as the newlyweds regaled her with stories from their wonderful two weeks away.

Eventually, the conversation turned to Ceri's new job, and how she was settling into her new role.

'I feel like a fish out of water,' she admitted, when Rowena asked how she was enjoying it. 'I've been growing things since forever, but teaching other people to do it is a whole new packet of seeds.' Determined to keep things light and not let too much of her worry show, she smirked and said, 'See what I did there?'

'Please, no more gardening puns,' Huw begged. 'I don't think I can *stake* it.'

Ceri rolled her eyes and shook her head. As puns went, that was so tenuous.

Rowena giggled. 'I think she might be trying to *hedge* her bets – if gardening doesn't work out, she's thinking about being a comedian.'

'Stop putting ideas in my shed,' Ceri quipped, and there were groans all round. 'Seriously, I was so scared that first day, I nearly packed it in. Mark, the Head of Faculty, has been great, though. Very supportive.'

Huw raised his eyebrows. 'How supportive?'

'Get lost, Huw; he's my line manager. Just because you're all loved up…'

'I thought I'd sow a few seeds, that's all.'

'And I thought you didn't want any more gardening puns?'

Huw persisted, 'So? Or should I say *sow* – s. o. w.?'

'Huw, stop it!' Ceri couldn't help laughing, though. Her brother had drunk one glass of wine too many. Or was he simply drunk on happiness? She had never seen him so playful and lighthearted, and once again she felt a twinge of envy.

'Anyway,' she said, 'he's probably married or in a relationship.'

'See! You do fancy him!' Huw cried.

'I do not.' There was only one man she fancied, and that was Damon.

'Leave her alone, Huw,' Rowena chided. 'She'll find someone in her own time. She doesn't need any help from you!'

'Oh, but she does,' Huw protested. 'She's had so many boyfriends I've lost count. My sister is the queen of first dates.'

'A first date doesn't make a guy a boyfriend,' Ceri retorted, haughtily. 'It means I've checked him out and decided not to take things any further.'

'They can't all have had something wrong with them,' Rowena said.

'Believe me, they can,' Ceri replied. She wondered what was wrong with Damon – apart from the downright rudeness when she had knocked on his door, and she had already forgiven him for that.

Huw chuckled, 'My sister always finds a little something that irritates her, or that she simply can't put up with, like soup-slurping, or nicking a chip off her plate. She hates that.'

Ceri scowled at him. 'It's not always the little things,' she argued. 'What about the chap who was married, but conveniently forgot to mention it?'

'OK, I'll give you that one, but what was wrong with the guy who told a fib about his shoe size?'

Rowena snorted with laughter. 'What on earth…?'

Ceri took up the baton, anxious to explain why she had booted that particular guy into touch. 'He seemed to be under the impression that big feet, meant a big… you know.'

'And did it?' Rowena spluttered.

'I didn't give him the chance to show me. That he'd lied about being a size eleven, when he was clearly only an eight or nine, was enough to put me off. If he can lie about that, what else would he lie about?' Ceri felt quite indignant, the memory still fresh. She couldn't tolerate lying. There was simply no need for it.

'Miss Picky, that's you!' Huw chortled. 'Perhaps he was insecure about the size of his manhood.'

'Miss-I-want-to-get-it-right,' she shot back. 'Can we change the subject? What with my new job and the allotment, I've got plenty to keep me occupied. I don't need to complicate it any further with a fella.' But her treacherous mind brought an image of Damon to the forefront, along with the suspicion that she was kidding herself. If Damon was on offer, she suspected she would happily allow that particular complication into her life.

'What allotment?' Rowena's eyes lit up, and Ceri breathed a sigh of relief at the change of subject.

'Keep it under your hat for now, but Terry is letting me restore the allotment on Willow Tree Lane,' she said.

Huw asked, 'Isn't that the field where we held the reception?'

'The very same. It used to be an allotment years ago,' Ceri explained.

'I remember,' Rowena said. 'Hyacinth Rogers, a friend of Mrs Moxley's, used to oversee it. She lived in that big house at the end of the lane, but when she died, the allotment died with her.' Rowena tapped her chin, thoughtfully. 'Maybe Sero could sell any excess veggies? We've been looking for a local supplier.'

'It'll be a while yet,' Ceri warned. 'The plots haven't even been allocated. The allotment isn't going to produce much this year.'

Ceri's eyes widened as a thought struck her – the allotment mightn't, but the *orchard* would. And Damon had told her she could help herself. As she'd said to him, it would be a shame for all that fruit to go to waste.

When she had mentioned the possibility of Damon selling some fruit to Sero, he hadn't seemed keen, but maybe that was because he didn't want to go to all the hassle of picking it himself, especially since the rest of his property was in dire need of some TLC.

She would wait until the fruit had ripened and broach the subject with him again.

The fact that it would be an excuse to see him again was irrelevant, but Ceri couldn't help feeling excited at the thought. He was the only man she had felt so strongly attracted to.

No one else had even come close.

Chapter 9

Damon smiled sadly when he saw the photo Sadie had sent him. It was one of her and Aiden when they were kids. Aiden had a guitar in his hand and a goofy grin on his face, and Sadie was clutching a violin.

Just like her brother, Sadie had always been musical, starting with learning the piano, then having a go at the violin, before settling on classical guitar when Aiden had discovered he had a talent for playing bass. Aiden had been able to sing too, which had been handy, because it meant that Damon didn't have to carry the vocals on his own.

But Sadie was an even better singer. Her vocal range was exceptional. Her voice was remarkably like Stevie Nicks' in Fleetwood Mac, and Damon often wondered why she hadn't gone into the music business alongside her brother. When Black Hyacinth had first formed back when they were in university, Sadie sometimes used to join them for rehearsals, and at one point Damon thought she might have become the band's fourth member.

He was just about to send her a message, saying 'Nice pic,' when he decided to phone her instead. He loved Sadie like a sister, and speaking to her would tell him more about how she was coping, than swapping messages ever would. Seeing her in person would be better again, but he'd settle for a phone call.

'How are you?' he asked softly, when she picked up.

'I'm—' she hesitated, '—getting there.'

'Good, I…' Damon pressed his lips together, not knowing what to say, remembering the funeral and her grief-stricken expression, the desperation in her eyes, and the way she had clung to him, sobs wracking her too-thin body.

He swallowed down the memory, not wanting to cry. It was six weeks since Aiden had been killed. It felt like yesterday.

She sniffed, 'Yeah, I know. There's nothing anyone can say, is there?'

'How is your mum?'

'Not good. She tries to hide it, but I can tell. Dad's bumbling along, keeping busy, but I don't think it's sunk in yet for any of us. I think I'm finding it harder to come to terms with it because Aiden was away such a lot. I still keep expecting to get a stupid meme from him or a drunken text. It might be different if we'd lived in each other's pockets, but I only saw him a couple of times a year and my parents didn't see much more of him. Black Hyacinth was always on the road…'

Damon heard the tears in her voice, and he blinked away tears of his own. 'Are you going to join Luke in India?' A holiday would do her good.

'Probably not.'

Pity, he thought. She needed to get away for a bit, just like he and Luke had done. 'Why don't you come here?' he blurted, the suggestion popping into his head. Warming to his theme, he said, 'Even if it's only for a couple of days, it'll give you a break.'

'I don't know…'

'Think about it, yeah? But come soon, because I don't know how much longer I'll be here.'

'I did hear that Frank wants the band to finish laying down the new album.'

'He's not wasting any time.' Damon's tone was bitter. He was about to say more, but his heart began to thump wildly and a familiar roaring, screeching noise filled his head.

Gasping, his vision turning inwards as the memory drew him in, he stammered out a mumbled, 'Gotta go, love you,' and heard her echo 'Love you, too,' before he abruptly ended the call as the flashback took hold.

Afterwards, drained and troubled, he stumbled outside, needing the solace of nature to calm him, and he inhaled deeply as his heart rate slowly returned to normal.

The garden was warm and perfumed, full of birdsong and the hum of insects, and when Damon found himself near the potting shed, he immediately knew what had drawn him there.

Inside was hot and stuffy, the air full of dust motes that circled lazily when he opened the door. Leaving it ajar, he gazed around, memories of his grandmother invading his mind. He could see her standing at the bench, the radio on as she pricked out seedlings, a cup of coffee lying forgotten beside her, smoke curling from the illicit cigarettes she used to smoke when she thought no one was watching.

He breathed deeply, letting the memories flow, peace embracing him in sepia-tinted arms.

This place was timeless. No matter what went on in the outside world, his gran's potting shed had remained unchanged, and being there immediately took him back to his boyhood and the simpler pleasures of chasing butterflies and grubbing for worms in the rich soft earth.

Hyacinth's presence was still here in the now-silent radio, and the dried-out tub of potting mixture, and in the chair in the corner with her scruffy old jacket slung over the back.

'Oh, Gran,' he murmured, wishing he had spent more time with her, wishing he had told her he loved her more often. He would give anything to feel her arms around him again, to hear her gentle voice soothing his cares away. He could almost feel her dirt-creased hand on his shoulder, and he placed his own hand over where hers had so often rested.

Feeling closer to her than he had since she'd passed away, he reached for the journals, then sat in his gran's chair and balanced them on his knees.

They were in chronological order, the topmost one being the most recent, and he decided to leave that until last. He wanted to start at the beginning of his gran's journey, the way Hyacinth herself had begun, and he was soon lost in the pages of her elegant, cursive handwriting – pages that brought her back to life, that spoke of a woman whose past he hadn't truly known.

–

'Ceri Morgan?' A woman was standing in the doorway of the classroom, her head tilted to one side and a frown creasing her forehead. Her face suggested she might be in her early forties, but her dress sense suggested someone much younger. Ceri had no idea who she was, but assumed she must be a member of staff.

Smiling she said, 'That's me. Can I help you?' She was about to nip to the staffroom for some lunch, and she was hoping this woman wouldn't delay her for long. The lesson she'd just taught had been particularly gruelling, and she was desperate for a coffee.

She'd hoped that with the youngsters no longer being in formal education and having chosen to be on the course, that they would *want* to learn. Today they had been based in the classroom, which was rare because most of her work with them was hands-on in the polytunnels or the beds. However, despite the practical side of the course, there was still an element of written work to be done, so a couple of sessions per week were spent in the classroom, catching up on their notes and making sure their coursework was up to date. She was very aware that there was only a month to go until the end of term, at which time she would have to assess and grade their work. It wasn't something she was looking forward to, having had no experience of this kind of thing – she didn't think that being on the other side of the desk when she was a student herself counted.

She'd discovered that she much preferred the hands-on practical lessons to the theory classroom-based ones, and was very aware that her delivery and presentation of these lessons needed some work. As did her classroom management, because she had a suspicion the teenagers were running rings around her.

It felt like she was the one who had a lot to learn, because she had spent most of the two-hour session today trying to persuade them to complete the task she'd set them. They, on the other hand (and by 'they' she didn't mean all of them, but it was a significant number), seemed to have had other ideas.

The woman drew herself up and pursed her lips. 'Portia told me I'd find you here. I'm her mother.'

'Oh, um, nice to meet you, Mrs Selway.' Ceri was nonplussed. Portia hadn't been in college for the past three days and she hoped there wasn't anything wrong.

'I wish I could say the same. And the name is Mrs Drake. I've remarried.'

'Oh… right. Is Portia OK?'

'She is, no thanks to you.'

'Excuse me?'

'You made her eat *dirt*.' Mrs Drake's mouth twisted in disgust.

Ceri was taken aback, and it took her a second to realise what the woman meant. The very first session she had taught seemed a long time ago. 'I didn't, I—'

'Don't lie to me. I've got video evidence.' Mrs Drake shook a mobile phone at her.

Ceri's mouth dropped open. Someone had been videoing her, *without her consent?* 'Did Portia—?' she began but she was cut off.

'Never mind where I got it from. I'll be taking this to the authorities. I just wanted to tell you that you can't get away with treating kids like animals. Disgusting, that's what it is. People like you shouldn't be teachers.'

Shaking with shock, Ceri watched the woman waltz out of the room and listened to her heels clip-clopping along the corridor, before sinking into her chair. Tears welled and she gulped them back, biting her lip with the effort as her chin wobbled.

She couldn't believe what had just happened. Half of her wanted to sob, and the other half wanted to confront Portia and demand an explanation.

Ceri forced herself to calm down and think back to that first day. She could see the students in her mind's eye, gathered around the wooden bench with the fake soil in a small tub behind her, and she squinted as she tried to recall who, if anyone, had been messing around with their phone.

It hadn't been Portia. Ceri was certain of it. Although Portia had her phone out at the start, Ceri was convinced the girl had slipped it into the back pocket of her jeans before the 'soil-eating' incident. So it had to be one of the others. But who?

Argh! Did it matter who filmed it? The damage was done and it was probably all over the college by now.

Shakily, she got to her feet and went to find Mark. He needed to know about this – if he didn't already.

–

Damon wrestled the garage doors open, coughing as dust rose in a cloud, threatening to choke him. The doors were old and wooden, and would need replacing if he intended to keep a car in there. It would also need a good clean out.

Living in London, he hadn't bothered owning a vehicle, but if he was intending to pop back to Foxmore more regularly (he would have to, if he wanted to keep an eye on the garden), he should invest in a car of some description. His flat in London had an underground garage, so he could store it there when he was in the capital, and it would also come in handy if he decided to pay his parents a visit. He couldn't remember the last time he'd seen them. Certainly not since Aiden had died. They'd sent flowers, of course, and he had spoken to them, to tell them he would be living in Willow Tree House for a while. They had made all the right noises, but he could tell that they hadn't been overly interested.

He shouldn't have been surprised. His parents had never been particularly interested in him. Their passion was archaeology. Digging around in the past had always taken precedence over the present and their son.

Thank God for his grandmother: she had loved him so very fiercely.

Brushing away thoughts of his parents, along with the dust he brushed off his T-shirt and jeans, Damon squinted into the gloom of the garage.

He had been expecting to see an empty space, containing little more than dust motes and spiders; he hadn't expected to see a car.

And not just *any* car. This was Hyacinth's beloved Austin Morris 1100.

Damon grabbed the doorframe for support. He'd assumed that she had got rid of it years ago, but here it was, rather the worse for wear, covered in grime and sitting on at least two flat tyres. It had once been a thing of beauty, but not any longer.

He stood there for a while, staring at it, wondering whether this might be the same car she had referred to in her journals, the same one that V had bought her, which she had wanted to return. Then he slowly closed the garage doors, knowing that he didn't have the heart to get rid of it, but neither did he have the heart to restore it. Maybe one day...

With the garage no longer a viable option, Damon would have to park whatever vehicle he bought on the drive, which was also not looking its best. The whole of the front garden had been gravelled many years ago, the individual chippings firmly embedded in the ground. But now weeds were growing through it with determined abandon, and the trees, bushes and shrubs that enclosed the space were threatening to overrun it completely.

There should be enough room to park half a dozen cars comfortably, but in its current state Damon would be reluctant to park even one. There was the bindweed to deal with for a start, plus he was concerned that some of the larger trees might need a branch or two lopping off. That wasn't something he could do himself; it would need a tree surgeon with the right equipment and a good head for heights.

He was about to search for 'tree surgeons near me' on his phone, when he wondered whether Ceri could recommend one. She was bound to know someone who could take a look at his trees for him.

And at the same time, he would ask her if she wanted any compost.

—

Damon left it until the afternoon had eased into evening to call on Ceri, feeling oddly nervous and excited about seeing her again.

As he approached the end of the lane and turned towards Rosehip Cottage, his steps slowed as he drew near. Her house was double-fronted with climbers growing around the door, and the tiny garden at the front, which was little more than a bailey, was full of pots. The scent of flowers carried on the breeze and he sniffed appreciatively, wondering if there was any sweet rocket contributing to the fragrance.

He knocked, and when she answered she seemed surprised to see him but quickly rallied.

'Have you come to pick my brains?' She raised an eyebrow.

'I have, and to ask whether you could make use of any compost.'

'You know the way to a gardener's heart. Come in.'

The thought popped into his head that he wished he *did* know the way to her heart, and it made him hesitate as he suddenly realised that he would like to get to know her better. A great deal better.

Pushing the unexpected thought away, he stepped over the threshold and looked around curiously.

Rosehip Cottage was small; the whole of the downstairs living space could fit into his parlour, but it was quaint. There was an open-plan living and dining area, with a set of stairs directly opposite the front door, separating the two distinct spaces, and it had a cosy, lived-in vibe, making him feel instantly at home. A squishy sofa was to his right, sitting atop wooden floorboards, and two of the main walls in the living area were exposed stone. A wood burner was recessed into one of them and shelves lined the walls on both sides of the chimney breast. A TV was propped on an artist's easel in one corner, and there was a log store in another.

Damon took all this in with a glance as Ceri led him through the dining area, which contained an old scarred table and a typical Welsh dresser at the far end, and into the kitchen.

He didn't know why he had expected something modern, but the butler sink and the cupboards were totally original, possibly unchanged since the cottage was built, and he guessed the house would have been constructed well over a hundred years ago, if not two. His grandmother would have felt very much at home here.

Ceri snagged a glass from a shelf and carried on walking into a brightly lit garden, where he was immediately hit by a wall of colour.

'Park your backside,' she instructed, sitting at a bistro-style table on which a bottle of wine and a half-full glass of red liquid sat. She poured another measure as he dropped down into a chair and handed it to him.

'Thanks.' He took a sip, and the smoky, fruitiness of the Malbec exploded on his tongue. It was a nice wine, and he drank some more, rolling it around his mouth before swallowing.

She took a deep draught of hers, closing her eyes for a moment, and he noticed that her face looked pinched and there was a worry line etched between her brows. It didn't detract from her beauty, but he wished he could make whatever was troubling her go away.

Opening her eyes, she stared back at him and he wondered whether he should ask if she was all right.

Before he could, she said, 'You wanted to pick my brains?' and the moment was lost.

'I think I need a tree surgeon and I was hoping you could recommend someone.'

'Unfortunately, I can't. I'm quite new to the area – but I know a man who might be able to. Which tree is it?'

'All of them, I think. I need to make sure they're not going to come crashing down in the next big storm.'

'Very wise,' she said, over the rim of her glass. 'You don't want to take that kind of risk. If a tree lands on a building, it can do a terrific amount of damage.'

'I hadn't considered that,' he admitted. 'I was more concerned about a rotten branch falling on my car, but now you've given me something else to worry about.'

'Sorry,' she said. 'I doubt it's in any immediate danger, though, so you can safely carry on parking it on your driveway.'

'I haven't bought it yet,' he confessed. 'I was hoping to park it in the garage, but my gran's Morris 1100 is already in there.'

Ceri stared at him blankly.

'It's a car,' he explained. 'An old one. Probably vintage by now. It's in a bit of a state. I was thinking of something a bit more modern, preferably with power steering and hydraulic brakes.'

'A petrolhead, are you?' she asked.

'Not at all,' Damon said. 'I'm not overly interested in cars. As long as it gets me from A to B, I'm happy.' Aiden was the one who had loved cars. They had been his downfall.

There was silence for a while, the only sounds being the buzz and hum of bees as they flitted from flower to flower, intent on their last meal of the day, and he wondered what he could say to fill it.

'Compost!' he blurted.

'Ah, yes, you wondered if I could make use of some? How much have you got?'

'Three heaps worth.'

Ceri's eyes widened. 'The three heaps I was drooling over?'

'The very same.'

'All of it?'

'All of it,' he confirmed. 'I'm not going to be able to use it this year, so I thought maybe you could.'

'It's good stuff,' she said, 'well rotted. Are you sure you don't need it?'

'I'm sure. Anyway, I need the space. I've got a load more stuff to compost.'

'In that case, thank you.' She topped up his glass. 'I take it you've been busy. Got lots of fresh material?'

Damon froze. How could she possibly know that? No one knew he had been composing new songs, not even Luke. He closed his eyes, then slowly opened them again, feeling a prat when he realised she was referring to fresh material for the *compost heap*. What an idiot.

'Are you OK?' She had a wary expression on her face.

'Yeah, sorry, I was miles away for a second. Um, yeah, I have been busy. I've cut back the rhododendrons and the hydrangeas, and a few other things, too. And I've bought a shredder.'

Ceri sat forward. 'Which one? I love a shredder.'

Damon uttered a surprised laugh. He hadn't expected his shredder purchase to elicit such an enthusiastic response.

'I couldn't decide between a chipper or a shredder at first,' he began, and proceeded to explain his reasoning, and tell her the make and model he had ended up buying.

'Good choice,' she declared. 'I always tell people that if they've regularly got a lot of green waste to dispose of, then a shredder is the way to go. Chopping up your hedge clippings or brambles before you pop them on the compost heap means they will break down far more quickly.'

'You do realise you're preaching to the converted,' he teased.

'Sorry. Until I moved to Foxmore, I used to work in a garden centre and I would often be asked advice on which tools to buy.'

'I thought you might be on commission, for a minute.'

'The way you thought I was touting for business when I suggested you might want to think about employing a professional gardener?' she shot back.

Damon flinched. 'I'm sorry about that. I just assumed... You said you've got a job – would that be as a gardener?'

'Why? Do you want to employ me?'

Damon, not sure what to say to that, opened his mouth, then closed it again.

'Just kidding,' she said, with a wry twist of her lips. 'I teach horticulture at the agricultural college.' A frown marred her brow. 'At least, that's what I'm employed to do. I feel like a fraud though. I *am* just a gardener, not a proper teacher.'

'I bet you're a great teacher,' he replied, gallantly.

'I'm a scared teacher,' she retorted. 'I'm as far out of my comfort zone as a tortoise up a tree would be. I've had the day from hell and I'm this close to packing it in.' She held her index finger and thumb a centimetre apart.

That explains the wine, the pinched expression and the frown line, Damon thought.

Hoping to make her smile, he said, 'Have you heard of *tortoisus clamberosus*? No? It's a rare breed of tree-climbing tortoise… Seriously, they wouldn't have employed you if they didn't believe you could do the job.'

'That's what Huw says. But he's my brother, so he's biased.'

'He's right, though.'

'I hope so. It's all so new to me: schemes of work, assessments, pastoral support. When I first heard that term, I thought it had something to do with pastures and fields, but it refers to the students' wellbeing outside of their actual course.'

'Are you enjoying it?' he asked.

'Not really. I've bitten off far more than I can chew, I haven't got a clue what I'm supposed to be doing, and to top it all off I had a run-in with a parent today. But it's a job and I need the money. At least it pays well, so if I can stick at it, one day I might save up enough to open my own nursery.' She sighed. 'I'm not sure how realistic that is, but I'm kind of making a start, so your compost offer will come in very handy. Thank you.'

'In what way are you making a start?' Damon was curious.

'It's only a small start, because I'll only have one plot just like everyone else, but I know from experience that I'll grow more than I can use myself, whether it be vegetables or flowers, so I'm hoping to be able to sell the surplus.'

'What plot?' he asked.

'Keep it to yourself for the time being,' she said, her eyes lighting up, making her whole face glow, 'but Foxmore is going to have an allotment once again. You're probably aware that your grandmother was the driving force behind the allotment on Willow Tree Lane, but when she passed away I believe it fell into disuse; at least, that's what Terry told me.'

It took Damon a moment to recall that Terry was the name of Foxmore's vicar. Hyacinth used to think the world of him, and when she died Terry had presided over her funeral. Damon couldn't remember a great deal about it, he had been too upset, but he did recall how kindly the man had been.

Ceri was saying, 'I had hoped to use the field myself, but Terry wanted it to be a community space, and he's happy for me to have a plot as long as the field is turned back into an allotment. So that's what I mean by starting small.'

Damon was horrified. The last thing he wanted was a load of people grubbing about in the field behind his house. He knew it was selfish, because he remembered how much joy the allotment had brought his grand-mother, and he was sure it would bring the same amount of pleasure to numerous other people, but the events of the recent past were still very raw and very much in the forefront of his mind. The thought of people being so close to his house made him shiver. What if one of them recognised him, and the press or the band's fans found out where he was hiding?

'Why do I need to keep it to myself for the time being?' he asked, hoping that the deal wasn't done and dusted. Maybe there was some legality with the church and the use of the land that had to be worked through first? By the time that happened, he would probably have returned to London, even though the thought made him feel sick.

Ceri said, 'I'm hoping for a couple of weeks of peace before the plotters descend on it, because I'm planning on giving my students an assignment which would involve designing an allotment. Plus, I'm going to have to measure up and stake out the various plots before they are allocated. You can't just have people turning up and starting to dig willy-nilly. Ideally all the plots would need to be the same size, equidistant, and some will be more desirable than others.'

Despite his aversion to having the field on Willow Tree Lane turned back into an allotment, Damon was curious. His grandmother had lived and breathed this stuff, and a part of him would like to see the allotment come back to life. He knew that Hyacinth, if she was looking down, would be nodding her approval of Ceri's plan.

'I take it the plot nearer the hedgerows would be the least desirable ones?' he guessed.

'Some, but not all. It depends on how much sunlight they get. Yes, the plots around the perimeter of the field will be shaded for some part of the day, but some are more shaded than others, and there's also the issue of some of the larger hedges taking all the nutrients and moisture, so the soil around them will be somewhat depleted.'

'Hence the compost?'

'It won't be nearly enough, but it will be a start. The good thing is that the field has been left alone since it ceased being an allotment. It's not as though it's been used to grow crops, although it would have been handy if sheep or cattle had been allowed to graze it. Never mind, I'm sure Alex Harris from the farm up the road will be more than happy for me to get rid of some of his slurry for him.'

Damon shuddered: slurry was not a nice word. But he understood that manure would improve the soil quality immensely. 'You're going to need barrowloads of the stuff,' he predicted.

'Probably. I'm hoping I can sweet-talk him into bringing a few tractor-loads down, and if I promise him a couple of pints in The Jolly Fox, he might even spread it over the plots for me. On second thoughts, your compost is too nice to dig into the soil. It should be used for sowing seedlings, or for potting on. Don't worry, I don't expect you to shift it. I'll do it. Can you give me a couple of days? I've got to sort out somewhere to put it.'

'I assume it will be going onto the field?'

'That's the plan, but I want to put it out of the way until I'm ready to use it.'

'Why don't you drop by tomorrow and we can make a start?' he suggested. 'It'll be quicker with two.'

'In that case, you must let me help you with your driveway.' Smiling, she echoed, 'It will be quicker with two. I'll ask about a tree surgeon at work on Monday, and if you give me your phone number, I'll send you their details. In the meantime, we can carry on cutting the bushes back and digging up that damned bindweed.

It'll take more than a day, but we can make a good start tomorrow.'

A whole day with her? Damon's heart skipped a beat. She must like him if she wanted to spend a whole day with him, he mused, before common sense grabbed him by the shoulders and gave him a good shake. She was merely being friendly and returning a favour. His gran used to say that gardeners were the best people: if you gave one a cutting from your favourite shrub, they'd give you some of their summer bulbs when they forked them up. He had offered her his compost and told her she could pick all the fruit she wanted, so she was returning the favour by helping him knock his drive back into shape, that was all.

Anyway, he wasn't in any position to think about romance, he had too many other things going on…

He swirled the wine around in the glass, and asked, 'Is the allotment the reason you wanted to know who owns the orchard?'

'It would have been wonderful if it was part of it,' she replied. 'The plotters wouldn't need to plant their own fruit trees.'

'Are you going to be in charge of the allotment?'

'It seems so. I honestly don't mind, because they do tend to run themselves most of the time, although I suppose if it's to be done properly I should set up an Allotment Association and hold meetings and stuff. But as the land the allotment is on is owned by the church and not the council, Terry will have the final say if there are any disputes.'

Damon finished the rest of his wine and got to his feet. It was time he was on his way; the bottle was empty and he didn't want to outstay his welcome.

'I'll see you tomorrow,' he said, his spirits soaring at the thought of seeing her again so soon, and as she showed him out, he had to rein in the sudden urge to kiss her. 'Bye, then.'

'Bye,' she echoed, leaning against the doorjamb.

He thought he could feel her gaze on his back all the way to the end of the road. However, when he turned the corner into Willow Tree Lane and glanced over his shoulder, he was disappointed to see that she had gone back inside.

But neither her apparent lack of interest nor his awareness that he didn't need a romantic interlude right now, prevented him from thinking about her for the rest of the evening.

Chapter 10

Ceri was up with the lark this morning, or the sparrow to be exact, because there was a bunch of them squabbling in her little lilac bush, observed by a pair of wood pigeons whose cooing calls seemed to be egging them on and adding to the cacophony.

Wishing that she had agreed a time with Damon, she hoped nine o'clock wasn't too early to show up on his doorstep, but that was two-and-a-half hours away and in the meantime she had better find something to do to stop her obsessing over him. So, she made some breakfast, then checked her lesson plans for the following week, sent an email to Mark asking him if she could take her first-year students on a field trip, and finally she prepared the assignment she would set them if the trip to the allotment was agreed. And all the while she tried not to think of that awful parent. If there were more like her out there, Ceri would definitely throw in the towel and get a job at a supermarket check-out. It might not pay as much, but at least she would be able to do her shift, then go home and not have to work for hours in the evening on things like lesson plans, and neither would she have to worry about setting assignments or parents accosting her.

Despite Mark's assurances that everything was all right and that no harm had been done, Ceri had been awake half the night fretting. He had assured her that parents often got hold of the wrong end of the stick, and he had taken it upon himself to speak to Mrs Drake and explain that the video she had seen had only been half the story, but Ceri couldn't help the niggling worry.

Scowling at the laptop and the piles of papers strewn over the dining table, she took herself off for a shower, even going as far as putting on makeup afterwards despite knowing she would be a dirty, sweaty mess within an hour. Then she set about making her and Damon a picnic lunch. If she was going to be at Willow Tree House all day, she would need something to eat and she didn't expect Damon to feed her.

Lunch prepared, she packed it into a backpack, grabbed her extendable secateurs, a couple of pairs of thick gardening gloves and a lighter, and set off.

It was another glorious day, and as she passed the entrance to the allotment she smiled at the sight of the wildflowers blooming among the grass. It would be a shame to lose them, and she intended to make sure that didn't happen. Some would have to be removed obviously, to make way for the vegetable beds but enough would remain, and she would also gather seeds later in the year, which she would scatter on the verges of the lanes and down by the river.

Ceri heard the music – an old seventies rock ballad – long before she saw where it was coming from, and she was humming to herself as she turned the corner into Damon's drive.

To her surprise, he was already hard at work pulling up weeds. And was that swearing she could hear? It was, and she tried not to giggle.

He had his back to her, but he must either have sensed her presence or caught movement out of the corner of his eye, because he straightened up and turned around, his eyes wide with shock until he realised who it was.

'There's an easier way to get rid of weeds,' she told him. 'Stick the kettle on and I'll show you.'

'You've only just got here, and you want a cup of tea already?' he teased, turning the music off, which pleased her. Although she enjoyed music, she preferred listening to the sounds of nature when she was outside.

'It's not for me, it's for the weeds,' she explained.

'The weeds want a cup of tea?'

'No, silly. You can kill them with boiling water. You'll see them wither and wilt immediately, and it only takes a few days for the plant to go brown and die.'

'What about the bindweed? Can we use the same method on that?'

'You can, but you've got quite a lot of it and it's rather well established. Those roots will go down a fair way and they'll have spread. We'll cut it back as much as possible, then try the boiling water method, but if that doesn't work I'm afraid it'll either be the good old-fashioned digging method or weed killer.'

'I don't fancy using weed killer,' he said, and Ceri breathed a sigh of relief. She hated weed killers and pesticides. They did more harm than good, in her opinion.

'I'll hack at the bindweed while you keep the boiling water flowing,' Damon suggested, and Ceri was about to protest that she was perfectly capable of cutting bindweed back, when she decided that she'd got the better end of the bargain.

'You may as well make a coffee, seeing as you're boiling the kettle,' he added with a grin, and she rolled her eyes as she went into the house, hearing him call, 'Mine's strong with a splash of milk, please.'

This time Ceri didn't try to keep her curiosity in check, and she gazed around nosily, even going as far as to peep into a room as she walked down the hall. It was a cosy snug, with a fireplace and deep shelves on either side lined with books. The decor was from another era, but it suited the house; oddly enough, it suited also Damon, despite the heavy metal, biker vibe he gave off, and she hoped he wasn't planning on stripping all the period features out.

Abruptly aware she was invading his privacy, she hastened into the kitchen, where she found two mugs, a jar of coffee, some tea bags, sugar and a packet of digestive biscuits next to the kettle, so she quickly made the drinks and carried them outside.

'You intended for me to make the coffee all along, didn't you?' she accused. 'If you think I'm keeping you supplied with hot drinks and biscuits all day, you're sadly mistaken. I'm not going to sit around while you get to do all the fun stuff.'

'You call this *fun*?' He jerked his chin at the pile of cuttings at his feet.

'I do, and I tell you what's really fun: using the shredder. Where is it?' She glanced around the drive with avaricious eyes but didn't see it.

'No you don't, lady! That shredder is *mine*.'

'Go on, give us a go. Don't be mean.'

The gentle, almost flirtatious banter was reminiscent of the Damon she had met in the field on the night of Huw's wedding, and she welcomed him back. She already fancied the pants off him – grumpy or accusing, he was a sexy guy – but this version was one she could easily lose her heart to. And a short while later, when he brought out the shredder and put her in charge of it, she thought she already had.

Ceri was in her element, feeding small branches and long stems into its hungry maw and watching it spit out useable mulch at the other end, but she didn't get too carried away and put the bindweed cuttings in. Those, she told him, would have to be burnt.

He had been surprised when she informed him that he owned a small incinerator, and even more surprised to discover that the galvanised steel container was still useable and hadn't rusted through. Ceri had spied it, half-covered in vines, near the compost heaps, and together they retrieved it and carried it to the front of the house, where she sited it on top of a couple of rogue paving slabs.

'Shall we have lunch first before we start burning this lot?' she suggested.

Damon looked taken aback. 'Er, OK. It's only eleven thirty, though,' he pointed out.

'Don't care. I'm starving.'

'I see.' His lips twitched. 'In that case, I'd better rustle up a couple of sandwiches.'

Ceri patted her rucksack. 'No need, they've already been rustled.'

And when she unpacked their lunch and he saw the spread she'd provided, he blurted, 'Wow! Look at this! You're definitely a keeper.'

Ceri guessed he didn't mean it, because he pulled a face and looked away awkwardly, so she was relieved when he asked, 'Fancy a cold glass of pear and elderflower cordial to go with it?'

'Yes, please.' Ceri fancied something stronger, because his words, no matter that they were unintentional, had caused her heart to flutter.

When he returned with the drinks, they munched on the ham salad sandwiches she had made, along with the slab of cake she had packed. She'd also thrown in a packet of breadsticks, some dips, and a few other bits and pieces. They ate in silence, and Ceri was glad when he turned the music back on, allowing a rather eclectic playlist to fill the void.

But gradually, the conversation returned, tentative at first, like a wary bird, and by the time he'd enthused over a slice of the Provençal veggie tart that she had bought from the deli yesterday and which was supposed to have been for her dinner tonight but which she had thrown into her backpack at the last minute, the awkward moment had passed.

After every last crumb had been devoured, Damon patted his stomach. 'I didn't realise how hungry I was. That was delicious – better than anything I would have made. Thank you.'

'Gardening can be hard work, especially clearing and pruning.' Her gaze roamed around the drive as she said, 'It's looking better already, isn't it?'

She was pleased with their progress so far. Many of the weeds had already visibly wilted, although some were more stubborn than others and would require a further dousing with boiling water. Much of the bindweed was now in piles on the ground, and what was left was about to have its own hot-water experience, and many of the bushes and shrubs had been trimmed back. There was still some way to go, but the driveway was beginning to look better already. Bigger, too.

'Let's get rid of this bindweed before we do any more pruning,' she suggested, producing the lighter with a flourish. 'Have you got some old newspaper we can use to get the fire started?'

'No, but I'm sure I can find something.'

Whilst Damon popped back indoors, Ceri prepared the base of the incinerator, rooting around underneath the bushes for dry twigs, and arranging them in a lattice at the bottom.

When he returned with a handful of paper, she instructed him to scrunch it up and put it in the gaps between the twigs, and when he only had a few sheets left, she passed him the lighter and said, 'Roll a piece of paper into a taper, then light it, wait for it to catch and drop it in.'

Damon rolled the sheet of paper lengthways and flicked the lighter. The paper caught immediately, and after a second or two he popped it into the incinerator. Then the pair of them leant forward and peered inside, their heads almost touching.

Ceri was so close she could smell the deodorant he used and the mildly intoxicating aroma that was his own personal scent. She was also acutely conscious that his face was a hair's breadth from hers, and that if she turned her head, her lips would caress the stubbled skin on his cheek. His hair was tied back, but some strands had escaped to tickle her ear, and she itched to run her hands through his long curls.

Her pulse leapt and she bit her lip as she sneaked a glance at him out of the corner of her eye. She would dearly like to find out where that tattoo ended...

To Ceri's relief, before she could do something she might regret, the slowly burning paper ignited a scrunched-up piece underneath, and a small flame erupted, swiftly growing as it latched onto the dry wood.

'Can I start putting stuff on?' he asked, eagerly.

'Give it a minute and add some more kindling first,' she advised. 'That bindweed is very green and contains a lot of moisture in its leaves and stems. We'll need to make sure the fire is well established before we go dumping loads of leaves on it, otherwise we might smother it and it'll go out. And be warned, it's going to smoke like the devil.'

After supervising Damon as he put the first few bind-weed stems onto the fire, she stepped back. She wasn't a fan of getting smoke in her eyes, but Damon didn't seem to mind, and she studied his face as he fed the flames. It shimmered in the heat, partly obscured by smoke, and with the grand old house behind him, he could be audi-tioning to play Oliver Mellors in Lady Chatterley's Lover.

Heat rushed into her cheeks that had nothing to do with the warmth of the fire, and she swallowed hard as a bolt of desire hit her in the solar plexus.

'I can't remember my gran doing this,' he said, his eyes alight as he shoved another handful in.

'I don't expect she did it very often,' Ceri said, her voice sounding strange. She cleared her throat. 'I guess she only ever burned the weeds. Everything else would probably have gone on the compost heap.'

'Strewth, it gives out a fair amount of heat, doesn't it?' he said. Then he took his T-shirt off.

Ceri uttered a strangled yelp, which she hastily muffled. Oh. My. God.

Her eyes roamed over his chest and flat stomach, and her breath caught in her throat. Toned, muscled, inked – he was gorgeous. She imagined how it would feel to stroke his chest, to trace her fingers over that stomach, to let her hand drop lower to the waistband of his jeans...

She drew in a deep breath.

Unfortunately, he caught her staring, but thankfully he must have thought she was looking at his tattoos, because he said, 'Misspent youth.'

He raised his hand, the one that was still holding his T-shirt, and she guessed he might be regretting taking it off and was considering putting it back on. He didn't. Instead, he tossed it to the side and bent down to pick up some more bindweed.

Ooh! What was he doing to her? This was torture!

Realising she had to say something, she forced out a laugh. 'We've all been there. I've got a sprig of lavender here.' She touched her left hip. Not wanting to get into a comparing tattoos discussion in case she let slip that she had a vine of ivy curling down her back and he asked to see it, she grabbed the shears and went back to work.

But no amount of savage snipping could erase the thought of his hands on her skin, as they followed that trail of ivy leaves...

—

'That's the last of it,' Ceri announced, as Damion upended the wheelbarrow and tipped the final load of compost onto the heap they had created in Willow Tree Field – or *Willow Tree Allotment* as she was now starting to think of it.

She had chosen the corner nearest the gate leading to Damon's garden as a suitable spot – it was both out of the way and meant they hadn't had to barrow it too far. She already knew that her plot would be situated on this part of the allotment (and not just because it would have sun all day long), so the heap of ready-to-use compost would be convenient for her, too.

Ceri eased the kinks out of her back and watched Damon do the same. They had taken it in turns to shovel and barrow, Ceri insisting on doing her fair share; she was no drooping wallflower who didn't have the strength to wield a spade. Actually she had a sneaking suspicion she was in better shape than Damon when it came to gardening. Even if he went to the gym every day or ran a marathon every month, the kind of activity they had done today used different sets of muscles – and she had been using hers since she was big enough to hold a trowel.

Once again, she wondered what he did for a living, and assumed he must be a desk-jockey of some kind. He certainly wasn't used to manual work, not with hands like those.

Dragging her eyes away from him, she instructed, 'You put the barrow away and I'll go check on the incinerator. The fire should have gone out by now, but the metal will still be hot, and it probably won't be cool enough to move until the morning. You can throw the ashes on your new compost pile,' she added over her shoulder as she trotted along the path, heading for the side gate.

She was right; the fire in the bin was out, but enough heat radiated from it to make her double-check that nothing was smouldering in the depths of those ashes. Reaching for a stick, she poked and prodded them, releasing a cloud of fine ash, residual smoke and tiny bits of charred paper into the air, making her cough. When it settled, she peered inside again and, satisfied that the fire was definitely out, she popped the funnel-shaped lid back on.

A fragment of paper floated serenely to the ground, landing at her feet, and she bent to pick it up. But before she returned it to the metal bin, she casually glanced at it.

Expecting it to be a shopping list or an old invoice or something similar, she was surprised to discover that it was a piece of sheet music, the kind she had written on herself in school when her music teacher had been trying to get the class to notate what they heard. It had been an impossible task as far as Ceri was concerned, and she had nothing but admiration for those people who could write music, because she couldn't read a single note.

Hearing footsteps behind her, she dropped the fragment of paper into the incinerator and glanced around to see Damon walking towards her.

When he caught sight of her, he began to laugh. 'You look as though you've been having a wallow in that thing,' he chuckled. 'You're covered in ash.'

'You can talk,' she shot back. He had dirt streaks all over his face, arms and neck. Thankfully he had put his T-shirt back on a while ago, so she could only imagine the state of his chest.

Yeah, she could imagine just fine... and her heart fluttered at the memory of him without his top on.

'We both need a shower,' he said, and she smirked when he realised how it sounded and blustered, 'Not together, you understand. I meant—' He broke off when she burst out laughing.

She was laughing purely to hide the image his comment had conjured, of Damon and her with water sluicing over their naked bodies, limbs entwined...

Ceri blew out a breath. Dear God, she didn't think she could take any more of this. She certainly *did* need a shower – a freezing cold one!

To cover her discomfort, she glanced up at the sky, taking in the position of the sun. It would be a few hours before it set, but she guessed it was either very late afternoon or early evening. Time she went home for that shower and some food.

'We've done a good day's work,' she said, gathering her backpack from the porch where she had left it. 'Thanks for the compost.'

'Thanks for the help with the drive. And for the picnic.' He paused, staring at her. 'How about I make us some dinner?'

'I need a shower,' she reminded him. The offer was tempting, though.

'You can have one here.'

No, no, not a good idea. Not unless he was going to hop into it with her. She swallowed, her mouth dry. 'I need clean clothes.'

'Fair enough. But will you come back? I owe you for your help today. I think I got the better end of the bargain.'

'You don't owe me anything,' she protested.

'Even so, will you let me make you dinner anyway?'

'It depends,' she hedged. She wanted this. She wanted *him*. But maybe having dinner with Damon after she had spent all day in his company wasn't wise.

'On what?'

'What you are going to cook.'

'A chicken stir fry, with salad?'

'Sounds good.' Her tummy rumbled. 'OK, thanks. I'd like that. I'll be back in half an hour. Do you want me to bring anything?'

'Just yourself,' he replied, and the way he gazed at her made her think that maybe he *was* interested in her after all.

Chapter 11

Damon never would have thought that a woman covered in smoky ash could be so darned cute. He hadn't wanted her to leave, he hadn't wanted the day to end, so offering to cook dinner for her was the only thing he could think of to entice her to stay. But why did he have to make that ridiculous comment of them both needing a shower, and then make it worse as he tried to dig himself out of it by explaining that he hadn't meant for them to take a shower together?

Although, as he soaped himself down and rinsed off the evidence of today's hard work, his treacherous mind imagined her in there with him and he quickly turned the temperature down to cold until his ardour was well and truly cooled. Skin tingling, he towelled himself dry and hastily got dressed. He had a meal to prepare.

'I've brought the wine,' Ceri announced, after ringing the doorbell and walking into the kitchen.

'I've got some, there wasn't any need to bring your own,' he said, opening a packet of chicken fillets.

'This is chilled.'

'So is mine.'

'I'm not doubting your word, but I didn't see any in the fridge when I made the coffee.'

'It's in the cellar.'

Ceri wrinkled her nose. 'You have a *cellar*? I'm not sure whether that's cool or scary.'

'It's cool,' he said. 'If you don't believe me, check the temperature of the wine.'

'Very funny. Don't give up the day job, will you? By the way, what *do* you do for a living?'

Damon had kind of been expecting this. 'I'm living off my investments at the moment.' It wasn't an outright lie – he did have savings and investments, and royalties were still coming in and would continue to do so, although the amount would decrease over time if the band didn't put out new material to fuel sales. Which made him remember those half-finished tracks. He needed to tell Frank when he was coming back, but he couldn't face it. Not just yet. Anyway, Luke was still in India as far as Damon knew, so nothing could be done until he returned.

An image of him and Luke in the recording studio, an empty space where Aiden should be, flashed into his mind and he swallowed hard. Nothing about that picture was right. Nothing about *any* of it was right.

The room started to become fuzzy around the edges and his heart rate rose sharply. When he heard blood whooshing in his ears and realised he was having difficulty catching his breath, he began to gasp.

'What's wrong?'

Ceri's voice sounded far off, and he fought hard not to give in to the blackness threatening to overwhelm him.

'Damon? Speak to me – are you OK?'

'Yeah.' He forced out the word, concentrating on her voice, on the hand he felt on his arm, on the tiled floor beneath his feet and the flowery scent of her perfume, and he willed the screech of metal and Aiden's desperate screams to fade.

Gradually he won the battle, and as his pulse slowed and his breathing returned to normal, he became aware that Ceri was gazing at him in concern, worry in her eyes.

'I'm fine.' It came out as a croak and he coughed once to clear his throat.

'Are you sure? What happened?'

Damon shrugged. 'Dunno. I get this… kind of… it's…' He shrugged again. How could he explain to someone else, when he himself wasn't sure what was happening? 'It's nothing. Just a thing that happens sometimes.'

She was looking at him curiously and he tried to smile, but guessed it was more of a grimace.

'I'm OK.' He turned back to the stove, thankful that he hadn't switched the hob on yet. 'I could use a glass of wine, though,' he said, uncorking the bottle and pouring a couple of glasses.

He handed one to Ceri, and she leant against the table, sipping it.

Damon took a quick glug, then turned his attention back to the chicken that he had been slicing into strips ready to pop into his gran's enormous frying pan. He noticed that Ceri's hair was still damp, and he hastily looked away.

'I thought we'd eat outside,' he said, throwing the chicken in hot oil. The sizzle as it hit the pan was quite gratifying, and the aroma of frying meat filled the air. 'It's too nice to eat indoors.'

'Good idea. Can I do anything to help?'

'No, thanks, it's all under control.'

He was aware of her watching him, and he felt self-conscious. It was weird to think he had been on stage in front of thousands and hadn't felt as nervous, yet this one woman could make him feel so incredibly self-aware. He suspected he could quite easily fall for her, if he let himself.

The food was soon ready and he grabbed a bowl of ready-prepared salad from the fridge, threw in a couple of cherry tomatoes, and got a loaf of wholemeal seeded bread out of the cupboard. It was a quick and simple meal, but it would be filling. He was no cook and didn't profess to be; this was about as good as it got.

Ceri helped him carry everything outside, and they took their seats at the table. The sun hadn't yet set and it was still quite warm, a perfect evening for al fresco dining.

Tucking in with enthusiasm, Ceri ate as voraciously as he, and he guessed that all the exercise and working outdoors had made her hungry. He was ravenous, and he tore off a large chunk of bread, spreading it thickly with slightly salted Welsh butter.

As usual, he had music playing in the background, but when one of Black Hyacinth's tracks came on, he quickly asked for a shuffle. He couldn't in all conscience sit here with Ceri, not really lying about who he was or what he did but not being truthful with her either, whilst listening to his own band's music.

'Aw, leave it on. I like that one,' she said.

'I've heard it too many times. I'm a bit fed up with it, if I'm honest.'

'Actually, I think I heard you playing this not so long ago. I was in the allotment, scoping it out. I did wonder if I was imagining it, because everyone said that your house was empty.'

'You heard me playing it?' he echoed, warily.

'Yes, although it sounded different so I think you must have been streaming the live version.'

Abruptly Damon pushed his chair back and got to his feet. 'Forgot the salad dressing,' he said, desperate to put an end to the conversation. It was a miracle Ceri hadn't put two and two together already, and although he suspected it was probably only a matter of time, he didn't want to let her in on his secret just yet. The anonymity was refreshing. Not only that, neither did he want to think too far ahead. He was enjoying the present too much and he didn't want anything to spoil it. There would be time enough to come clean when he had to leave.

He hurried inside and spent a couple of minutes rooting around in the fridge and hoping Ceri would have forgotten all about it by the time he went back outside.

Thankfully, she had. She was busy throwing tiny pieces of bread to a small brown bird. The thrush took one look at Damon and flew off.

He laughed self-consciously. 'I'm not that scary, am I?'

Ceri said. 'Not at all. I reckon if you sat still long enough and did a little breadcrumb thing, you might be able to get it to eat out of your hand in time.'

'Is that what you would do?'

'There's something quite magical about having a bird eat out of your hand. Robins tend to be the cheekiest and the easiest to persuade that you're not a threat. I love the way they follow me around the garden whenever I'm doing any weeding. The minute I turn my back, one hops in to grab a juicy bug or worm, and then flies off to eat it before coming back for more.'

'You really love what you do, don't you?' he observed.

He had been watching her face, the way her eyes lit up as she described the robin. In fact, he had been watching her all day, mostly out of the corner of his eye, but occasionally he had gazed at her directly, only turning away when there was a risk of her noticing.

'I love gardening, and anything plant-y,' she said.

'Yet you work in a college?'

'Yeah, I'm not so sure about teaching. I don't know whether I'm cut out for it, but at least I still get to work with plants and it pays more than working in a garden centre, which is what I did before I moved to Foxmore. I'm hoping to be able to save enough out of my wages to buy a small piece of land in a few years.'

'This is for your nursery, yes?'

She nodded. 'But for now, I'll have to make do with the allotment.'

Oh yes, the allotment. How could Damon forget? He still wasn't keen on the idea of having half of Foxmore in the field next door to his house, but at least there was a fairly substantial hedge separating his property from the plot of land. The only thing he needed to worry about was that gate. Maybe he should padlock it? It wouldn't prevent anyone from climbing over, but it should deter the casual nosy parker.

Using a piece of bread to mop up the last of the juice from the stir fry and popping it in his mouth, he asked, 'More wine?' He picked up the bottle to top up her glass.

Ceri shook her head. 'Not for me, thanks. I've got lots of lessons to prepare in the morning, and I can't think of anything worse than facing a group of teenagers when I've not got a clue what I'm doing.'

She got to her feet and began gathering the dishes, but Damon waved her away.

'I think you've done enough for one day,' he said. 'You must be exhausted.'

'No more than usual,' she said. 'Don't forget, I'm used to being active all day, every day.'

'That's as maybe, but you've done me a huge favour in helping me with the drive, so there's no way you're going to clear up.'

'In that case, I think I'll love you and leave you,' she said. 'My bed is calling to me.'

Please, not that, Damon thought. He didn't need an image of her in bed to keep him awake tonight. It had been bad enough imagining her in the shower.

'I'll walk you home,' he offered, and Ceri gave him a look.

'I'm perfectly capable of walking home by myself,' she retorted.

'I didn't mean to suggest that you weren't, but it is starting to get dark.'

'I've got one word to say to you,' she said. 'Graveyard.'

'Pardon?'

'It was dark then, but you didn't offer to walk me home.'

'I didn't know you.'

'Yet you'd already kissed me.' She stared him straight in the eye, her lips slightly parted, and he felt heat surge through him.

'So I had,' he replied slowly. His gaze locked onto hers and for several heartbeats neither of them said anything.

It was Ceri who broke the contact, looking away and biting her bottom lip, and Damon wasn't sure whether she had expected him to kiss her again, or whether she had been concerned in case he was going to.

'Thanks for dinner,' she said. 'And thanks again for the compost.'

'I think I had the better end of the bargain,' he chuckled, to hide his discomposure.

'I'll let you know about the tree surgeon,' she added.

He had expected her to walk into the kitchen and leave by the front door, but instead she trotted off down the path, heading towards the little wooden gate and the allotment beyond.

Resisting the urge to follow her to the gate to watch as she danced across the field, he allowed himself to picture her slim figure fading into the twilight.

With the clearing up done, Damon took the rest of the wine into the parlour, opened the French doors, and picked up his guitar. He played his latest composition from memory, polishing it and fine-tuning it until he was as happy as he could be, thinking of Ceri as he played…

It had been a close call when she'd asked him about his music. It didn't feel right lying to her, even if it was by omission, but he didn't see what else he could have done if he wanted to remain anonymous.

His hands stung from all the cutting and clipping, his back and the muscles in his thighs and shoulders ached, and his forearms were covered in scratches, but he had to admit that he'd enjoyed himself today. And the reason was Ceri. If he had done the work on his own, without her by his side, it would have been a satisfying task but not nearly as enjoyable.

Having spent all day in her company, Damon was asking himself why he was holding back. He should have kissed her. Aiden wouldn't have hesitated. But Damon wasn't as fancy-free as his friend had been. Despite having kissed a total stranger in a meadow, Damon wasn't the type of man to make a habit of casual sex. He preferred it to mean something, and Ceri was beginning to mean more to him than was wise, considering he would be returning to London shortly. It wasn't a good idea to get involved when he wasn't able to commit to her.

A memory from when he was a teenager flashed across his mind. It had been one of the rare occasions when he had flown out to goodness-knows-where to spend a couple of weeks with his parents. It might have been naïve of him, but he had hoped they would have stopped grubbing about in the dirt for long enough to spend some time with him, but that hadn't been the case. He had been expected to do his bit on the dig, joining in with the other volunteers. Except, he hadn't been a volunteer. He had been railroaded into it in order to spend some time with his mum and dad, and also not to be bored out of his mind. He couldn't even remember where the dig had been – somewhere hot, sandy and dusty. All he could remember was the baking sun, the flies, and a deep sense of disappointment.

Damon abruptly realised he wanted what his parents had. They were utterly devoted to one another. Although they had taken it to the extreme in that he had felt excluded – both by their love for each other and their intense passion for their profession – he nevertheless wanted to experience that kind of love for himself.

Until now, he had not met anyone who he thought might stir such feelings in him. Could Ceri be that woman?

And did he have the courage to find out?

Chapter 12

Ceri clapped her hands together to bring the attention of her students back to her. 'Listen up,' she called, waiting for silence. It was a trick Mark had imparted. 'Don't shout over them,' he'd advised. 'Tell them once, then wait. They'll soon pay attention.'

It worked, and the class fell silent. She gazed at her students and wondered, not for the first time in the past couple of days, whether the video footage that one of them had taken of the soil-eating incident had been malicious, or whether it had merely been youthful indiscretion.

None of the faces staring back at her were giving anything away, and she tried to put it out of her head – although the incident had preyed on her mind over the weekend, and especially on Sunday when she had been up to her eyes in college work.

Taking a deep breath, she carried on, saying, 'You've got one final assignment before the end of term.' She ignored the groans. 'This will make up part of your coursework grade for this academic year. However,' she waved a hand for silence, 'it does mean that we get to go on a field trip.'

Once again, she had to wait for the class to settle, but it didn't take long.

'Where are we going?' the boy who had volunteered to eat the mock soil asked.

'Foxmore. It's a village about ten miles away. Do any of you know it?' One or two nodded, and she continued, 'Foxmore used to have an allotment, but it fell into disuse several years ago. I've been tasked with setting up a new one, and I thought it might be nice for you to get in at the grassroots, as it were, and see how to set up an allotment from scratch. Some of you may end up being part of an allotment association when you're older, but even if you don't, this exercise will still be invaluable.'

She went on to explain how they would have to consider where to site the individual plots, taking particular note of any areas of shade, the direction of the sun, the prevailing winds, and so on. She added the instruction that they would need to maintain as much diversity as possible in the field, and that they would have to take wildlife into account, especially the bees and other pollinators. It was a substantial brief, which would hopefully stretch them.

She also explained that although the plotters would be responsible for breaking their own ground, plus the ongoing maintenance of their plots and erecting any sheds, greenhouses or small polytunnels, she wanted the students to produce a piece of work that showed where the ideal positioning for these kinds of structures would be for each plot. She also told them that she wanted them to do some soil sampling and devise a programme of soil improvement measures. And, if there was enough time, she suggested that they may even be able to help with staking out the plots.

'You just want free labour,' one of the cheekier lads called out.

'Of course I do! I've got to get some reward out of teaching you horrible lot,' she joked. 'Seriously, guys, the trip will take place on Thursday. Bring a packed lunch, hats, sunscreen, and plenty of water. Try not to forget your notebooks, pens and pencils, please,' she added, knowing from even relatively short experience that there were always one or two who were totally unprepared.

She finished with, 'Before you go, I want you to do some research regarding the rules and regulations around setting up an allotment,' but she wasn't sure how much of this last piece of information they'd heard, because they were too busy putting their books away and getting ready to leave.

She envied them. She wished she could leave too, but she had a departmental meeting this afternoon. With another day drawing to a close, Ceri blew out her cheeks, congratulating herself on getting through it, yet realising that a couple of weeks was hardly long enough to begin to feel comfortable in any job, let alone one that was so radically different to anything she had done previously.

Telling herself that it would get better, she made a coffee in the staffroom and then headed to Mark's office. On the way, she quickly checked her phone. She hadn't been expecting to see any messages from Damon, but she was disappointed, nevertheless. As promised, she had sent him details of a couple of tree surgeons in the area, and he had messaged her back to thank her. It had all been very friendly and polite, and she honestly didn't know what she had been expecting. She'd helped him with his driveway and he'd given her about twenty barrowloads of compost, so their deal was done.

But for a moment, just as she had been taking her leave of him on Saturday evening, she'd got the impression he was about to kiss her. He hadn't, and although there was no further reason for him to contact her, somehow she had expected more. It was typical that the only man she hadn't found fault with was the one who wasn't interested in her.

Oh, well, so be it. It was probably for the best: she had enough to keep her occupied with this new job and the allotment. She was rushed off her feet as it was, so trying to shoehorn a romance into her hectic life wouldn't be a good idea.

However, she couldn't shake the feeling that she had missed an opportunity. If only she had been a little bolder and had kissed him, rather than hoping he would kiss her…

—

'Hi, I've come about your trees,' a woman said when Damon answered the door. A van was on the drive with the word 'Treemendous' emblazoned on the side.

'Great! Thanks for coming at such short notice,' he said, stepping outside. He had taken the precaution of shoving his hair up inside a baseball cap, and he had a pair of reading glasses on his nose. He hadn't shaved for a few days, and dark stubble blurred the lines of his face, so he hoped he wouldn't be recognised.

He said, 'As I told you on the phone, I'm not worried about any one tree in particular – I just want to make sure they're safe and not going to come crashing down in the next high wind.'

'Very wise. Although I can't guarantee that there won't be any casualties, I'll do my very best to ensure their health and stability. If it's OK with you, I'll remove any dead or decaying branches now, and if I see any tree that I think needs to be lopped, I'll discuss it with you first.'

'Lopped? As in chopped down?'

'Tidied up. Some species can get top heavy and run the risk of toppling, so it's better to lop off a few branches now to give it more stability, rather than waiting until the damage is done.' She wasn't looking at him as she spoke; her attention was on the trees flanking the drive. 'If I deem anything to be dangerous, I'll remove it immediately, but if not, I'll come back later in the year, around October time, and do the rest of the work then,' adding, 'birds are still nesting,' when she noticed his frown.

'Of course! I didn't think of that. As long as a branch doesn't fall on the guy who delivers my groceries, that's all I'm worried about.'

'Leave it to me,' she said. 'I'll give you a shout when I've done my initial assessment.'

Damon took the hint and went back indoors. She didn't need him peering over her shoulder. And while he waited for her to do her thing, he sent a message to Ceri.

Tree surgeon arrived. Waiting for verdict.

Followed by a worried-face emoji.

Her response was instantaneous – a couple of tree emojis and a fingers-crossed one.

OK, so at least she hadn't ignored him. It wasn't the most promising start to the conversation, though.

He tried again.

> Can I buy you dinner on Friday? As a thank you?

> No need to thank me.

> Can I buy you dinner anyway?

Ceri's reply took a little longer, but when it came, his spirits soared: she'd said yes.

And now he was left to wonder whether he was playing with fire, because his reaction had told him that he was far more invested in her than was wise.

–

On Thursday morning, Ceri jumped out of the mini-bus and opened the gate to allow Mark to drive the vehicle onto the field. She was feeling nervous because this was her show – Mark was only here to drive the bus – and she was dreadfully conscious that he would be observing her teach and she was scared of being found wanting. What if he thought she was no good? What if she made a total hash of it?

Her students tumbled out, chattering excitedly, and she was pleased to see them already making observations, so maybe this wouldn't be so bad after all...

Ceri began by reminding them of the parameters of their assignment and setting some expectations, and then she let them loose, trusting them to get on with it by themselves. She would be around to help or to answer any questions, but she wanted this to be their own work as much as possible.

'It's got a good open aspect,' Mark said, gazing around the field. 'I wouldn't mind a plot here, myself.'

'Do you live nearby?'

'No, three miles outside Dolgellau.'

'That's a shame. I could have asked the vicar to put your name down for one.'

He said, 'I haven't been to Foxmore in years. My husband and I used to do a lot of walking in the area, and Foxmore is the nearest place to Aran Fawddwy.'

'I've hiked up that!' Ceri exclaimed, remembering when Huw had persuaded her to scale the mountain's steep flanks. Her thigh muscles and her knees had ached for days afterwards. 'It's a long way to the top.'

'But the views are worth it,' Mark said. 'Have you been up Cader Idris?'

Ceri said she hadn't, and Mark proceeded to describe the fantastic views from one of Wales's highest peaks. She wouldn't mind seeing them for herself, but she didn't fancy the hike to the top.

Their chat came to an end when Portia, ironically, needed some help with the soil sampling kit, but at least Ceri felt she had got to know her head of department a little better. She could also report back to her match-making brother that the man was out of bounds on a second front: not only was Mark her line manager, but he was also married. What she *wouldn't* tell Huw, however, was that she was going to dinner with Damon, because if she did she'd never hear the end of it. He would jump to the wrong conclusion and think it was a date, despite Damon making it clear that it was nothing more than a thank-you dinner.

Her eyes strayed to the little wooden gate separating the allotment from his garden, and as she strolled around the field, she found herself gravitating towards it.

Ostensibly, she appeared to be checking the pile of rich compost that she and Damon had dumped there, but in reality, she was hoping to catch a glimpse of him. To her disappointment, he was nowhere in sight.

'Is it time for lunch yet?' one of the boys asked, and Ceri checked the time, surprised to see that the kids had been working hard for a couple of hours. From what she had seen and heard, they were making good progress.

'Shall we stop for a break?' she announced to the group, equally eager to unwrap her sandwiches and have a coffee from the flask she had brought with her.

'I haven't got a drink,' someone said. 'Can I get one from the shop?'

She'd heard the kids pointing out the shops in the village as the minibus had trundled along the main street earlier, so she had half been expecting this. 'Kyle, what did I tell you: *don't forget to bring a packed lunch, and plenty of water.*'

'I did, but I've drunk it all. See?' He held up an empty bottle.

Ceri looked to Mark for direction, who shrugged.

'I don't see why not.' He turned his attention to the students. 'Make sure you're back here by one thirty. I don't want to have to send out a search party. And behave yourselves,' he called after them, as the majority headed towards the gate and the village beyond.

'I wasn't sure whether I could let them go,' Ceri said.

'They're a sensible bunch. And they're not children, they're young adults,' he added, 'although they don't always act like it.'

With a final, worried look at her students' retreating backs, Ceri sat down in the grass and took out her lunch. It wasn't nearly as sumptuous as the picnic she had made for her and Damon, but she wolfed her sarnies down anyway. And as she ate, her gaze kept returning to the wooden gate and what lay beyond.

She couldn't wait for tomorrow, and she wondered where he was taking her. Actually, she didn't much care. The fact that she was going to dinner with him at all, was enough to make her pulse soar.

To her surprise and relief, all the students made it back to the allotment on time and in one piece. It seemed that some of them had found a fish and chip shop and had indulged in chips and curry sauce, and Portia and two of her friends had gone a bit more upmarket and had sampled the paninis in Pen's Pantry, the bistro-style cafe on the green.

So much for Ceri telling them to bring a packed lunch!

'It *was*,' Portia was saying, as Ceri attempted to get the students to refocus on their assignment.

'It *wasn't*,' her friend, Eleanor, insisted. 'As if someone like him is going to be hanging around a dump like Foxmore.'

Ceri blinked. Foxmore, a *dump*? Hardly! The village was small, quaint and unspoilt. But maybe that was what her young charges didn't like, preferring the bright lights of Dolgellau. Not that the town had many bright lights from what she had seen of it, but it was larger than Foxmore and boasted several bars, pubs and restaurants.

'It was definitely him. I should know, I've seen them in concert,' Portia argued.

Eleanor pursed her lips. 'I don't believe you.'

'It's true! I *did* see—'

Ceri called, 'OK, guys! Can we get back to work, please? You've got an hour and twenty minutes to complete your observations, make any notes and take any photos you need. Don't forget, this assignment will contribute to your overall qualification.'

Eleanor stuck out her chin. 'But Portia said—'

'Is it about the assignment?' Ceri demanded.

'No, but—'

'Then it isn't relevant. You can carry on your discussion in your own time.'

Sullenly the two girls stalked off. Ceri could still hear them arguing, but at least they were making some attempt to get back on task, so she left them to it. As long as they handed in a decent assignment, she didn't care what they were squabbling about. Knowing teenage girls, it would quickly blow over and soon be forgotten.

—

Damon hung back for a moment to admire his latest purchase.

The car, a Volkswagen, wasn't new – it was four years old – but he'd just picked it up from the dealer and it was all shiny and polished, gleaming in the afternoon sun. He'd gone for reliability and the four-wheel drive function, because he remembered being snowed in when he was younger, Foxmore's roads having been impassable for most vehicles. It was hardly a rock star car, but it suited him just fine.

He had parked it in one of the spaces on the road encircling the green, feeling immensely pleased with himself. *He had wheels!* He should have bought it weeks ago; it would have made life so much easier.

Grinning, he slung his purchases on the backseat. He had treated himself to a freshly baked loaf of seeded bread from the bakery on the high street, and several slices of smoked bacon and a wedge of caramelised onion quiche from the deli. The salad that he had bought from the convenience shop wasn't the best though, the lettuce being rather limp and sorry-looking, and the tomatoes were on the squishy side, but it was all they had, and would be fine to go in the BLT that he had planned for his late lunch.

As he pulled out of his parking space and drove around the green, he mused that Foxmore hadn't changed much since he was a child, when his gran used to send him to the shops for bread and milk, packets of seeds and bottles of cherry pop. Some things were different, though. The cafe was now called Pen's Pantry, when it had once been called Draper's and had been owned by an elderly couple of the same name, and the antique shop was new, as was the estate agent and the shop on the corner that had once sold shoes but was now a zero waste shop.

But other things had stayed the same. The church still had a rickety lived-in look, which he supposed was only to be expected since it was goodness knows how many hundreds of years old, and apart from the whitewash on The Jolly Fox and the addition of planters bursting with pretty spring blooms, the pub was as he remembered.

Thinking of the pub got him pondering where to take Ceri for dinner. Somewhere nice, but not too far away, as he didn't want to spend half the evening driving.

Still thinking and singing along to one of the tracks on his eclectic playlist as he drove, his good mood soured when he turned into Willow Tree Lane and saw a load of people in the field next to his house.

Don't tell me work has already started on the allotment, he thought with dismay. He knew it was only a matter of time, but he had hoped for another couple of weeks of solitude before he went back to London. The villagers could work on it as much as they liked after that, because he wouldn't be around to see it.

Slowing as he passed the gate, he spotted a minibus just inside the field and noticed that the people were teenagers. When he caught sight of Ceri, he realised they must be her students and were on the field trip she had told him about. The knowledge didn't make him feel any better; he still wasn't keen on having strangers so close to his property. But what choice did he have? He'd just have to put up with it and hope the allotment didn't affect him too much. It shouldn't, he told himself, considering he wouldn't be here more than a few times a year, and when he was at the house, growing vegetables was hardly going to lead to raucous behaviour. He had known his gran to be rather lively on occasion, though!

Making a mental note to fit a padlock to the little wooden gate, he swung his car into the drive and cut the engine.

The front of the house looked so much better after his and Ceri's hard work, and the car sat nicely on the drive, although it did look rather new and shiny in contrast. Maybe, in time, he would get the old Austin running again, which would be far more in keeping with the age and condition of the house, and he grinned as he imagined him and Ceri pootling along the lanes around Foxmore in it.

Pootling, indeed! That was something his gran would have said.

Then his face fell as he remembered that he wouldn't be in Foxmore for much longer and that by the time he returned, Ceri might have found someone else to have dinner with.

Unless… he came clean and told her who was and what he did for a living?

But even then, would it make any difference? He could hardly expect her to wait around for him. Despite vowing to return as often as he could, it might be another eight years before he stepped foot in Foxmore again.

Chapter 13

'Nice car,' Ceri said. 'Is it yours?' She had just stepped out of her cottage having seen Damon pull up and was feeling excited about having dinner with him, yet inexplicably nervous, too. She wanted this evening to go well, and she also really hoped that this meal wasn't just about expressing his gratitude. She hoped he would kiss her at the end of it.

Damon halted in the act of emerging from the vehicle, the driver's door open, his head appearing above the roof. 'I bought it yesterday,' he said, waiting for her to get in.

She clicked her seatbelt on and settled back as she scanned the interior. 'I'm surprised you didn't go for something a little flashier,' she teased.

He started the engine, shooting her a quick look. 'Why do you say that?'

She could hear tension in his voice and she hoped she hadn't hit a nerve. 'Look at you,' she said lightly. 'Long hair, tattoos… A Volkswagen is very—' she hunted for the right word '—respectable.'

'Are you saying I'm not respectable? I'm hurt.' He put on a wounded expression, and she giggled.

'Sorry, I take it back. You look *very* respectable.' What he actually looked was delectable. He was wearing jeans as usual, but these were black, without a tear or a rip in sight. Topped with a simple white shirt, the sleeves rolled up to reveal his inked forearms, he looked good enough to eat, and she tried not to drool.

'Where are we going?' she asked.

'The Pen y Graig. It's a gastro pub, a twenty-minute drive away. It has some really good reviews. Let's hope it lives up to them.'

'I'm sure it will. Apart from going to work and back, I've hardly been out of Foxmore, so I'm looking forward to it.'

What she was looking forward to more was a whole evening with Damon. Despite telling herself that she didn't have time for a relationship, she was very much hoping this would develop into one.

After spending all day Saturday with him, he was now in her thoughts constantly. When he had asked her out to dinner, she'd found it hard to contain her excitement and this evening hadn't come quickly enough. Take yesterday, for instance; she should have been concentrating on her students, but half her attention had been on the house next to the allotment and the gorgeous guy who lived in it. And now here she was, sitting next to said gorgeous guy and trying to keep her desire for him in check.

'Even when you're at work you can't keep away from the village,' he joked. 'I saw you in the field yesterday with a bunch of teenagers.'

'Ah, yes. That was my sneaky way of picking their young minds. I'm pretty sure how the allotment is going to be laid out – along the lines it was previously – but this assignment might throw a curve ball. I'm going to have to pull my finger out and finalise the design though, because Terry is opening up applications for the plots soon.'

'It sounds rather formal,' Damon said.

'Actually, I think it's more of a first come, first served kind of the thing. Terry says that loads of people are interested in having one.'

A scowl flashed across Damon's handsome face, but it was gone so fast she must have imagined it.

'Do you want one?' she asked, wondering if he was aggrieved that he hadn't been asked.

'I think I've got more than I can handle with my own garden,' he replied.

'How is it going?'

'The front of the house is looking good, thanks to you,' he said, giving her a sideways smile. 'But as for the rest...'

'I still think you should hire someone to help you knock it into shape. And no, I don't mean me,' she teased.

Damon groaned. 'Sorry about that.'

'It was an easy assumption to make. Wait, I've got an idea!' she exclaimed. 'I could let my students loose on it! It would be a great experience for them and you'd get all that free labour as well.'

'No thanks.' He sounded stiff, and she sensed that the tension of a few moments ago was back. 'I don't need any help.'

That told her, didn't it.

She turned her head to stare out of the side window, feeling hurt. He hadn't minded her help when it came to tidying up his drive, so why had he gone all weird on her now?

The rest of the journey passed in silence, and Ceri was beginning to regret agreeing to have dinner with him. But when they pulled into the pub's car park and got out, Damon touched her arm. The feel of his hand on her bare skin electrified her, sending tingles through her body.

'I didn't mean that the way it sounded,' he said. 'I probably do need help with the garden, but I want to do as much of it as I can myself. With some guidance from my favourite horticulturist – if she's still speaking to me.'

'How many other horticulturists do you know?' Her eyes were on his mouth. He was standing so close that if she leant forward a little, she would be able to kiss him.

'Loads, but you're the only one I want in my bed.' He caught his bottom lip between his teeth. '*Flower* bed. *Beds*.' He emphasised the plural and groaned. 'Oh, buggeration.'

Ceri burst out laughing. His embarrassment was so sweet. He was blushing, too.

But her mirth quickly dissolved at the seriousness of his expression. 'Actually, I take that last bit back,' he said. 'I *do* want you in my bed.'

She froze, the words burning a trail through her mind, fanning the desire she had been trying so hard to control. She swallowed. 'Then maybe you should do something about it,' she suggested, and a tremble began in her knees, working its way up her legs.

His eyes bored into hers. 'I'd love to. I should take you to dinner first, though.'

Ceri almost told him to get in the car, drive back to Foxmore and take her to bed instead, but they were here now, and she was hungry. Or, she *had* been – her appetite seemed to have deserted her.

It felt rather surreal as they were shown to a table and their drinks order was taken.

All Ceri could think about was what might happen after dinner, and she picked the first thing her gaze alighted on when she looked at the menu, hardly tasting her meal when it arrived.

Damon seemed equally distracted, pushing his food around the plate, and every time his eyes met hers, her heart missed a beat at the naked desire she saw in them. Dinner was exquisite torture, for her at least, and she couldn't wait for it to end.

Eventually, Ceri couldn't stand it any longer, and when the waiter cleared their plates away and asked whether they would like to see the dessert menu, she waited for the man to leave, then said, 'What I want for dessert isn't on the menu.'

Damon's eyes smouldered and Ceri inhaled sharply as she heard his low growl of acquiescence. Her pulse throbbing in her throat, he took her by the hand and led her outside to the car, but before they got in, he turned to face her.

'I've wanted to do this all evening,' he murmured.

Then he kissed her, a light brush of his lips against hers, which was over far too soon but held a promise of wonderful things to come.

—

Damon pulled over and the car came to a halt directly outside Ceri's cottage. She got out and he quickly followed her inside, his heart thudding as desire caught him in its grasp.

Her eyes never leaving his face, Ceri reached around him to push the door shut, and he could feel the warmth of her skin through his shirt and the scent of her invaded his nostrils.

He wanted her so badly it hurt.

She seemed to be waiting for him to make the first move, so he did.

Tracing a finger down her neck and along her collar-bone, he eased the strap of her summer dress to one side, baring her shoulder. Her skin was soft, golden, and incredibly inviting.

She stiffened and gasped when he kissed the very same spot his finger had touched, and he groaned in response, fighting the desperate urge to make love to her there and then, hungry and fast. Although it might satisfy his immediate desire, and possibly even hers, she deserved better – she deserved to be worshipped, to have every part of her adored.

Ceri remained immobile as his tongue licked a path from her shoulder to her neck, but her breathing had quickened, and when he glanced at her face, her lips were parted and her eyes were closed. Tilting her head to the side, she invited him to carry on kissing her neck, and when his mouth reached the delicate skin beneath her ear, she gasped again and squirmed in delight.

'Upstairs,' she breathed. 'Please…'

Damon didn't need telling twice. Without waiting for her to lead the way, he scooped her into his arms, settling her against his chest, and headed for the stairs, stumbling halfway up as she nibbled and kissed his neck, her soft murmured laughter telling him that she was getting her own back.

He reached the tiny landing, glanced to the right, then the left, saw a double bed with a pair of slippers poking out from under the metal frame and aimed for it.

Lowering her down gently, he paused for a moment, drinking her in.

She was so beautiful, lying there dishevelled and wanton, her eyes dark with desire, a hint of rose spreading across her cheeks. He wanted to remember it, to savour this moment before she became his and he became hers. They were on the cusp of something wonderful, and he didn't want to rush it.

Slowly, slowly, he peeled off her clothes, then his own, his eyes never leaving hers, then he kissed her and knew his life would never be the same again.

–

'Helloooo? Ceri? Are you there?' Huw's voice floated up the stairs, and Ceri's eyes snapped open.

Oh, God, it was her brother, and from the sound of it, he was downstairs.

Slowly, she looked into the face of the man whose arms she was wrapped in. He was wide awake and gazing solemnly back at her.

'It's my brother. I'll get rid of him,' she whispered. 'Stay here.' She slipped out of bed and grabbed her dressing gown. 'Coming!'

As she trotted downstairs, she could hear Huw in the kitchen and she found him standing near the back door.

'There you are,' he said. 'I thought you might have been in the garden. Have you only just got up?'

'Yes. Huw, you could have knocked.'

'I did, but when I didn't get any answer, I assumed you were outside.'

'If you do that again, I'm going to ask for my key back,' she grumbled. 'You can't just let yourself in whenever you feel like it. This is *my* house now.'

'Ooh, get her,' he drawled. 'Who's got out of the wrong side of the bed this morning? Anyway, I didn't let myself in; the door wasn't locked.'

Ruddy hell, she had forgotten to lock it last night, although she supposed she could be forgiven, as she'd had something else on her mind at the time.

Ceri went on the defensive. 'So that means you tried the handle,' she argued.

Huw looked smug. 'I didn't have to. I can tell when the door is unlocked because the handle isn't all the way up.'

'Smart arse. What do you want anyway?'

'Mrs Moxley wants to know if she can have one of the plots on your allotment.'

'It's not *my* allotment. Tell her to speak to Terry. He's organising that side of things.'

'Apparently, she did and he told her to speak to you. First come, first served, he said, so she wanted to make sure she was the first. She would have come to see you herself, but she's doing a shift in Sero. Have you got any bacon? I'm starving.'

'No. Go home and make breakfast in your own house.'

'Grumpy-guts. How about you get dressed and we'll have breakfast in Pen's Pantry? It'll be more like lunch, though.' He peered at her. 'Are you OK? Not feeling ill, are you? You look a bit flushed.' He backed away. 'Whatever you've got, don't give it to me. I don't want to catch it.'

Ceri thought he already had... Ever since he'd met Rowena he'd had an acute case of love-itus. And after last night, Ceri was beginning to feel she might be heading in that direction herself. It had been... *wonderful*. She hugged herself, remembering. No wonder they had slept in this morning, because neither she nor Damon had managed much sleep last night. The thought made her giggle.

'Have you got a temperature?' Huw asked suspiciously. 'I think you've got a rash – your face has gone all red and blotchy.'

'I am not red and blotchy.' She checked her appearance in the mirror hanging above the fireplace. Damn it! She *was* blotchy. It was probably from Damon's stubbly chin on her sensitive skin. It wasn't a rash she had, it was beard burn caused by too much kissing.

A noise from upstairs made her flinch and she glanced at the ceiling.

'What was that?' Huw began, then a knowing expression stole across his face. 'You've got someone here, haven't you? Who does that car belong to?'

'What car?'

'The one parked outside your house. I'd assumed one of the neighbours had changed their car, or they've got a visitor, but I'm beginning to suspect that it's *you* who's got a visitor… one who stayed all night.'

Ceri scowled and blushed furiously.

'I'm right, aren't I?' he crowed. Lowering his voice, he said, 'Who is it? Someone from the college? *Mark?*'

'Aside from him being my boss, Mark is married, so no, not Mark.'

'Who then?'

'Me.' Damon had appeared at the bottom of the stairs, fully dressed. He looked far less ruffled than she did, and she felt quite put out. He didn't look as though he'd made love all night and then some! He looked gorgeous, and Ceri wanted nothing more than to take him to bed again.

Huw's mouth dropped open. He glanced at Ceri, who rolled her eyes. 'Damon, this is my annoying older brother, Huw. Huw, meet Damon. And close your mouth, Huw. It's not your best look.'

'Um, nice to meet you,' Huw said. He was staring at Damon, his eyes wide.

Damon said, 'You, too. I'll be off, Ceri.' He took a step towards the door. 'Can I call you?'

'I'll be cheesed off if you don't.' She walked over to him, and whispered, 'Sorry about this.'

He stroked her cheek. 'Later?'

'Definitely.' She lifted her face to be kissed. It might have gone on a little longer than she intended because Huw coughed loudly.

Ceri saw Damon out and prepared herself for the barrage of questions she knew was about to come her way. 'I'll get dressed, then you can take me for brunch,' she said to her incredibly annoying brother. 'You're paying.'

—

Damon could smell her on him. Ceri's unique scent clung to his skin, his hair, his clothes. If he closed his eyes he could still see her sprawled naked across the bed, could still hear the murmured noises of pleasure she'd made, could still feel the softness of her skin under his hands.

He missed her already and he had only just parted from her.

How had she got under his skin so deeply in such a short amount of time? And how had he let it happen, knowing that he would be out of her life within the next few weeks?

Fidgety, unused to feeling this way, he did what he always did when he was restless or out-of-sorts – he turned to music and before long he had lost himself in another composition. Ceri was at the heart of this one, too…

She had also managed to wriggle her way into his actual heart, and it was a strange feeling. Excitement coiled in his belly at the thought of seeing her later, and his pulse leapt. He had to call her now, this minute. He needed to hear her voice. He needed to check that last night hadn't been a one-off.

Powerlessly he dialled her number and the relief when she answered was worrying. He was in so, so deep...

'Hi, you,' she said, softly.

'Hi. What are you doing?'

'Nothing much. You?'

'Nothing much, playing music,' he said, knowing she would assume he was listening to it, not composing it. He took a deep breath. 'And missing you.'

'That's good, because I'm missing you, too.'

'Can I see you again?'

'When?'

'Now?'

'I'll be there in ten minutes.'

Damon put the phone down. Ten minutes. Even that was too long to wait, but at least it gave him time to stash his guitar and his sheet music. He would tell her, but not just yet. At the moment he was luxuriating in his anonymity and he didn't want anything to alter her opinion of him. Deep down he knew she wasn't like that, but it was too soon, their relationship too new... And he was all too aware of its fragility. He would be returning to London shortly, and he had no idea how to deal with that.

Chapter 14

The church hall was bustling with noise as people took their seats. Ceri was surprised and somewhat alarmed by how well attended the meeting was. Terry had invited all the villagers who were interested in renting a plot on the allotment, and the turnout was considerably larger than Ceri had anticipated for a Tuesday evening.

'There aren't enough plots to go round,' she hissed to Terry out of the corner of her mouth. She and the vicar were perched on the raised dais at the front of the hall, and she felt hideously conspicuous. This was worse than the first time she had stood in front of a class.

'It'll be fine,' he said, airily. 'Although there may well be one or two disappointed people.'

'One or two? There'll be loads.'

'See Mrs Moxley?'

Ceri scanned the room, then nodded when she spotted the old lady. Mrs Moxley beamed at her and gave her a thumbs up. Ceri smiled weakly back.

Terry said, 'She wants a plot – I told her to speak to you, by the way – but she's brought her daughter, her granddaughter and great-grandkids with her for moral support. And for the tea and biscuits afterwards, and because it's something to do on a Tuesday evening – although you would have thought that those kiddies should be in bed. What was I saying? Oh, yes... you can rule her lot out. Only Mrs Moxley wants a plot. I suspect the rest of the family will be roped in to help though, as I can't see her doing all that digging on her own.' He scanned the room. 'And there are plenty of others who'll want to have a plot as a family. Take Ianto Phelps, for instance.' Terry pointed to an elderly chap wearing a flat cap. 'He's here with his wife, and I dare say they'll be working their plot together, as will a good many others. So, it's not as bad as it looks,' he finished.

Thank goodness for that – Ceri had feared she was about to be lynched.

At seven o'clock on the dot, Terry yelled, 'Order! Order!' and the noise subsided. 'Thank you for coming. I'll now hand you over to the woman behind the allotment's resurrection, Ceri Morgan.'

Ceri gulped. She hadn't expected to be thrown to the wolves – she had assumed Terry was going to lead the meeting.

Getting shakily to her feet, she said, 'Er, hello, everyone. I understand you're here because you want a plot in the allotment? Ha, ha, of course you are.' She swallowed nervously. 'Terry has passed on a list of names, and as you know, the plot allocation will be on a first come, first served basis.' A couple of boos were offset by a few cheers.

'Fix!' someone yelled.

Someone else called, 'Shut up, Aled. Why are you here anyway? You don't need an allotment, you've got a ruddy great farm.'

Terry leant nearer to Ceri and whispered in her ear, 'He's one of those who is only here for the refreshments.'

Ceri took a drink of water, her mouth dry, then carried on. 'There are sixteen plots available, roughly twenty-five square metres each, and mostly rectangular.'

'Who gets first dibs?' Mrs Moxley called. 'I don't want just any old plot.'

Ceri had been thinking about this. 'We're going to number the plots, then draw names out of a hat,' she said, firmly.

'All except Ceri herself,' Terry interrupted. 'If it wasn't for her, there wouldn't *be* an allotment, so I reckon she should have her pick.'

Ceri blushed furiously. She had been planning on choosing her plot first anyway, and it simply hadn't occurred to her that she wasn't being democratic.

To her relief, there were lots of nodding heads in the room, so she felt able to continue. 'I'll mark out the plots,' she said, 'and when that's done and they've been allocated, Terry will be performing a little opening ceremony, which you are all welcome to attend. But you'll have to bring your own drinks and biscuits, I'm afraid...' Laugher followed, and after several questions, the meeting broke up as people headed for Betsan, who was presiding over the tea urn and the plates of biscuits.

'Do you need any help marking out the plots?' Terry asked, after he had fetched them both a cup of tea.

'I'm going to ask my head of department if he can spare a couple of hours and the minibus, as I thought my students might like to do it. They handed in an assignment today with their plans for the allotment and I must say, I'm rather impressed. I haven't had a chance to grade them yet, but I've had a quick look and a couple of them have got it spot on, the way it was when Hyacinth Rogers ran it. Whoever laid it out originally knew what they were doing.'

'That would have been Hyacinth herself.' Mrs Moxley had sneaked up on them unawares and inserted herself between them. 'She used to love that allotment. Took great pride in it, she did. And her garden. It's such a shame it's been allowed to go to rack and ruin. It was lovely, it was. A proper cottage garden with proper flowers. You could have taken a photo of it and put it on a chocolate box.' She slurped her tea. 'What about the orchard? Those apples could have given the ones in the Garden of Eden a run for their money.'

'I'm afraid the orchard isn't part of the deal.' Ceri was disappointed about that, too, but if she owned an orchard as lovely as Damon's, she probably wouldn't want loads of people trampling through it either.

Mrs Moxley's eyes lit up at the possibility of some gossip. 'I've heard rumours that someone is living in Willow Tree House.'

Terry said, 'I believe Hyacinth's grandson has moved back in.'

'Oh, I do hope so!' the old lady exclaimed. 'She left the house to him, you know. And all her money. Her son didn't get a look in. Mind you, I don't blame her – that son of hers was always off gallivanting. All over the world he's been, digging here and digging there. Neither him nor that wife of his could lift their noses out of the dirt long enough to pay that boy any attention. Packed him off to boarding school as soon as he was old enough, the poor little sod. If it wasn't for Hyacinth, young Damon wouldn't have had a home life. He used to spend every summer with her and most of the other school holidays, too. He was a lovely boy. Very polite.' She sighed

184

dramatically. 'Hyacinth missed him dreadfully when he stopped coming so often, but I suppose he got too old for Foxmore. I bet our Rachel's kids won't want to hang about once they hit their teenage years. They'll be off like rats up a drainpipe.'

Ceri wasn't sure she approved of Mrs Moxley talking so freely about Damon's past, and she suspected he would be mortified if he knew. But then, from what Mrs Moxley had said, he had lived in Foxmore long enough to know what the village was like. Everyone knew everyone else's business, and no one could keep anything secret for long. He had been away for quite a few years, though, so maybe he had forgotten how gossipy it could get.

She thought back to the comment Eleanor had made about Foxmore being a dump. It was ironic that so many teenagers couldn't wait to leave a village like this, yet when they had families of their own, they often couldn't wait to come back. She was certainly glad she'd made the move. Cardiff had been a great place to live and she'd had such a lot of fun, but now she was ready to settle down. And what better place to settle down in than Foxmore? And what better man to settle down with than Damon?

Silently she chided herself for such thoughts. Their relationship was far too new to be doodling Mrs Ceri Rogers on the back page of an exercise book, the way she used to write Ceri Sharples when she was in Year 9 and had a major crush on Wayne Sharples. She and Damon had to get to know one another properly first. Even though they had slept together and had explored each other's bodies, she had yet to explore his mind and there was so much she didn't know about him.

One of the things – one that had been niggling at her for a while – was what he did for a living. He'd told her that he was living off his investments, which was all well and good, but she still hadn't established what he did to have amassed those investments in the first place. Or had he inherited them from Hyacinth, as Mrs Moxley had suggested? Despite knowing him intimately, she didn't feel she could ask. Not just yet. Give it a couple of weeks, and maybe she would.

She had learned a little about his childhood this evening though, and her heart went out to him as she thought about what Mrs Moxley had said. How awful that he'd been shunted off to his grandma's house in the country because his parents were too busy. It was also a shame that he hadn't been back in a while... But he was here now, and that was what mattered.

They had spent all weekend together, mostly in bed. She couldn't get enough of him, and she hugged herself as she remembered how perfect it had been.

Almost perfect...

Damon was an attentive and generous lover, passionate yet considerate, giving freely of himself. Physically, at least. Emotionally, though... she sensed he was holding back and she wondered whether it had anything to do with the strange episode he'd had on the day she had helped him clear his drive.

As for her, Ceri hadn't held back – she hadn't been able to, because she had never felt this way about anyone before.

–

Damon felt very conspicuous sitting in The Jolly Fox by himself. He felt as though people were staring at him. But Foxmore was a busy little place, thronging with walkers, climbers and campers throughout the summer months, and he hoped that if anyone did notice him, they would assume he was a tourist, here to enjoy the great outdoors and a pint in the pub after a day in the mountains.

He was aware he was taking a risk being here, but when Ceri had suggested having a meal in the pub after the meeting, she'd caught him unawares and he hadn't been quick enough to think of an excuse. Besides, he had ventured into the heart of the village on several occasions, and nobody had recognised him so far, so he was hopeful that would also be the case this evening.

Keeping his eyes fixed on the door, Damon's heart leapt when he caught sight of Ceri. Her face was glowing and her eyes shone, and he waved to gain her attention. Her beaming smile when she saw him and hurried over, made it leap again.

'I take it the meeting went well,' he said, after fetching her a drink from the bar. So far so good, he thought: the barman hadn't looked at him twice, and neither had anyone else. Damon had a couple of menus tucked under his arm, and he handed one to her.

She said, 'I'm famished. I haven't eaten a thing since one o'clock. Yes, it went really well. Terry threw me in at the deep end and got me to do all the talking, but I didn't make a fool of myself, thank goodness. It's going to be hard work breaking the ground, and the rest of this year will be spent preparing the plots ready for spring planting,' she added. 'I doubt if much will be grown from now until then, although if people get a move on they could sow spinach, spring cabbage, turnips, and some autumn salad leaves. If they are sensible, they'll do a bit at a time, and not try to do it all in one go. Twenty-five square metres doesn't sound very much, and it doesn't look particularly large until you have to work it. Managed well, it should feed a family of four all year round. But as I said, it won't be producing much for a while.'

She stopped to take a drink, and he studied her. The glow was still there, and he realised she was in her element. She lived and breathed plants, and they were as vital to her as oxygen.

'I've been thinking,' Ceri said. There was a hopeful look on her face with a hint of pleading behind it, and he had a feeling he wasn't going to like what she was about to say.

'The orchard… Mrs Moxley asked me about it. I told her it wasn't part of the allotment, but it got me thinking.' She put a hand on his. 'With the allotment not producing anything significant for a while, I thought it might be nice for the plotters to pick some of your fruit. It would save it from going to waste, and they could help tidy the orchard up and cut the brambles back in exchange.'

Damon didn't hesitate. 'Definitely not.'

Ceri's eyes widened and he realised he had been rather abrupt.

'Sorry, Ceri, but I don't think I can face seeing people in Gran's orchard.' He couldn't face seeing anyone on any part of his property. The risk of being recognised was too great. Maybe after he left…? But even then, he wasn't keen.

'Not even me?' Her voice was small.

'You aren't *people*.'

'What am I?'

Damon struggled to answer.

'A friend with benefits?' Ceri asked archly.

'No!' Did she really think that? 'You are far more to me than a friend.' He reached out a hand to brush a strand of hair away from her face. 'Far, far more,' he murmured.

She gazed deeply into his eyes and he stared back, willing her to believe him. Oh, God, it was going to be so hard when the time came for him to leave, and he feared that the more time he spent with her, the harder it was going to be.

But what was the alternative – end it now?

He couldn't even contemplate it.

A strident voice made him flinch, breaking the mood and he looked up to see an old lady bearing down on their table. His heart sank as he recognised her. It was Mrs Moxley, an old friend of his grandmother's, and he prayed she didn't recognise him.

'Ooh, look at them curls,' she cried, and it took a second for Damon to realise she was speaking to him. 'Our Rachel's got hair just like that, but hers is more frizz and less curl. Is it natural?' The woman put out a hand to stroke his hair.

Damon jerked back in alarm. He caught Ceri's eye and saw her trying not to laugh.

Mrs Moxley said, 'Aw, don't be a spoilsport. Let me have a feel. It looks well lush, as our Rachel would say. She's my granddaughter.'

'*Well lush?*'

'Thick and shiny,' the old lady said.

She was staring at him expectantly, so in the hope that once she got what she wanted she would leave him in peace, he said, 'Go on then, but I don't let just anyone touch my hair.'

'A bit of a prima donna, are you?' she chortled, grasping a handful of curls.

'Not at all.' He was the least prima donna-ish member of the band. Aiden had been the most. He swallowed hard, enduring her touch as she stroked his hair.

'Ooh, it's so soft!' she cried. 'Have you felt it?' This was aimed at Ceri.

Ceri shot him an amused look, before saying, 'Yes, I have.'

Damon's expression was pained. He was sorely tempted to cut it all off.

'What do you use on it?' Mrs Moxley asked.

'Er, nothing special.'

'Don't let our Rachel hear you say that – she spends a fortune on hers. Aren't you going to introduce me?' she demanded. She had asked Ceri the question, but her gaze was trained on him.

Damon's heart sank.

Ceri was happy to oblige, and she was smiling as she said, 'This is Damon, Hyacinth's grandson.'

'Well, I never!' she exclaimed. 'I knew you when you was a boy. Remember me? I'm Mrs Moxley. I used to dangle you on my knee once upon a time. So...' She fixed him with a beady-eyed stare. 'You've moved back to Foxmore, have you? I must say, it's about time. Your gran would be pleased, God rest her soul, although she probably wouldn't recognise you. I certainly didn't. He's changed a fair bit, has Damon.' She directed this last comment to Ceri, then turned back to Damon. 'Come here, let me give you a hug.' She held her arms open, lurched forward and almost fell into his lap in her eager-ness.

When Mrs Moxley eventually straightened up, she said, 'Hyacinth was so proud of you. By the way, how is that band of yours doing?' She said to Ceri, 'He was always playing his guitar when he was a nipper, and Hyacinth told me that he and some of his friends were in a band.' She switched her attention back to Damon, whose heart was in his mouth. 'I expect you've grown out of all that by now, so what do you do with yourself these days?' She looked at him expectantly.

He inhaled slowly, trying to stay calm, and berated himself for his stupidity in thinking he could remain anonymous in a place like Foxmore. He should have anticipated that people would expect to be introduced to him. He should never have come out this evening; he should have stayed at home and ordered a takeaway if Ceri was fed up with his cooking.

'Excuse me.' He got to his feet and stumbled in the direction of the gents' toilets, and when he reached them he leant against one of the wash hand basins and stared at his reflection in dismay. How did Mrs Moxley know about the band? Black Hyacinth had only formed a short while before his gran died, and he'd mentioned it to her just a handful of times. He had been in his final year of university and about to start work for an insurance company on their graduate fast-track programme, and the band had been more of a hobby and a pipedream than a real possibility. He'd got the impression that Gran had been more pleased with the prospect of him having steady employment than listening to him chuntering on about music. She'd passed away before Black Hyacinth had signed their first record deal, when the only things the band had been known for were YouTube videos and the occasional gig in a sticky-floored pub or a student union bar. It had hardly been the big time.

Tears prickled as he replayed Mrs Moxley's words in his head. *Gran had been proud of him*. He wished with all his heart that she could have seen him in concert. She would have complained bitterly about the noise, would have griped about the lack of lighting (Black Hyacinth's sets were *dark*) and she wouldn't have approved of the tattoos, either – but she would have been thrilled, nevertheless.

Angrily, he brushed away the moisture from his eyes. The last place he wanted to cry was in the toilets of a pub. Pulling himself together, Damon splashed water on his face, dabbed his cheeks dry with a paper towel, and straightened his shoulders.

It was time he told Ceri the truth.

–

Ceri watched Damon leave the table, worry niggling at her. She had no idea what Mrs Moxley had said to upset him – unless it was talking about his gran.

With one eye on the door leading to the loos, she carried on a desultory conversation with Mrs Moxley, not really listening to what the elderly woman was saying, and when she saw him emerge, she noticed that his jaw was clenched and he looked tense.

When he jerked his head towards the exit, Ceri made her excuses.

'What's wrong?' she asked as soon as they were outside.

'We need to talk. Do you mind if we take a walk?'

Someone saying 'we need to talk' was never a good sign, especially when those words were uttered by the person you were in a relationship with. Taking hold of his arm, she made him stop and turn to face her. 'What is it?'

'Not here.'

The pain in his eyes made her flinch. Whatever this was, it wasn't good.

Ceri was so focused on Damon that when a large white SUV slowed to a crawl alongside them, it took her a second to notice.

'Damon! Over here. *Damon!*'

His head shot up, a shocked expression on his face. Ceri thought she saw a hint of fear in it, too, but she must have imagined it, because he immediately broke into a beaming grin and headed for the car and the woman who was leaning out of the driver's window. She had her arms outstretched and was making 'come here' gestures.

In three strides, Damon reached the vehicle and the woman's arms wrapped around his neck. Ceri didn't think they were actually kissing, but they were certainly pleased to see each other.

Awkwardly, she remained where she was, wondering what to do. Who was this woman, and what was she to Damon? She clearly knew him well, because she had clambered out of the car and was now throwing herself at him again.

In her mid-twenties, with long blond hair tumbling to her waist, she was dressed in grey faded skinny jeans and a cropped black T-shirt with a logo splashed across it which showed off her washboard stomach. One arm sported a full sleeve of tattoos, the other was festooned with black leather straps and armbands. Her makeup was skilfully applied, although heavier and darker than Ceri favoured (if she bothered to wear any at all) and to complete the picture, the woman wore scuffed black calf-length boots, despite the warmth of the evening.

She looked amazing and Ceri felt drab and ordinary in comparison.

Finally they parted, and as Damon stepped back Ceri realised that he must have forgotten all about her, because when he glanced over his shoulder his expression closed in as he noticed her hovering awkwardly on the pavement.

'Don't worry, I'm going,' she muttered, a lump forming in her throat and her eyes stinging. She couldn't believe she had been so gullible. Of *course* a man like Damon would have a girlfriend.

The girlfriend was gazing at her curiously. 'Who's this?' she asked him.

'Er, Ceri.' It was little more than a mutter. Damon was obviously embarrassed. And so he should be.

'Ceri? Hi.' The woman stepped forward and held out her hand.

Ceri stared at it, then good manners kicked in and she shook it.

'I'm Sadie, Aiden's sister.' The woman swallowed and dropped her gaze to the pavement.

Ceri had no idea who Aiden was and neither did she care. But she had a fair idea who Sadie might be, though, and she felt sick to think that he was in a relationship. She shook her head in disbelief, the pain of his betrayal stabbing her in the solar plexus.

Sadie's eyes shot to Damon, then back to Ceri. 'Aiden… the bass player in Black Hyacinth?' She looked at Damon again and said, 'Don't tell me she doesn't know?'

Ceri found her voice. 'Know what? That you two are an item? I think I've managed to work that out for myself.'

Damon glanced at Sadie, before turning back to Ceri. His expression was unreadable. 'We are not an item.'

Ceri frowned. He sounded so emphatic that she wondered if she'd got it wrong. 'What, then? What don't I know?'

Damon caught his bottom lip between his teeth. He looked uncomfortable. 'That was what I wanted to talk to you about. I'm, um, in a band.'

Sadie interjected, 'He's the lead singer in Black Hyacinth.'

Her mind blank, all Ceri could think about were the flowers on his grandmother's grave.

Sadie hummed a few bars of something familiar, and suddenly Ceri got it and everything slotted into place.

'*"Dark Dimension"*,' she whispered. '*You* are in *Black Hyacinth*?'

'Yeah, I wanted to—'

Ceri didn't care what he wanted: she'd heard and seen enough.

Black Hyacinth was famous. *Damon* was famous. And he had just made a total fool of her.

Furious, hurt, and embarrassed, Ceri turned on her heel, and marched off up the pavement. Tears were gathering and there was no way she was going to let Damon see them fall. She refused to let him see how much he'd hurt her.

He should have told her. Not led her on, allowing her to believe they might have a future together when all he had been interested in was getting his leg over whilst he hid in Foxmore for a few weeks.

More fool her!

She'd thought she had found her perfect man, but he had lied to her and that was something she could never forgive.

Chapter 15

Damon knew he had to go after her right now. He had to make Ceri see things from his point of view. She needed to understand that he had been just about to tell her who he was when Sadie turned up.

He took a step, then felt Sadie catch hold of his arm.

'You said to come for a visit.' Her tone was plaintive and he hesitated.

Ceri was hurrying along the pavement and had almost reached the turn off to her road. He wanted to catch her before she got to her cottage.

'Here.' He yanked his keys out of his pocket. 'Left and left again. My house is at the end of the lane. I'll see you later.'

He was aware of Sadie's eyes on him as he broke into a run, but he didn't wait to see if she followed his instructions. His attention was wholly and utterly on the woman he was falling for.

'Ceri!' he yelled, and he saw her falter, so he knew she'd heard him. But she didn't stop, and he only caught up with her as she was about to open the little gate to Rosehip Cottage.

'Go away,' she said, refusing to look at him. Her cheeks were wet and he could see she was crying.

'Not until you let me explain,' he begged.

'You lied to me.'

'I didn't. Not exactly.'

'Semantics,' she spat, and he was forced to concede that she was right. He mightn't have lied, but he hadn't been entirely truthful either.

'Please let me explain.'

'Oh, bugger off, why don't you! Go back to London, or wherever it is you live. Go back to your rock star life and *leave me alone.*'

'No, I…' Damon's heart was racing and his head was starting to pound.

Not now, please, not now.

His chest was a ball of pain. He couldn't breathe and noise filled his ears until all he could hear was Aiden screaming, forever eternally screaming—

Gasping for breath, the world spinning around him, Damon knew he was about to pass out.

'Damon… *Damon!*'

He heard Ceri's voice and felt her tug on his arm, urging him to the ground. He sank down, the stone step cool underneath his clammy hands as his head was shoved roughly from behind, forcing his face between his knees.

'Breathe, breathe,' she commanded.

Damon breathed, one shaky inhalation at a time as he struggled not to gasp. There wasn't enough oxygen in the air and his vision began to blur.

'You're OK, I'm here, you'll be fine.' Her voice was calm and soothing, and he forced himself to focus on it, using her to tether him to the here and now, desperate not to let the past tighten its grip and drag him down.

Slowly, slowly, the darkness receded until, several long deep breaths later, he was able to sit up.

Ceri was gazing at him in concern. 'Just a thing that happens sometimes?'

He lifted a shoulder, feeling drained, emotionally and physically, and hoped he wouldn't cry, despite wanting to burst into tears. That was what he had said to her, *'Just a thing that happens sometimes'*. God, it was so much more than *a thing*… It was taking over his life and his sanity, and he feared he would never be free of it.

'Is it because of Aiden?' she asked.

He nodded, and she sat down beside him, forcing him to scoot over slightly so they could both fit on the step.

'You must think I'm a right wimp,' he said. He was trying to sound normal, but he knew she could see through him.

'Because you suffer from panic attacks? Not at all.'

'Is that what they are?'

'I'm no medical expert, but it sounds like it.'

He hadn't considered that possibility, but a panic attack made perfect sense. He certainly felt an overwhelming sense of panic whenever it happened, just as he had done that night when he'd heard Aiden's—

Nope, he wasn't going to think about it right now. One episode a day was enough, another might send him over the edge.

Ceri said, 'Do you want to talk about it?'

He didn't, but perhaps that was part of the problem – that he had been trying to keep it in. But he supposed the grief, the remorse and the guilt had to come out some way, and his subconscious mind had chosen the panic attack route.

Taking a deep breath, he reached for her hand, grateful when she didn't pull away. Then he began.

'We were on tour in Berlin, a city we'd played in twice before but had seen little of. The first time had been in an-and-out job: do the gig, then drive to the next venue straight after. I wish with all my heart that the second time had been just as hurried, but it was the last stop on the tour and most of us had wanted to let our hair down. Luke flew to England the next day because he wanted to see his family, but me, Aiden, Frank – our manager – and some of the roadies were still in the hotel, which might explain how details of where we were staying got out.'

He closed his eyes briefly, before opening them again and carrying on. 'Aiden had a new car and he wanted to try it out. One of the roadies had driven it over from the UK so Aiden could drive it back to London because those German motorways are fast. He asked me to go with him, but I wanted to stay and explore the city. Take a bit of a break, you know, because those last few months had been gruelling – constant travel, trying to kip in the bus, catching meals when we could. It had its upsides, too, of course.' He smiled sadly. 'Little can compare to the thrill of being onstage in front of several thousand fans.'

Ceri squeezed his hand for him to continue.

Damon blinked hard, blew out his cheeks and looked up at the sky. 'Aiden's car was in the basement car park of the hotel. He'd unlocked it to put his stuff in but had forgotten his passport, so he went back to the room. While he was gone a fan, a fifteen-year-old girl, snuck in the back and hid.' He swallowed and Ceri could see how hard this was for him.

'Maybe if Aiden had been going slower he would have stood a chance, but the girl panicked when she realised he wasn't just out for a joyride, but was heading to France. She tried to get in the front seat and Aiden lost control. He was killed. She walked away with scratches and a broken arm.' He pulled a face. 'He was on the phone to me when it happened. I heard the whole thing.'

'Oh, God, no wonder you're getting panic attacks. How awful – for all of you.' Ceri stroked his arm, her expression full of sympathy.

Damon scowled. 'He shouldn't have been driving on a German motorway in a car that was too powerful for its own good. He shouldn't have been on the phone. If I had agreed to go with him, the accident never would have happened. He would have watched his speed because I would have nagged him to slow down, and he definitely wouldn't have been on the phone. And if I had gone with him, that girl would never have been able to get near the car, let alone hide in it.'

'You can't blame yourself. It was an accident.'

'I can and I do.' His eyes were haunted when he turned his gaze on her. 'I always will.' Damon's voice was hoarse. 'I should have told you who I was, but I couldn't bear it if the press found out where I was. Or the fans.'

He shuddered with distaste as he remembered how he used to love the adoration, and how he used to love being in the limelight, despite his overriding passion being for the performance itself and not the associated fame. But not now.

Pain stabbed at his chest and he briefly closed his eyes. Was this it, was this the end of him and Ceri? He feared that whatever they had was over and he was shocked by how much it hurt. Without meaning to, he had fallen for this woman. He should never have let her into his garden…

But he strongly suspected he had let her into his heart way before that, when he had watched her dance under the stars in a flower-scented meadow.

Ceri stared into the distance, her expression guarded.

Night was falling and twilight lay heavily in the deepening shadows and the silhouettes of the trees in the churchyard opposite. Bats were looping and swooping in the air above their heads and a blackbird sang its final song of the evening before fading into silence.

Finally, she spoke. 'You named the band after your gran, didn't you?'

'Yes.'

'And the flower?'

He nodded. 'We also named our first proper hit after her favourite variety.'

'"Dark Dimension". I should have guessed. All the clues were there... the guitar, the sheet music. It wasn't the radio or a playlist I heard that night – it was *you*.' She twisted around to face him. 'I get why you didn't want anyone to know who you were, but you should have told me before we slept together.'

'That's the thing – I didn't *want* you to know. I was happy with you *not* knowing. You made me feel ordinary. You got to know me for myself, not because I'm Damon Rogers, lead singer of Black Hyacinth.'

She was studying him, a hint of pity in her eyes. 'Yes, I did.'

Her lips parted and his gaze dropped to her mouth. He desperately wanted to kiss her, but he was too scared to try. She might understand why he'd kept his identity from her, but he didn't believe she would forgive him.

But when she leant towards him and her arms wound around his neck, he knew that she had, and as he lost himself in the kiss he realised that he never wanted to let this wonderful woman go.

Ceri trailed her hand across the bowed heads of the poppies growing between the headstones as she made her way across the graveyard to the place where Hyacinth was buried.

The headstone was black marble, and it caught the light of the full moon as it shone through the trees, casting dappled shadows across its gleaming dark surface. The words were picked out in white, a stark contrast.

Ceri noticed fresh flowers and assumed Damon must have put them there. She also noticed that the hyacinths he had planted were fading fast. Soon the goodness in the leaves would be withdrawn into the bulbs and the plants would lie dormant until next spring.

Slowly sinking to the ground, she sat cross-legged next to Hyacinth's grave and wondered where to begin.

She wasn't entirely sure why she was here, but after they'd said their goodbyes and Damon had left to see to his guest, she had been too restless to sit still, and her feet had brought her to Hyacinth.

Sighing, she plucked one of the leaves and brushed it absently against her cheek.

'I don't know why I'm here,' she began, 'but although we've never met, I feel I can talk to you.' She had already felt an affinity to the woman who had created such a beautiful garden when she had been shown around it, and now they also had a shared concern for Damon in common.

'Mrs Moxley is right: you would have been proud of your grandson. Maybe not so much when it comes to your garden, though,' she added quietly. 'It's going to take more time and effort than Damon can give, to bring it back to its former glory. Actually, that's what I want to talk to you about...'

Ceri had no idea whether any good would come of sharing her feelings with an inanimate headstone, but she felt there was no one else she could talk to. And talking it through might help get things straight in her head, because right now she was a jumbled mess of conflicting emotions that she had no idea how to deal with, having never before felt this way about any man.

Damon had got under her skin from the very first moment she had seen him watching her dance in the meadow, and he had worked his way into her heart without her even realising. But it had taken the events of this evening, when she thought she had lost him, for her to understand that she had fallen in love.

How reckless of her.

It didn't take a genius to know that Damon Rogers of Black Hyacinth fame would never be content in a small place like Foxmore. He was here to heal and once he had, he'd be off, back to fame and stardom, and she'd be left with nothing but her memories.

Ceri didn't want him to go. She wanted to get to know him properly, to see where this brand new relationship of theirs might lead. But she knew he wouldn't give it up for her. And neither would she ask him to, because trying to keep him here would be like trying to hold on to starlight – impossible.

She should have ended it tonight, as soon as he'd told her the truth, but she hadn't been able to. Instead, she had forgiven him his deception and had kissed him until she was breathless and weak with longing.

'Oh, Hyacinth, what am I going to do?'

Was it her imagination, or did she hear the wind whisper, '*Follow your heart…*'

Getting to her feet, Ceri trailed her fingers across the smooth marble, lingering on the name of the woman who rested there, vowing to make the most of the time she and Damon had together. It was the only thing she could do.

–

Sadie had discovered the wine. When Damon entered the house, he found the door to the cellar ajar and Aiden's sister sitting in the corner of the sofa with her legs tucked underneath her bottom and a glass of red in her hand.

She leapt to her feet when she saw him, hastily put the glass down, slopping some of its contents on the little table, then flung her arms around his neck and clung to him. He could feel her trembling as she began to cry.

Damon held her for a long time as she sobbed, his own grief a hard ball in his chest, until she finally drew away, wiped her cheeks with her fingers, and dropped back onto the sofa. Picking up her wine, she croaked, 'Thanks for letting me stay.'

'Anytime. You know that.'

Sadie held up her glass. 'If you want some, the bottle is in the kitchen.'

Damon poured himself a decent measure, took a gulp, and then plonked down into one of the armchairs.

Sadie asked, 'Is Ceri all right? She looked upset. Sorry, I didn't mean to land you in it.'

Damon shrugged. 'I know you didn't.'

'Is it serious between you?'

'Yeah, I think it might be.'

She drank more of her wine. 'I'm glad. You need someone special in your life.'

'You're special.' He was trying to lighten the mood.

'I know, but I'm not in love with you. And I'm fairly sure you're not in love with me.'

Damon spilled his wine. '*Love?*' he spluttered.

'I saw the way you were looking at her, which was why I assumed she knew.'

'I didn't tell her because it was none of her business at first, then when it should have become her business, I didn't tell her because I wanted her to like me *for me*. I was just about to come clean, when you rocked up and stole my thunder.'

'Sorry.' Her expression was contrite.

'No harm done.' At least, he didn't *think* there was…

Sadie said, 'Luke will be back in the UK next week. He's grumbling that Frank's been on at him to finish those new tracks. Has Frank been nagging you too?'

'He's mentioned it once or twice.' Frank had messaged him several times, and each time Damon had brushed him off.

He dropped his gaze, the thought of returning to the studio filling him with dread.

God, not again… He could sense darkness hovering at the mere thought of it, and his heart began to thud uncomfortably. It felt as though it was banging against his ribcage and would burst out of his chest at any moment.

Sadie drained her glass. 'Want a refill?'

Numbly, he shook his head, and was only dimly aware of her getting off the sofa and walking out of the room.

No, no, no, he prayed, his jaw tensing as he gritted his teeth.

But just as the sound of tortured metal filled his ears, an image of Ceri floated into his mind and he grabbed it, holding onto it the way a drowning man would clutch a lifebuoy. Concentrating hard on her face, he thought about the depths in her eyes, the way she smiled, the little line between her eyebrows when she frowned, and gradually the panic attack receded.

Taking a deep breath, he realised that what had felt like minutes had only been a matter of seconds. He could hear Sadie in the kitchen, the clink of the bottle against the glass as she poured more wine, and elation slammed into him.

He'd beaten it!

He had driven the panic attack away by focusing so deeply on Ceri that it hadn't been able to overwhelm him.

The relief he felt was incredible and he had Ceri to thank.

Maybe he was over the worst, and perhaps he *would* be able to go back to performing live after all? But just as quickly, common sense kicked in and he told himself to slow down. He might have managed to beat it once, but that didn't mean he would beat it again. He'd give it a couple of weeks. Besides, he wasn't ready to leave Foxmore quite yet.

It was then that the realisation struck him: it wasn't the thought of suffering further panic attacks that was responsible for his reluctance to get back to work – it was the thought of leaving *Ceri*.

Chapter 16

Ceri straightened up and arched her spine. It was Thursday morning and she and a dozen or so students were in the middle of marking out plots in the allotment, ready for the opening ceremony on the weekend.

Her back ached from where she had been crouching over, holding a small wooden stake in position whilst one of her students wielded a hammer. It had taken all her willpower to hold the stake firm as the lad drove it into position.

The field had recently been mowed by a delighted Terry on his sit-on mower, and the first thing the students had done when they'd arrived on site this morning was to rake the cut grass into a huge pile in the shadiest corner. It could sit there and slowly decompose, and as it did so it would provide a home for all kinds of creatures.

Next had come the tricky part of marking out the plots and this involved a great deal of measuring. Ceri wanted to make sure each plot was the same square meterage (although not all would be the same shape) and that they were equidistant, with paths between them. At present, the paths were little more than trampled grass, but over time they may be paved or gravelled. The allotment was a work in progress and would evolve and adapt over the coming years.

Ceri had provided the students with a plan for the plots, and she was trying to let them get on with laying them out by themselves, only lending a hand now and again but, in reality, she was supervising them closely.

'This has been a brilliant exercise for them,' Mark said, as he watched the last stake being hammered home. 'Hands-on experience is invaluable. Well done.'

It was great to get such positive feedback regarding her teaching and although she still felt out of her depth, she wasn't quite as anxious as she had been in the beginning.

'Thanks, everyone,' she said, when the tools were stowed in the boot of the minibus. 'You've done a sterling job. The plotters will be pleased, and I know I am. There's going to be an allotment opening ceremony on Sunday, so if any of you fancy coming along you'll be more than welcome.' However, from their bored looks and their rolled eyes, Ceri assumed that her students wouldn't be showing their faces on the day.

'I'll see you tomorrow,' she added, as they gathered their things together. 'Don't forget, we'll be in polytunnel number two.' She was about to tell them what they would be doing in there, when her phone rang. It was Damon, and her heart skipped a beat. She hadn't seen him since he had confessed to being a famous rock star, because he had been entertaining Sadie, but they had messaged each other several times a day, and she was missing him like crazy.

'Damon, hi,' she said, turning away in a vain attempt to grab some privacy.

'What time will you be home from work?'

'Actually, I'm at the allotment. We've just finished marking out the plots.'

'I want to see you. Would you like to join us for dinner? Sadie would love to meet you.'

'Not tonight. Maybe another time?'

'Oh… OK.'

He sounded disappointed and Ceri nearly changed her mind, but she knew she would feel awkward.

'Can I at least kiss you?' he asked. 'I'm at the gate. Come over, please – I need to hold you.'

Ceri's gaze shot to the little wooden gate separating the allotment from Damon's house and her pulse leapt when she saw him standing on the other side of it. Her lips were already tingling at the thought of his mouth on hers, and she couldn't wait to feel his arms around her. She gave him a small wave and he waved back.

Taking a step in his direction she suddenly became aware that she had a load of students gawping at her, and she hastily said, 'Gotta go, I need to finish up here. I'll see you in about ten minutes.'

Thankfully Mark had loaded the kids onto the bus, so she trotted up the steps to say goodbye. She guessed they must have had enough of her for one day when only a couple of them acknowledged her; the others were either on their phones or chatting. To her surprise Portia and Eleanor still seemed to have their minds on the allotment because they were staring out of the window, their heads together as they examined their handiwork. Portia's layout had been almost the exact match to the way the allotment had been laid out before it had fallen into disuse, and Ceri made a mental note to remember to congratulate her on handing in a good assignment.

Ceri watched the minibus bump its way out of the field and onto the lane, then she shouldered her rucksack and headed across the allotment, picking her way around the newly laid out plots.

Damon was waiting for her just inside the gate and she fell into his embrace, his lips finding hers as she closed her eyes in bliss. Being in his arms was like coming home. It felt so right, so natural, as though she belonged there.

The thought flitted through her head that it was dangerous to feel like this about a man who might be out of her life in a few weeks. The past three days since Sadie had arrived had been endless, and had left her with a physical ache in her chest, giving her a taste of what would be in store for her when he left. But she was addicted to him, so she would take what she could get now and deal with the heartache later.

And she had no doubt that her heart *would* be broken. It was merely a question of *when*.

–

Damon hadn't jammed with anyone for ages, not since before the tour, and he was enjoying himself immensely. Like any jam session, it hadn't been planned. He had been in the kitchen, clearing away the remnants of their meal, when he'd heard Sadie strumming some chords.

She was using one of his other guitars and when she saw him standing in the doorway, watching her, she'd jerked her chin at the Gibson.

Intrigued, he'd picked it up and began to play, and soon the two of them were running through an eclectic range of music, from soul to jazz.

But when Sadie began playing "Into the Sun", one of the tracks on the *Dark Dimension* album, Damon hesitated.

She looked up when he didn't follow along. 'What's wrong?'

Damon pulled a face. 'It doesn't feel right.'

'Playing without Aiden?'

He lifted a shoulder. 'I suppose.'

She gazed at him steadily. 'You're going to have to get used to it,' she said gently. 'He's not coming back.'

'I know...'

'And you've got those tracks to finish,' she reminded him.

He settled the Gibson on his knee, his fingers absently plucking out a tune as he considered how to answer. He knew he needed to focus on the new album and putting the unfinished tracks to bed, but his heart simply wasn't in it.

'What's that?' Sadie's voice cut into his thoughts.

'Huh? Oh...' His fingers stilled as he realised he had been playing one of his recent compositions. 'I've been messing about. It's nothing.'

'It's most definitely *something*,' she argued. 'Go on, play it for me.'

'It isn't finished.'

'Don't care. *Pleeease*?' She gave him a pleading look, and he shook his head.

Aiden's sister had always been able to wrap him and Luke around her little finger and after she'd pouted at him and pleaded some more, Damon found himself closing his eyes as he began to play.

The music flowed through him, the notes filling his heart and his mind. The lyrics came from his soul, and he meant every single word of them. And when he strummed the final chord, his fingers reached for the next song, and the next, until he had sung every song he'd composed since the day he'd watched an ethereal woman dancing under the stars in a flower-strewn meadow.

The last note hung in the air before fading to silence, and Damon slumped back in his chair. He was done: strung out, wrung out, empty. Yet his heart was full of joy, his mind was calm, and a wonderful serenity filled his soul.

This was the first time he had played all the songs in one set, and they hung together perfectly. They were the best he had ever written.

'Wow...' Sadie's whisper made him jump. He had given himself to his music so completely that he had forgotten she was there.

Sitting up self-consciously, he put the Gibson back in its case, then risked a glance at her.

To his consternation, she had tears trickling down her face. But she didn't look sad, she looked entranced.

'That was so incredibly beautiful,' she said, shaking her head slowly. 'Powerful, moving, intense.'

'Which song?' He caught his bottom lip between his teeth. Her opinion mattered to him.

'All of them. Shit, Damon, they are brilliant.' She paused. 'But they're hardly Black Hyacinth material.'

'I didn't write them for Black Hyacinth, I wrote them for...' He hesitated.

'Ceri?' Sadie stared knowingly at him. 'Are you really going to finish the album?'

'I think I have to. I owe it to Aiden.'

'And what about after?'

'What do you mean?'

'Black Hyacinth will need a bass player.'

Damon inhaled sharply. The thought of bringing someone else in to replace Aiden was untenable. Ever since he had fled to Foxmore he had been shying away from thinking about it, but the time had come.

'How about me?' she added.

'You?'

'Why not? I can play your stuff almost as well as Aiden.'

'I don't doubt it.'

'Let me help you and Luke finish the album. When you see how good I am—'

'I *know* how good you are. Your vocals are amazing, but… I'm done.' He hadn't known he was going to say those words until they were out of his mouth, but as soon as he'd uttered them he realised it was true.

He didn't want to be in the band without Aiden. That part of his life was over.

The problem was, he didn't have a clue what he was going to do instead, because the only thing he wanted to do, the only thing he knew anything about was making music.

–

Sadie eyed Damon with caution as he wandered into the kitchen the following morning. He was surprised to see her up and dressed this early.

'Coffee?' He flicked the machine on.

'Yes, please.' She took a seat at the scrubbed pine table and began to fiddle with one of the placemats.

'Spit it out,' he instructed. It was obvious she had something on her mind.

'Are you still serious about leaving the band?' she asked.

'I am.'

'Have you really thought about it?'

'I've been awake all night thinking about it, and I haven't changed my mind.'

'But you've put your heart and soul into the band! You all have.'

He leant against the countertop. 'I can't do it anymore. Or to be more accurate, I don't *want* to do it anymore.' It was ironic to think that he'd been battling his panic attacks ever since Aiden had died, fearing that he wouldn't be able to perform again, yet now that he possibly had the means to control them, he'd discovered that he didn't have the heart for it anymore. Maybe his subconscious had already known, and the panic attacks had been his body's way of showing him.

Sadie got to her feet and walked across the kitchen to put her arms around him. With her face in his chest, she asked in a muffled voice, 'What are you going to do?'

He knew he could never give up music. How could he, when it was as essential to him as the breath that filled his lungs? It was part of him, in the same way that working the soil had been part of his gran, and the same way that sifting through the earth to search for buried clues to the past was part of his parents.

'I'm going to write music,' he said, and he was abruptly filled with the certainty that he was doing the right thing.

Both Luke and Aiden had known that he loved his music more than he loved the lifestyle that went with it — everything else had merely been a by-product. He didn't miss the hype in the slightest, and from now on if he could get his music fix by writing instead of performing, that was all he wanted.

Actually, he wasn't being completely truthful, because there *was* something else he wanted. Ceri.

Sadie gave him a squeeze then released him, and Damon reached for his phone, turning it over in his hands. He now knew exactly how he wanted the next few years of his career to pan out, but he wasn't sure how well the news would be received.

Frank, he suspected, would be less than happy; he would probably be aghast.

Damon blew out his cheeks and brought the phone to life. He wouldn't say anything to Frank just yet – it was only fair that he spoke to Luke first.

Luke sounded upbeat when he answered the call. 'Damon, my man! Is rural Wales getting you down yet?'

'Not yet. Um, Luke, I need to speak to you about something important. I... er... want to quit the band.'

Silence.

'Luke, did you hear what I said?'

'I heard.' There was a long pause, and Damon prayed his friend could forgive him. But when Luke finally said, 'I'm glad, mate, because I've been thinking the same. I've been like... derailed, you know?' Damon sighed with relief.

Derailed – that perfectly described how he'd been feeling, as though the track that his life had been running on had buckled and snapped. But after last night, Damon hoped he had found another set of rails, ones that would lead him in a new and exciting direction.

'Have you told Frank?' Luke asked.

'No, I wanted to sound you out first. Have you?'

'Nah, *I* wanted to speak to *you* first. Are we going to finish that album?'

Damon met Sadie's eyes. 'I think we should. How do you feel about Sadie playing bass? She's up for it, if we are.'

'Stonking idea. And having her name on the album will give her a leg up, if she wants it.'

'I think she might.' He smiled at her. 'It would be criminal to let a voice like hers go to waste.' Sadie beamed back, the first proper smile he'd seen from her since she lost her brother.

'What are you going to do with the rest of your life?' Damon asked Luke. 'Bum around India?'

'Oi, don't knock it until you've tried it. Not just India, the world is a big place. Wanna come with me?'

'No, but thanks for the offer.'

'What about you? Don't tell me you're going to lounge around in your garden for the rest of your life?'

'Actually, I've written a few songs,' he confessed.

'Are they any good?'

'I think so.'

Sadie gave him a thumbs up, and shouted, 'They're bloody brilliant.'

Luke chuckled. 'Good for you! Music's in your blood. You've gotta do what you've gotta do, man, and if that means writing songs, you go write them. Do you want me to have a listen?'

'Thanks, Luke. I'm hoping Frank will continue to be my agent and flog them for me. What do you think? Will he say yes?'

'He'll be pissed off about the band, but I expect he'll come round. Having songs to sell isn't as good as having records to sell, but it's better than nothing – and he knows you're an effing good songwriter.'

Damon ran a hand through his hair. 'You should reserve judgement until you hear them.'

'How many have you got?'

'Five.'

Luke gave a low whistle. 'You *have* been busy. Must be all that Welsh air. Send them over.'

Damon did, and when Luke told him how much he loved them, it was music to Damon's ears.

Chapter 17

Extricating herself from the tangled sheets, Ceri said, 'I can't stay in bed all day, I'm going to make a start on my plot.'

Damon propped himself up on an elbow. 'You really want to do that *now*?'

'Uh huh.' It was Friday and with Sadie having left this morning, Damon had dragged Ceri off to bed as soon as he'd waved her off. Ceri was lucky not to be teaching today as classes had been cancelled due to a library event, so she'd stayed home, ostensibly to work, but in reality she had spent most of it in Damon's bed.

He said sadly, 'OK, you win. Your wish is my command.'

'You don't have to come with me,' she said, but hoping he would, nevertheless.

She might want to spend as much time with him as possible (because who knew when he would decide he'd had enough of Foxmore?), but she was also keenly aware that the soil wouldn't dig itself. And she got restless if she didn't have her hands in dirt at least once a day. After a day spent mostly indoors, she was eager to go outside. She also wanted to make a start on her plot to set an example, because the opening ceremony was on Sunday.

He said, 'You can't wait to get planting, can you?'

'It's in my genes.'

'It was in my gran's, too.' He sighed and sat up. 'I'll fetch my spade.'

She got out of bed and picked up her scattered clothing, pulling her knickers up over her thighs and stepping into her jeans, dancing out of the way as he reached for her. 'Oh, no, you don't.'

'Spoilsport.'

Ceri sniffed haughtily. 'You'll enjoy it all the more if you have to wait for it.'

'You're a tease,' he grumbled, pulling his jeans on. His T-shirt was dangling from the end of the brass bedstead, and he drew it towards him.

If he thought that was teasing, she'd show him what teasing really was. Licking her lips, she tilted her head to the side as she slowly and deliberately scanned his body from head to toe.

Damon groaned. 'Stop it, unless you want me to pin you down on the bed and...' He smirked suggestively.

'You wouldn't dare.'

The look in his eyes told her that he would, and with a squeal, she yanked her top over her head, then whirled around and dashed out of the bedroom. She managed to get down the stairs, out of the kitchen door and halfway down the garden path before he caught her, and they collapsed in a heap on the ground, giggling, until he stifled her laughter with a kiss.

'Go fetch a couple of shovels and a wheelbarrow,' she instructed, after he finally released her, and whilst she waited for him to return she strolled over to the allotment and studied the plot she had chosen.

It was the one nearest to the gate that separated Damon's garden from the allotment, but that wasn't the sole reason she had picked it. The plot was at the top of the field and received a substantial amount of sunlight, unshaded by the surrounding hedgerows. It was also the furthest away from the main gate, which meant less footfall around her veggies, but it did mean it was one of the furthest from the standpipe. She would have to see if she could source an old bath or a water trough to put next to the one already there, because one wouldn't be enough until the water butts were established, and she took out her phone and made a note before she forgot.

'Where do you want to start?' Damon asked, handing her a spade and taking the opportunity to nibble the back of her neck.

'We'll do a bit at a time,' she said, squirming in delight. 'Start at this end and work our way down. The best thing to do is to cut into the sod like this.' She demonstrated what she meant, digging the spade vertically into the grass on four sides to make a square cut. 'Then you slide the spade under and lift. If you do it right and go deep enough, you should get a good proportion of the roots out. Then pop the turves in the wheelbarrow, and once we've got a load we'll dump them over there.' She pointed to a spot next to the mound of compost. 'They need to be stacked so the grass is on the bottom and the soil is on the top. In about a year, the grass and roots will have died, and we'll have loads more lovely compost.'

Damon set to work, and Ceri watched him – not to check that he was doing it right, but because she liked seeing the ripple and bunch of the muscles in his back and shoulders, and she imagined caressing them later.

Pulling herself together, she hefted her spade and joined him, soon developing a smooth, satisfying rhythm of dig, slide, lift, and by the time the clock struck six, the plot was nearly half dug.

'I'm starving,' Damon declared. 'How about I make us some dinner while you put everything away?'

'Deal!' She much preferred cleaning the tools off and stowing them away to cooking.

He tossed his spade into the wheelbarrow and together they strolled through the little wooden gate, parting ways when the path forked, Ceri heading towards the shed and Damon heading to the house.

As the barrow bounced over the old cobbled path, Ceri thought that his grandmother's garden, even in its current state, was one of the loveliest she'd ever seen. Hyacinth had devoted her life to it and it showed. Ceri was under no illusion that it would take a gargantuan effort to bring it back to where it was, but it could be done with time and effort. Some new plants wouldn't go amiss, either. A garden like this would eat money though, and you could buy a hundred plants and make only the smallest of dents.

Damon had done more work on it, mostly chopping and cutting back, and as the overgrown shrubs, climbers and bushes were gradually being tamed, other smaller plants were coming into focus. Ceri was thrilled to see so many different varieties of annuals and perennials showing their flowery little faces. Many of them had spread or self-seeded, and quite a few were in the wrong place, although they seemed to be growing happily enough.

When Ceri arrived at the engine room of many a garden – the potting shed – she remembered Hyacinth's journals. Curiously she stepped inside and saw that the tin containing them was still on the shelf, so she picked it up and prised the lid off.

Intending to only have a quick glance through them, before long she was immersed in Hyacinth's description of a tulip bed and the new variety she had bought, and she lost track of time until Damon appeared in the doorway, blocking the light.

'What are you doing in here?'

'Being nosy. Have you read any of these?'

He came to stand next to her and gently took the journal out of her hand. Feeling guilty that he'd caught her reading it without asking permission, she hoped he didn't think she was invading his privacy.

'One or two,' he said. 'She's got such a wonderful way with words. I love how she describes the garden.'

To Ceri's relief he didn't seem at all bothered.

She said, 'I've only had a quick glance at a couple of pages, but from the descriptions, I think in its heyday it might have been as lovely as many of today's show gardens.' Her eyes widened as an idea occurred to her. 'How do you fancy a day out tomorrow?'

'Where are you thinking of going?'

'To visit a garden, where else?'

Damon shook his head. 'Trust you! Come on, dinner's almost ready.'

'What are we having?'

'Chilli con carne.' He placed the slim notebook back in the tin and popped the lid back on, stroking it reverentially. 'I can almost feel her. She's here, in this shed, and in this garden.'

Ceri placed a hand on his arm. 'I can feel her, too. I suppose she put so much of herself into her garden that you can't help it. And this—' she indicated the potting shed '—was her domain, her sanctuary.'

'It's swiftly becoming my sanctuary, too.'

It might be true, but Ceri knew in her heart that sanctuary or not, it wouldn't be enough to keep him here.

Damon had no idea what had roused him but once he was awake he couldn't get back to sleep. Excitement about the future vied with concern whether he was doing the right thing, making him twitchy and restless. If Luke had been upset on hearing that Damon wanted to leave the band, Damon wasn't entirely sure he could have gone through with it; however, knowing that his bandmate felt the same way had reassured him. It was natural to have some reservations, he guessed, and he knew it would take time to get used to the idea that after the new album was released, Black Hyacinth would be no more.

He would hang fire saying anything to Ceri just yet, though, because it was only fair that he informed Frank and the record label first.

Damon turned onto his side and tried spooning her, in an attempt to go back to sleep, but after lying there for over twenty minutes listening to her soft, even breathing, he decided to get up for a while, worried that he might wake her.

Unwilling to pick up his guitar, because playing it would most certainly disturb her, he wandered into the kitchen. The faint aroma of chilli lingered in the air, and he opened a window to dispel it. As he did so he thought back to seeing Ceri in the potting shed with one of his grandmother's journals in her hand, and he felt a sudden urge to read them.

The night was quiet and still, with not a hint of a breeze to rustle the leaves as he crept down the path towards the potting shed. No owl broke the silence, no bats flew overhead. Even the fox was absent. It was as though the world held its breath, waiting for the sun to return.

The shed was warm, holding onto the heat of the day. He left the door open and lit a candle, wondering how often his gran used to work in the potting shed in the dark. The flame was feeble, but when he picked up a journal and opened it there was just enough light to read by, and it didn't take him long to get lost in the pages. He was soon immersed in his grandmother's life and that of the garden, but when he came to one particular section, what he read both shocked and delighted him. The church didn't own the field next to the house: *he did*. The allotment on Willow Tree Lane had belonged to Hyacinth all along.

Laughing softly at the discovery, his first instinct was to dash back to the house and wake Ceri with kisses to tell her the good news.

His second was to say nothing for the time being. He needed to sort the band out first and get those tracks finished. And when that was done and Black Hyacinth was officially disbanded, he intended to gift the field to Ceri so she could make her dream of owning a nursery come true.

–

'Tell me about Plas yn Rhiw.' Damon was sitting in the passenger seat of Ceri's car, looking forward to his day out.

'It's a manor house near Abersoch, with the most gorgeous gardens,' she replied.

Abersoch was a small town at the furthest end of the Llŷn Peninsular, and from what he could remember the area was wild and beautiful. He hadn't been to that particular part of north Wales for years. 'Talk about a busman's day out,' he joked.

She stuck her nose in the air. 'This is more for your benefit than mine – although I'm perfectly happy to have another look around the gardens. You're going to love them.'

'For *my* benefit?'

'It'll give you some inspiration for your own garden, and believe me, you're going to need it when you start to flag.'

Inspiration wasn't his major concern today. What was at the forefront of his mind was spending the whole day with Ceri. This felt like their first proper date and he was more than happy to sit back and watch the glorious countryside flow past the window as the car turned towards the coast and followed the road as it skirted past seaside towns such as Criccieth and Pwllheli.

The views were fantastic, impossibly blue sea on one side with the sun glittering on the water, and on the other rolling green fields interspersed by patches of woodland, small villages and hamlets. The further west they went the more rural the landscape became, with nothing but farms and the occasional house to be seen.

Plas yn Rhiw's manor house was situated in an elevated position surrounded by a broadleaf woodland with stunning views across Cardigan Bay, and when Damon unfurled himself from the car he inhaled deeply. The air was fresh and fragrant, perfumed with growing things and a hint of the sea. He was loving it already, and he hadn't even seen the house or the gardens yet.

They walked along the lane to the entrance to the property and when Damon spied a chalkboard propped up beside the tree-lined driveway, he slung his arm around Ceri's shoulders. 'There's a tearoom. Fancy a coffee and a cake before we start?' he suggested.

'Good idea!'

Ceri's eyes were everywhere, drinking in the sight of each and every plant, whilst he drank in the sight of *her*. He couldn't get enough of looking at her, of touching her, and kissing her. And it wasn't just physical – he loved talking to her too, loved her humour and her sass.

He loved her.

Faltering, he almost stumbled as he abruptly realised that he was in love, and the knowledge shocked him to his core. He knew he had been falling for her, but to discover that he had already *fallen*… It made his heart sing, and he didn't think he had ever been as happy.

Ceri's squeal of glee when they approached the tea rooms and she saw a shop selling plants next to it, made him laugh. Her enthusiasm and delight was catching, and he found himself just as enthused and delighted.

'We'll come back to these later,' he said, dragging her away. 'We don't want to be carting plants around with us.' He had to kiss her to persuade her he was right, but he suspected that she wanted to be kissed anyway. When he'd got her full attention, he reluctantly withdrew. There would be plenty of time for that this evening when they got home.

After a restorative slice of the most delicious Battenberg cake he had ever tasted (it had been a favourite of the sisters who had bought the property in 1937) and a pot of tea, Damon was ready for a look around the house and gardens. Ceri opted for the gardens first (no surprise there) so, holding hands, they wandered among the more formal part of the grounds.

Formal wasn't strictly correct, however. Although some of the garden was reminiscent of a Tudor hedge garden, most of it was an English cottage garden. It was so very like his own had been in its heyday, that it took his breath away.

Visitors could be mistaken for thinking that Plas yn Rhiw's grounds had been left to its own devices, but he was well aware of how much hard work went into making a garden look as beautiful as this. It was bursting with colour, and not just from the flowers. Ceri pointed out the huge variety of leaves in so many vibrant shades of green, from tiny feathery ones to magnificent palmate ones larger than a child's padding pool, plus the many coloured stems ranging from green and brown, through to yellow, red and even black. The garden was also brimming with insects, bees and butterflies primarily, and he ducked when an enormous bumblebee sailed past his head.

This was what his grandmother's garden used to look like when he was younger, and this was how he wanted it to look like again. Ceri's prediction that the visit would revitalise his enthusiasm, which had waned slightly due to the sheer enormity of the task ahead of him, was correct.

Arms around each other's waists, Damon and Ceri explored the wildflower meadow and native fruit orchard at the back of the house, then finally strolled around the manor house itself.

Damon vowed to come back. He had a suspicion he hadn't seen everything, and although he might have gained an overall impression of the garden, most of the details had escaped him as there had simply been far too much to take in all at once.

'I'm not ready to go home yet,' Ceri announced, snuggling into him as they retraced their steps to the car. 'Besides, I'm hungry. How about we stop off somewhere for a late lunch?'

'Sounds good to me.' He didn't want to go home yet, either.

'Fish and chips on the beach?' she suggested.

'Perfect.'

Damon expected Ceri to drive to the nearest seaside town, which happened to be Abersoch, but they sailed on past. They also drove straight past Pwllheli, and he had begun to wonder whether she had changed her mind and was taking them back to Foxmore, when she finally turned off into the lovely town of Criccieth.

'Why Criccieth?' he asked, as she hunted for a parking space.

'It's got a ruined castle and a beach,' she informed him.

'A ruined castle, eh? Very romantic,' he teased. 'You just want to kiss me on the battlements. Ow!'

Ceri had punched him on the arm, and he rubbed the spot ruefully. She had a mean right hook on her and he didn't think she had put her full weight behind it, either. Must be all that spadework she did.

'There's nothing wrong with romance,' she said pointedly. 'You ought to try it sometime.'

'Are you accusing me of being unromantic?'

'If the cap fits…' She arched a brow.

'I can be romantic,' he protested, but his reply was ruined when his tummy rumbled loudly.

Ceri burst out laughing. 'Of course you can,' she giggled. 'Let's get you fed before you fade away.'

Damon was too hungry to object, so they went in search of a fish and chip shop, then found a bench on a grassy area overlooking the beach with a view of the castle to sit and eat their belated lunch, washing down the hot vinegary chips and fluffy battered cod with cold cans of fizzy pop.

'This takes me back,' he said. 'I haven't had fish and chips at the seaside since I was a boy.'

'Usually eat in fancy restaurants, do you?'

'I wish!' If he was honest, upmarket restaurants didn't appeal to him much, apart from special occasions. This was far more fun and just as tasty.

Ceri licked her fingers, then bundled up the remains of her meal.

He said, 'Wait, you've got…' He was about to brush some grains of salt from her lips when he decided to kiss them away instead. 'Mmm, salty,' he said, eventually coming up for air.

'Shut up and kiss me again,' she ordered, digging her fingers into his hair and tugging his head back down to hers.

'I think we'd better carry on with this at home,' Damon said after a few minutes. 'We're a bit too old to be snogging on a bench.'

'Who says?'

'People are staring.'

'Let them,' Ceri said, but she glanced around to check. 'No one is taking the slightest bit of notice,' she argued. 'You just want to take me to bed.'

'Guilty as charged.' Now that his stomach was full, he was free to turn his attention to another kind of hunger.

'We've got a castle to explore,' she admonished. 'I love a ruined castle.'

Once again her enthusiasm was catching, so he let her drag him up the hill to the monolith at the top, and when he got there Damon had to admit that it was rather impressive. Perched on an outcrop of rock between two beaches, the castle dominated the landscape and he could easily picture how magnificent it must have been when it was a fully functioning fortress.

Built by Llewelyn the Great in the thirteenth century in response to England's invasion of Wales, Damon guessed it must have struck fear into anyone who saw it. But all that was left of it now were two massive conical towers flanking the main arched gateway, and a huge curtain wall.

'Isn't it magnificent!' Ceri exclaimed, gazing around in awe.

'It's certainly impressive,' he agreed. The massive lump of rock it sat on rose majestically out of the sea and was striking enough on its own, without a gigantic castle perched on the top of it.

He pulled her close and kissed the top of her windswept head, spluttering as a strand of hair found its way into his mouth. It was breezy up here, and his own locks also kept blowing into his face. To get out of the wind, he dragged her down behind a wall where it was more sheltered, then sat on a lump of rock and pulled her onto his lap.

'That's better,' he said, and kissed her properly.

She smelled of the flowery perfume she favoured, but she also smelled of fresh air and the sea, and a scent that was uniquely hers. She tasted pretty darned good too, and he wished he didn't have to stop. Damon was utterly besotted – all he could think about was Ceri. She made his heart sing and his soul soar, and he ached for her whenever they were apart.

'Would it scare you if I told you I think I'm falling in love with you?' he asked, and immediately regretted it.

'Would it scare you if I told you I think *I'm* falling in love with *you*?' she echoed. She was staring deeply into his eyes and the world abruptly stopped.

He bit his lip. 'I love you, Ceri.'

Ceri swallowed and closed her eyes, and when she opened them again what he saw in them mirrored what was in his heart. *Love.*

'I love you, too,' she whispered, and those words were the most wonderful sounds he had ever heard.

Chapter 18

"Reasons to be Cheerful, Part Three", Ceri had no idea why that particular song was cycling through her brain this morning, especially considering the only lyrics she knew were the title and the line about getting back into bed.

She should take the song's advice and return to Damon's nice warm bed, but her sleep had been fitful and as the first rays of the morning sun had slanted through a gap in the thick curtains, she finally admitted defeat and got up.

Damon didn't stir, so she quietly slipped downstairs, made a coffee and brought it outside into the garden.

Even at this ungodly hour, it was already warm, the day promising to be bright and glorious, perfect for the official allotment-opening ceremony which would take place later today after Terry had led the Sunday morning service.

Birds were in full song, the air filled with their fluttering and chatter, and although she appreciated the dawn chorus, Ian Dury's lyrics continued to play over and over.

She had many reasons to be cheerful, but she couldn't help that her heart felt so heavy that she wanted to cry.

Damon loved her.

She loved Damon.

But that didn't change a goddam thing.

She knew she would lose him. It was inevitable. He was still the lead singer in Black Hyacinth. He was still going to return to his former way of life soon. He was still going to leave, and the thought of him not being in Foxmore made her heart ache with sadness.

Even if he did ask her to go to London with him – which was incredibly unlikely – would she go? From the snippets he had shared with her, she understood that being in the band was a nomadic lifestyle. He had a base in London, a flat which, by his own admission, he was hardly ever in because he spent most of the time on the road.

That wasn't for her. And neither would she fit in.

She uttered a small, sad laugh, realising how silly she was being to even think he might ask in the first place.

When he left, it would be without her, and would be for good.

So telling her he loved her didn't change a thing.

–

Ceri walked softly into the bedroom. Damon was still asleep, one arm above his head, his face turned to the side. He looked so peaceful that she was tempted to leave without waking him, but he stirred, opened one bleary eye and mumbled, 'What time is it?'

'Nine thirty-seven.'

'Too early.' He pulled the duvet over his head. In a muffled voice, he said, 'Come back to bed.'

'I can't. Terry will be presiding over the allotment opening ceremony in a couple of hours, and I want to make sure everything is ready.'

Yawning, he sat up slowly. 'At least let me make you breakfast.'

'I've already eaten,' she lied. She hadn't been able to face food. Pecking him on the forehead, she told him she would see him later, and went home to get ready.

Over another cup of coffee, she tried to turn her thoughts to the day ahead.

Terry had allocated the plots and had informed everyone who was getting one. As soon as she had told him how many plots there would be, he had put the plot numbers in one bowl, the names in another and Betsan, who had worn one of those sleep masks to cover her eyes so she hadn't been able to see, had randomly married up plotters with plots.

By half-past eleven, Ceri was pleased to see plotters beginning to gather. Most of them came prepared for gardening, and she noted the assortment of wheelbarrows, spades, shovels and rakes. One lady had even brought a tray of seedling tomatoes with her, which Ceri thought might be slightly optimistic, but she cheered the woman on anyway.

A white van pulled into the lane and two people began unloading a flat-packed shed and concrete slabs. They clearly intended to get a head start. There were several children amongst the assembled plotters, which also pleased her no end. If kids caught the gardening bug early enough, it would most likely stay with them for the rest of their lives, and in Ceri's opinion the world could never have too many gardeners.

Someone – Terry, she presumed – had tied a length of ribbon across the gate before she'd arrived, but what was really lovely and had touched her deeply, was the wooden sign hanging from it that said, 'Willow Tree Lane Allotment'. Seeing it had brought tears to her eyes and a lump to her throat. She couldn't wait to tell Damon about it. She wished he was here for the ceremony, but they'd agreed it was better he stayed away in case anyone recognised him.

Ceri said hello to some familiar faces and chatted with one or two. The excitement and sense of anticipation was palpable, and it warmed her heart to think that she was, in part, responsible for it. Of course, Terry had played a vital role too, because without him the allotment would never have come into being. It was on his insistence that the field was being used for the benefit of the community, and although Ceri was regretful that she didn't have it all to herself and that her nursery dreams had to wait a while longer, she was grateful to him nevertheless.

Eager for the ceremony to begin, she kept a keen lookout for the vicar. But when he arrived, Betsan at his side, Ceri blinked. What on earth were they *wearing*?

The pair of them had on what appeared to be large, upturned plant pots made of cardboard, from the shoulders to the tops of their thighs. Their legs were encased in a series of smaller plant pots, and they both had some weird hat thing on their heads.

'Ooh, Bill and Ben, the Flower Pot Men!' Mrs Moxley screeched. 'I used to love them when I was a babbie.'

Ceri had no idea what she was on about, but Terry and Betsan certainly looked very garden-ish.

Terry called for silence, taking centre stage directly in front of the gate. 'Friends, plotters, county folk, lend me your ears – of sweetcorn, that is,' he chortled. His opening joke was accompanied by groans, as he continued, 'God said, "Let the land produce vegetation: seed-bearing plants and trees on the land that bear fruit with seed in it, according to their various kinds. And it was so." Genesis, verse eleven!' he thundered, cutting across the tittering, as he held his arms in the air and gazed skywards.

His wife nudged him. 'That's enough, Terry. You're not in church now.'

'All of the great outdoors is God's Church,' he replied, but when she shook her head and glared at him, his shoulders drooped. 'Spoilsport. I've got a captive audience here,' he hissed loud enough for everyone to hear; and Ceri got the impression that she was watching a comedy double-act.

'Just get on with it,' Betsan said.

'Heathen.' He turned his attention back to his impromptu congregation. 'I declare this allotment well and truly open. God bless all those who garden in her.' His wife handed him a pair of shears and he cut through the ribbon to the sound of cheers and clapping.

He had barely managed to get the gate open before people were barrelling through, eager to reach their plots.

Ceri hung back. 'Bill and Ben?' she asked him.

'The Flower Pot Men. Watch with Mother? *Wee-e-eed*?' Terry sang, in a rather alarmingly high-pitched voice.

'Pardon?'

'*Wee-e-eed*,' he repeated, then more normally, 'Weed. It's what one of the characters was called. Weed.'

'Right. Okaay...' She hoped he hadn't been helping himself to the communion wine.

'It was a TV series in the sixties, aimed at children,' Betsan explained. 'Had a revival about twenty-odd years ago. Our kids used to watch it.'

'I like the outfits.' Ceri bit her lip, trying not to laugh. It was so sweet of them to dress up.

'I told you this was a daft idea,' Terry said to Betsan.

'You love my daft ideas.' His wife nudged him with her arm. Ceri noticed that she had oversized gardening gloves on her hands.

'You look very fetching,' Ceri said. 'I'm sure everyone loved it.'

'They're loving getting stuck in more,' Terry observed.

The allotment was a hive of activity already, and when she gazed at it, Ceri felt a surge of pride.

'Can we go in, Miss?'

Startled, she looked around to see Portia and Eleanor behind her.

'Hi!' she exclaimed. 'You came! How lovely. Of course you can go in. Those are a couple of my first-year students,' she explained to the vicar, as she watched them saunter away. Then she spotted someone else, and was equally as surprised and pleased.

Damon was standing a little way down the lane. He wasn't looking at Ceri, though – he was staring at Bill and Ben, his mouth open.

Ceri beckoned him over, and he walked towards her slowly.

'I was watching from my garden' he said. 'But I just had to come and see what *that* was.' He gestured to Terry and Betsan.

'They're Bill and Ben apparently. Don't ask.'

Terry had focused on Damon and was squinting at him. 'I don't know if you remember me? I'm Terry Pritchard, the vicar, and this is my wife, Betsan. I presided over your grandmother's funeral.' He stepped forward and held out his hand, remembered he was wearing gardening gloves and took them off. 'Thought I'd make a bit of an effort,' he said. 'Blame my wife – it was her idea.'

'Nice to meet you again,' Damon said formally, shaking the vicar's hand first, then Betsan's.

'I don't think we've seen you in Foxmore since her funeral.' Terry cocked his head to the side, clearly fishing for information. 'Are you back for long?'

'Foxmore has always been my home,' Damon said mildly, but his jaw was tense and Ceri knew it was a tell-tale sign that he wasn't happy with the conversation.

She gave him a sympathetic look, wondering whether she should intervene, then she noticed that Betsan had intercepted it and was studying her curiously. A smile played about her lips and Ceri realised Betsan had guessed that she and Damon knew each other better than they were letting on.

Betsan said, 'Come on, Terry, let's leave Ceri in peace. I'm sure some of your parishioners would like a chat.' She dragged her husband away, leaving Ceri and Damon alone.

Alone – apart from the two chaps ferrying bits of a shed from the white van in the lane to the far end of the allotment. Plus the students, who didn't seem quite as enthralled with the allotment after their initial look around. Ceri had spotted them near Damon's wooden gate a few minutes ago, but now they were heading in her direction.

'Thank you for being here,' she said to him in a soft voice. 'You don't know how much it means to me.'

'It looks like it's going to be a roaring success.'

'I hope so. I'd better show willing and go do some work,' she said. 'I'll see you later.'

He pulled her to him and gave her a swift kiss on the lips. 'I'm counting on it. I can't wait to take you back to bed.'

Ceri shivered with desire. The smouldering look he gave her made her insides melt, and she hastily turned away before she gave in to her lust and dragged him back to the house. She had an allotment to concentrate on!

—

Leaving Damon half-asleep hadn't been easy, but it was Monday morning and Ceri had to go to go work, so she didn't have any choice.

She crept out of his bed, dressed hastily and returned to her little cottage for a shower and some breakfast. Then she attempted to get her head into teaching mode as she drove into work. Although today wasn't arduous, she wasn't looking forward to it. Not only was she continuing to struggle with her role as a teacher, but she also now had the added distraction caused by Damon telling her he loved her.

Warning herself that she should put her private life to the back of her mind, she made a concerted effort to concentrate on her students. However difficult she might find her job, it would be unprofessional not to give it her best, and the kids deserved it, despite the soil-eating video incident.

Today they would be repotting the summer bedding plants ready for the college's annual plant sale. All manner of shrubs, climbers, annuals, fruit and vegetable plants would be sold off, and the campus was open to the general public. It promised to be a fun day, with people able to see the farm animals that were used to teach many of the courses, as well as various stalls selling food and other produce (the honey from the college's bee hives was particularly good), and Mark had told her that the college often had a surge of applications after these events.

She was busily sorting out the healthiest plants when Portia sidled up to her and asked, 'Do you live in that big house, the one next to your allotment?'

'It's not my allotment,' she said. 'It belongs to the village.'

'Yeah, but do you live in that house?'

'No, but I do live in Foxmore.' She wasn't about to tell them exactly where – she didn't think it appropriate.

'Do you know who does?' Eleanor asked.

'Why do you want to know?' Ceri scrutinised a weak-looking cotoneaster and put it to one side, hoping she might be able to nurse it back to health.

'You can see into their garden from the allotment. It looks lush.'

'It is,' Ceri agreed. She was the same – she always noticed the garden before she noticed the house it was attached to. Maybe she'd make gardeners out of these kids, after all. They didn't exactly live and breathe horticulture, but they were embracing it with much more enthusiasm lately. It made all her hard work and fear that she was out of her depth in this new teaching role of hers easier to bear. She still wasn't convinced she was any good at it and she still didn't particularly enjoy it, but maybe she would in time…?

Portia broke into her thoughts. 'Was that your boyfriend?' She was smirking, and Ceri cringed.

Oh, God, had the girls seen her and Damon snogging yesterday at the allotment? It hadn't been much of a snog – just a hug and a swift touch of the lips – but even that was too much. Hardly professional, was it?

She pursed her lips and decided not to answer. There was no way she was going to discuss her private life with her students. 'Shall we get on? We've got a lot to do today.'

But as Portia sloped off, Ceri was struck by the awful fear that the girl might have filmed the incident.

Ceri sincerely hoped not, and it took her until lunchtime to dispel the niggling worry that Mrs Drake might rock up and make a complaint about that, too.

–

Chatter from beyond the little wooden gate made Damon pause. Wandering over to see what was going on, he discovered two plotters calling to each other from across the allotment. They were discussing the merits of differing varieties of tomatoes, and he stopped to listen. Despite his lingering concern, he was coming around to the idea of having an allotment next door to his house.

Yesterday afternoon had been busy, with lots of noise and people coming and going (which he put down to the excitement of the opening ceremony and having been allocated a plot), but it had already settled down, and today only a couple of plots were being worked on.

The degree of progress some had made was striking though, and one plot was now totally bare of grass. Its owners must have worked like the devil yesterday. Another was a quarter dug, the exposed soil having been turned over, and several bamboo wigwams were visible. Damon wondered what they intended to grow; it wasn't too late for broad beans, or even runner beans or peas if the seedlings were already well established.

He smiled to himself when he realised he must have absorbed more than he'd thought from his gran. She had adored the allotment and had often roped him in to help. The bit he used to like best was picking whatever crop was harvestable, and he'd lost count of the number of times he had been scolded for slicing open ripe peapods with his thumb and eating the contents there and then, instead of waiting to have them cooked and served on a plate for his tea. They had been so sweet, and his mouth watered at the memory.

As Damon left the plotters to carry on with their tomato discussion and headed inside, he wondered whether Ceri would keep the field as an allotment after he gifted it to her. Somehow, he couldn't imagine her turfing the plotters out. From what he had seen yesterday, they were so delighted that the allotment had been resurrected that he didn't think she would have the heart.

His heart missed a beat as he thought of her. He'd not wanted her to go to work this morning, and was counting down the hours until she returned. The weekend had been so wonderful that he felt bereft without her. But on the upside, at least he would be able to phone Frank today and speak to him in private.

It was a task he wasn't looking forward to.

–

'Damon, Damon, don't make any hasty decisions, eh? Take as long as you need,' Frank urged.

'I've taken long enough. My mind is made up.' Damon felt awful breaking this kind of news to the band's agent and manager over the phone, but the sooner it was done the better. Black Hyacinth was over. It had run its course, no matter what Frank, the record label, or any of the legal bods he might rope in, had to say. Damon had no doubt that Frank felt Aiden's loss keenly, but Damon suspected it had more to do with the reduction in revenue if Black Hyacinth disbanded.

Not if – *when*.

Frank said, 'What about Luke? Surely he deserves a say in this?'

'He does, and he has. I've already spoken to him and he feels the same way. He said he'll ring you later.'

'I'm going to have to speak to the record label and the legal team—' Frank began, and Damon inhaled sharply then let the breath out in a whoosh.

He didn't want to go down this route, but if they forced his hand… 'If you want to take me and Luke to court, go ahead. I can see the headlines, "grieving members of rock band Black Hyacinth forced to—"'

'It won't come to that, Damon,' Frank broke in. 'No one will hold you to it under the circumstances. And for what it's worth, I completely understand. Between me and you, my heart's not in it, either. Black Hyacinth won't be the same without Aiden.'

Damon softened. 'Thanks, Frank.' Without Frank, Black Hyacinth wouldn't have enjoyed the success that it had. The band owed him a lot and Damon didn't want to part on bad terms.

Frank said, 'Can you keep this under wraps until I've had a chance to speak to the record company? There will be all kinds of legal things to be considered and I don't want the news leaking out prematurely. Not a word to anyone, OK? Not until we're given the go-ahead. I'll make sure Luke knows the score too.'

'No problem.'

'I mean it, Damon. They might be awkward, otherwise.'

'I promise I won't say a word to anyone. My lips are sealed.' There was no one he would want to tell anyway, apart from Ceri. His parents wouldn't give a toss.

'What about those unfinished tracks?' Frank asked.

'We'll get them done. We owe it to Aiden. Sadie has offered to take his place on bass, if necessary.'

'That's good. I'll have a word with her, too, make sure she knows the score about keeping it confidential for now.' Frank let out a sigh. 'Got any dates in mind? I'll need to book studio time.'

Damon said, 'I'm easy. Ask Luke when you speak to him. He'll be back in the country in a couple of days – I'll fit in with whatever you want.' He paused, then said cautiously, 'Um, Frank, I've got a favour to ask. I've been writing some songs and I wondered if you'd have a listen?'

'You have? That's fantastic news. Maybe we could tack them onto this new album?'

'No. Absolutely not! Believe me when I tell you that you wouldn't want Black Hyacinth to record this stuff.'

'Don't put yourself down,' Frank said. 'I know you used to bounce ideas off Aiden, but ultimately all of Black Hyacinth's music was written by you.'

'I don't think the fans would be too happy with *this*,' Damon said dryly.

Frank was silent for a moment, then he asked, 'Why not?'

'Let's say they're more ballad than rock.'

'So? Black Hyacinth have sung ballads before.'

'Not like this. Think more Eric Carmen's "All by Myself" and less "Dark Dimension".'

Although "Dark Dimension" was slightly more mainstream than most of their other stuff, it was still gritty and raw, more grunge than rock, and Damon was pretty sure that the band's die-hard fans would be less than pleased. Not only did he not want to add any fresh material to the new album, he also didn't want to dilute the band's memory by introducing work that Aidan hadn't been a part of.

Damon said, 'I was thinking that maybe you could continue to be my agent?'

'You're thinking of going in that direction?' Frank sounded surprised.

'Maybe, if they're any good.' If they weren't, Damon would have to come up with something else to do with the rest of his life.

'OK, look, send them over, yeah? I'll have a listen and tell you what I think. I'm not promising anything, you understand.'

Damon understood. Although he had written most of the material for Black Hyacinth, writing stuff to sell was a different market, especially in a genre he wasn't renowned for.

When he got off the phone, relief that the call had gone better than expected made him feel all hot and bothered, so he decided to take a shower.

Taking the stairs two at a time, he bounded onto the landing and was about to dive into his bedroom when a movement outside caught his eye, and he paused.

The landing window overlooked the allotment and, more importantly, the little wooden gate separating it from his own garden, and he could have sworn he had just seen someone slip through it. *Two* someone's in fact, and he scowled. He hadn't got around to putting a padlock on it yet, but he would remedy that tomorrow. And to make doubly sure that the plotters realised that this was private property and not part of the allotment, he would order a Keep Out, Private Property sign. That should do the trick. In the meantime, he needed to usher whoever it was out of his garden; he wasn't ready for his cover to be blown just yet.

Cross, he turned around and went back downstairs, but when he went outside there was no one to be seen.

Chapter 19

Ceri stuck her foot on the crossbars of the fork and lent all her weight on it, digging the tines deep into the soil and wiggling them around to try and loosen the damn dandelion root. She knew it was pointless leaving it there, because it would only regrow. It was better she removed it now, before she planted anything, rather than have to do it later.

She'd had a particularly trying day at work, so instead of going straight to Willow Tree House where Damon would be waiting for her, she was currently taking out her angst on this particularly stubborn root. She wanted to see him, but not while she felt so curmudgeonly, and she knew she would feel better after an hour or so of cross digging.

There was no single reason for her bad temper, just a cumulation of little things, from dropping her mug and breaking the handle, to being asked to redo her end-of-year reports because they didn't follow the college's format. Mark had apologised profusely for not giving her a template to work from, but she could see that he was up to his eyes in departmental reports, so she forgave him. It didn't make the situation any easier though; she had worked so hard on them over the previous week that being told they needed to be redone the minute she'd walked through the door this morning had sent her into another spiral of self-doubt. And that was the last thing she needed first thing on a Monday morning.

Which was why she was digging over the rest of her plot and getting madder by the second with this sodding root.

'I've got some runner beans in the ground,' an elderly gent said as he sauntered over, his hands on his hips. He had been watching her fight with the dandelion for the past few minutes. 'You wanna get that root out. You don't want to leave it there.'

She knew he meant well, but his advice irritated her. Couldn't he see that was what she was trying to do? She wondered how far the dandelion's tap root went down, and from the feel of it, she estimated it was halfway to Australia.

'Bernie Williams,' the man said.

'Ceri Morgan,' she panted, as she put her back into her task.

'I know. I was at the meeting and the opening whatchamacallit when the Reverend made a tit of himself. Bill and Ben, my arse – excuse my French.'

Ceri bit her lip and tried not to laugh. See, gardening was lifting her mood already.

'What are you thinking of putting in there?' he asked. 'I'm only asking coz I've got a couple of packets of peas going spare. They are last year's, so not all of them will germinate, but you're welcome to have them.'

Ceri was touched. She stopped digging and straightened up. 'That's very kind, thank you.'

It was getting a little late in the year to sow peas, but she might get a small crop, and even if she didn't, the plants themselves would lock nitrogen into the soil, giving a boost to anything she grew in that spot next year.

'Are you going to put a shed up?' he continued. 'You're going to need a shed or greenhouse.'

'Funny you should say that; I've got one of each being delivered next week.'

'If you need any help building them, I'm your man,' Bernie said. 'I can't do any heavy lifting, mind, but I can hold stuff and tell you where it goes. That's my plot over there.' He pointed, and Ceri's gaze followed his finger. She recognised it as one of the first to have had a shed erected.

'If you want a water butt, speak to the council,' he continued. 'That's where I got mine from. They're free, and if you're lucky they'll throw in a packet of wildflower seeds. They give away compost bins too, but you've got to be quick because they go like hotcakes. I prefer a wooden one myself, not them plastic things with lids.'

'I agree,' Ceri said. In her opinion, traditionally constructed compost bins did a far better job of breaking down waste vegetable matter, and she glanced at the pile of compost behind her plot.

Bernie noticed. 'Where did that lot come from, I've been wondering?'

'A friend donated it,' she said, not wanting to divulge its exact source in case it started a conversation that she wasn't prepared to get into. Damon hadn't been hiding away as much lately, but he still continued to guard his privacy jealously.

'Nice stuff, that,' Bernie said. 'Wouldn't mind a bit of it myself.'

Ceri took the hint. 'Help yourself to a barrowload,' she offered, hoping that word didn't get around, otherwise there would soon be none left. Then she chided herself for being mean. Allotments were all about community spirit, with a healthy dose of competition thrown in. Both of those things were already in evidence, the community spirit especially; while she worked, she had heard questions being asked and advice freely given, along with offers of help.

'I might take you up on that,' Bernie said, and she watched him trot sprightly back to his plot and grab his wheelbarrow.

A short while later someone else asked if they could have some compost and offered her rosemary and lavender cuttings in exchange.

Bernie, his barrow now full of compost, sauntered across the allotment, several packets of seeds in his hand. 'Here's the peas, and I've got some broad beans you might like. Only one packet of those, mind, but it should be enough for a couple of dinners.'

Ceri particularly liked them in a salad, and her mouth began to water at the thought. It would be several weeks before they were ready for picking though, and her thoughts turned to the more immediate subject of dinner this evening. Bless him, Damon had offered to do the cooking again, and she promised herself that she would make it up to him.

Returning to her dandelion problem, she grasped the foliage and yanked hard.

'Argh!' she yelled as the plant abruptly released its grip on the earth, and she stumbled backwards cursing under her breath.

Glad that it was finally out, she was about to call it a day and nip home for a shower and a change of clothes, when she saw Mrs Moxley heading in her direction. She had someone else with her – a woman in her fifties – and as they grew closer Ceri spotted the resemblance between the two and she guessed it must be her daughter.

'I've got the plot next to yours,' Mrs Moxley announced, picking her way around a partially turned over plot. She beamed. 'I do love an allotment. I never used to, but my husband had one for years – the very spot where you've got yours, actually. It would have broken his heart to see the allotment as it was before you took it on. I don't know how you managed to persuade—' She stopped abruptly as her attention was caught by Bernie Williams. He was waving at her, and she waved back.

Ceri was amused to see a blush spread across the old lady's face. Mrs Moxley appeared to have a soft spot for Bernie.

'I've got the kettle on the Primus,' he called, and she shouted back, 'I'll be there in a tick.'

She turned her attention back to Ceri. 'Where was I? Never mind, I just thought I'd introduce you to our Janice. She and her husband will be doing all the hard work. I'll be supervising. Our Janice doesn't know the first thing about plants, despite spending hours here with her father, God rest his soul.'

'I didn't spend hours here, Mam. Just now and again. We used to *tell* you I was here because you'd only have nagged if you knew I was down by the river with my friends.'

'Well, I never! You learn something new every day!' Mrs Moxley exclaimed. 'If I'd have known that, I would have given you a clip around the ear – and your dad, too. What was he thinking, letting you go down to the river on your own?'

'I expect he was thinking that he didn't want a bored kid mooching around and getting under his feet.'

Mrs Moxley pursed her lips. 'You didn't let your Rachel play down by the river.' She turned to Ceri. 'She's Janice's eldest.'

Janice rolled her eyes. 'They were different times when I was a kid, Mam. Anyway, I know what can happen, so no, she never went down there on her own. I remember falling in once, and Merton Rogers had to pull me out. We went back to his house so I could dry off, because I knew you'd do your nut if I came home soaked to the skin.'

'I can't believe Hyacinth used to let her Merton go down to the river by himself.'

'She didn't. He used to tell her that he was going to Sharon Williams's house to play, and Sharon used to tell *her* mum she was coming to *ours* – so if anyone's mam or dad asked, you would all think we were at someone else's house.'

'You sneaky little baggage. Wait until I see Sharon. Actually, I'll have a word with Bernie now – he can deal with her.'

'Mam, Sharon isn't a kid anymore, she's the same age as me.'

'A father can still tell his daughter off, no matter how old she gets. And so can a mam. Now, scoot, before I give you a clip around the ear for worrying me like that.'

Janice laughed. 'I didn't worry you! You didn't know a thing about it.'

'I do now, so I'm going to worry in retrospect.'

'Mams, eh?' Janice rolled her eyes again as she watched her mother totter across the field. 'They never stop worrying. You've not got any kids, have you?'

'Er, no, I haven't,' Ceri said, and caught her breath when an image of a curly-haired child with Damon's eyes and her nose, popped into her head.

Suddenly she was desperate to be held by him and to hear him say how much he loved her, but Janice was still speaking and Ceri didn't like to cut her off.

'Mam is so pleased to have an allotment on Willow Tree Lane again. She hasn't stopped talking about it. Not only did my dad love it here, so it brings back memories of him, but Mam and Hyacinth were really good friends, especially after my dad died. Heart attack,' she added. 'He smoked like a trooper and drank like a fish, but none of us expected him to go so soon. Well, you don't, do you?' Janice sighed, her gaze still on her mum. The old lady was laughing at something Bernie was saying, and Ceri smiled.

Finally, after some more small talk, Ceri was able to make her escape, and with her mood considerably improved, she dashed home for a shower.

If she hurried, she could be at Damon's house in fifteen minutes and in his bed a second or two after that...

–

Ceri skipped along the lane towards Willow Tree House, thinking that leaping into bed might have to wait because she was famished, and she hoped Damon had planned something nice for their tea. He was surprisingly good in the kitchen, and she was more than happy to have him cook for her.

But when she rang the bell there wasn't any answer, and trying the door revealed it to be locked. However, the gate at the side of the house leading to the garden wasn't, so she strolled through it and went around the back.

'Damon? Damon?' she called, but the only sounds came from a group of squabbling sparrows and the bees crawling over the honeysuckle growing around the kitchen door.

She stepped inside, but after a quick search she realised he must be in the garden and she finally found him sitting in the potting shed, one of Hyacinth's journals in his lap. He barely looked up when she appeared in the doorway.

'Hiya,' she said hesitantly, seeing how engrossed he was.

Damon blinked and he glanced up absently, before his gaze focused on her. 'Hi. Is it that time already?'

'Good reading?' she asked, surprised he had lost track of time. Although to be fair, she would have done the same if she had been reading them. How wonderful to be able to read the history of the garden like this.

'*Interesting* reading.' His expression was thoughtful.

'Oh?' she replied, inviting him to say more as she leant her bum against the potting bench.

'These journals aren't just about how well Gran's fuchsias coped with the summer of '76.' He held up the one in his lap. 'It contains snippets of her private life.' He put it down again. 'I never knew my grandad. My dad didn't know him, either. Gran told Dad that he'd died before he was born.' Damon hesitated, and she briefly wondered why the change of subject, until he continued... 'But according to this, he was still alive and kicking twenty years ago.' He tapped the journal's cover.

Ceri frowned. 'Any idea why she lied?'

'He was married. She was having an affair with him and got pregnant. My father was the result.'

'Who was he?'

'She only ever referred to him as 'V', as far as I can tell.' He shrugged. 'But I haven't read them all. There's one more to go, so all may well be revealed.' He stood up, putting the journal that he was holding back in the tin. 'I need a kiss. Come here.'

Ceri sank into his embrace, revelling in his scent, the strength with which he held her, and the urgency of his lips. When he withdrew, she groaned in frustration.

'Dinner first,' he scolded. 'You must be hungry.'

She was, but despite her hunger, food could wait. However, Damon didn't seem to agree, because when they reached the house he removed the arm that he had slung around her shoulder and opened the fridge.

As they worked side-by-side to prepare the meal, Damon said, 'I think I have an idea who V might be.'

Intrigued, Ceri gave him a nudge when he hesitated. 'Who?'

'Mrs Moxley's husband.'

Ceri gasped. '*Really?* What makes you think that?'

'My hair.'

She ceased dicing the pepper and put down the knife. He looked in need of a cuddle. 'Your hair?' she asked, stroking his curls. 'I don't understand.'

'Rachel and I have the same hair. Mrs. Moxley pointed it out.'

'But that doesn't mean—'

'It might,' he insisted. 'When I was a kid and in boarding school, my dad's career was starting to take off and Mam often joined him on his digs. They were hardly ever in the county, which is why I stayed with Gran for most of the school holidays.'

Ceri nodded. She'd already heard this from Mrs Moxley, and Damon had also told her that he used to spend his school holidays with Hyacinth.

He carried on, 'Gran wrote in her journal that me and Rachel were like two peas in a pod: we had the same eyes, *the same hair*. I think I can guess why she made me have so many haircuts, just in case someone twigged.'

'That's hardly conclusive evidence,' Ceri pointed out.

'No, but Gran mentions V's wife once by name. I thought she was referencing the month, but she wasn't. She was talking about his wife – *June*. That's Mrs Moxley's first name.'

Ceri's mouth dropped open. It was all starting to add up. Damon might be on the right track after all. 'I thought your Gran and Mrs Moxley were friends?'

'They were. Right up until she died.'

'Mrs Moxley couldn't have known about her husband and Hyacinth,' Ceri mused.

'I doubt if she did,' Damon agreed. 'Gran's dad, my great-grandfather was called Lloyd Jones. He made his money in slate. He lost most of it, but managed to hang on to Willow Tree House, and thankfully he'd had the foresight to put money in a trust for Hyacinth. He died from TB when Gran was in her late twenties. By then she was married to a chap called Charlie Rogers, but she moved back to Foxmore to look after her father when he became too ill to care for himself. According to her journal, she and Charlie had been estranged for a couple of years by then, and they divorced a year later. Gran wrote in her journal that she was relieved when the law on divorce changed, and that she and Charlie could finally go their separate ways.'

'So she became pregnant *after* she returned to Foxmore?'

'It appears that way.'

'But why did she tell your father that Charlie was dead?'

Damon shrugged. 'I expect it was easier that way. Everyone assumed the baby was Charlie's and if Dad knew that Charlie was still alive he might have wanted to contact him. And if he had done that he would have discovered that Charlie wasn't his real father.'

'I'm surprised she managed to keep it secret. You know what Foxmore is like.'

'I certainly do. Gran talks about meeting V and there being a connection between them that not even Noah's flood could extinguish. It was a miracle no one noticed.' He smiled sadly. 'It couldn't have been easy being a single parent in those days, but at least she didn't have the stigma of being an unmarried mother. A widowed one was considerably more respectable, so that might be another reason she told everyone Charlie was dead.'

'Are you going to say anything to your father?'

'It's all conjecture at this point, so before I do, I'd need proof. I should imagine it will come as a shock to him. And there's Mrs Moxley to consider. If V really was her husband, do I want to sully her memory of him? It's in the past, and maybe that's where it should stay.' Damon was silent for a moment, various emotions flitting across his face. 'It's weird to think that I have a... I'm not sure what to call Rachel. Would she be my cousin? And my father has a half-brother or sister that he doesn't even know about.'

'Would he be pleased, if he knew?'

'Actually, I don't think he would care one way or the other. I think it's probably better to let sleeping dogs lie. It's ancient history and although it's fascinating to read my gran's journals, I should be looking to the future and not the past. And on that note, I've got to go to London tomorrow. Luke is back in the UK, and we need to put the album to bed.'

Ceri froze. Pain shot through her and suddenly she didn't feel hungry anymore.

–

There were tears in Ceri's eyes, and she was utterly mesmerised as Damon played for her. The music swirled and swooped, making every cell in her body sing. She had listened to some Black Hyacinth tracks (of course she had) since she'd discovered who Damon was, but they hadn't appealed to her, although she would never admit it to him. "Dark Dimension" was the only song she liked, but it faded into significance compared to what he had played tonight.

Damon hadn't as much as picked up a guitar in her presence before, but this evening he had asked her if she minded. Not knowing what to expect, she had agreed.

And she'd been utterly blown away.

Finally, after he had wrung her out emotionally with the beauty of his music, he stopped strumming and put the guitar down.

Ceri was speechless, but she hoped the tears trickling down her face portrayed how deeply it had touched her.

'What do you think?' he asked. His uncertainty was so acute, that she scooted over, put her arms around him and smiled into his eyes. 'Beautiful. Totally and utterly beautiful. It was like "Bridge Over Troubled Water", "The Sound of Silence" – the Disturbed version – and Fleetwood Mac's "Rhiannon", all rolled into one.'

'Thank you.' Damon hugged her, holding her so tightly she couldn't breathe, and after a few moments she wriggled free.

'I'm going to miss you,' he said, his eyes dark, his expression sombre.

Not as much as she was going to miss him. Being back in London, picking up where he left off... he would soon forget her and Foxmore, as he lost himself in his music once more.

Her tears tonight hadn't just been for the songs he had played for her – they had been for the life they could have lived, the love they could have shared if he had simply been Damon Rogers and not the lead singer of a famous rock band.

'I would suggest you come with me,' he was saying, 'but it won't be any fun for you. I'll be in the recording studio for hours on end, and when I do come out for air I'll be knackered and drained. All I'll want to do is eat and sleep. You'll be bored out of your mind. Anyway, you've got work.'

That he had thought about taking her with him at all made her feel sick. She had no idea what his world was like. Her only frame of reference was the occasional documentary she had watched about bands like The Eagles (her dad liked music, especially Sixties and Seventies stuff) and to be honest, what she had seen made her heart sore. Even without the drugs and the alcohol, the lifestyle was a wild one. It must be a heady thing to have fans clamouring for you, both on stage and off, and she imagined the buzz might be addictive.

He had told her he would be back.

She knew he wouldn't.

She took his hand. 'It's late. Can we go to bed?'

All she wanted was to hold him until she could hold him no longer.

She would deal with her heartbreak afterwards, when all she had left of him were her memories.

–

Their lovemaking was as passionate and tender as ever, and he repeatedly told her how much he loved her; but even so, she had to work hard not to cry.

'It'll only be for a few days, a week at the most,' he said, taking hold of her face in his hands. 'I'll be back before you know it.'

But no matter how hard he tried to convince her, she knew she would probably never see him again. Music was as much a part of him as gardening was a part of her. He would never be free of it. He would get back in that studio and he would realise how much he missed it and how deeply it ran in his veins.

He was lost to her already, even if he didn't know it yet.

Curled up against him, Ceri listened to Damon's gentle breathing, wishing sleep would claim her as easily. She shifted restlessly, trying to get comfortable, and froze when he murmured and turned over.

Worried that she was disturbing him, she sidled to the edge of the bed and carefully slipped out from underneath the sheet.

The night was a warm one and the bedroom window was open, but she closed it softly when she heard the bark of a fox. Guessing it must be in the garden (it sounded as though it was immediately below the bedroom window), Ceri crept downstairs and into the parlour.

The view through the glass doors was of dappled darkness and shifting shadows, with a crescent moon hanging in a clear starlit sky. The fox barked again, fainter this time, and when she opened one of the tall French doors, it had gone.

Something flittered over her head and a bat jigged and swooped silently, so fast it was hard to keep track of, and she quickly lost sight of it against the black background of bushes and trees.

Leaving the door open, she wandered into the kitchen, hoping that maybe a glass of milk would settle her and soothe some of her fears. Hadn't Damon told her he loved her? Hadn't he told her he was coming back? She should try to believe him, and not allow her insecurities to overwhelm her. He wouldn't say those things if he didn't mean them. Damon wasn't a liar, despite withholding the truth about who he was and what he did. He'd had his reasons for doing so, and she accepted that.

Taking her milk with her, Ceri returned to the parlour. Sipping slowly, she wandered around the room, trailing her fingers across the photos on the dresser, the people in them indistinct in the gloom. Pausing by one, she picked up the silver frame and peered at the image of Hyacinth. She knew from memory that Damon's grandmother had her head thrown back in this one and was laughing at something or someone beyond the camera, and briefly she wondered who had taken the photo and what it was that Hyacinth had found so amusing. Could it have been the mysterious V who had wielded the camera?

Hyacinth's presence was still very much in evidence in this room, as it was throughout the rest of the house and the garden. As far as Ceri could tell, nothing much had changed since the woman's death, apart from the addition of some of Damon's possessions scattered around the house. She couldn't imagine this room being stripped of all its character and replaced with stark modern furniture. It was lovely just the way it was, and although Damon had spoken about modernising the kitchen and putting in a new bathroom, so far he had made no discernible changes.

It confirmed her fears.

He wouldn't be coming back.

A flash of light and the sound of buzzing startled her, until she realised it was Damon's phone. He had left it on the table next to a gold-covered winged back chair, and it was busily shuffling about with the force of the vibration from the incoming message.

Ceri didn't mean to look, her intention was only to stop the dratted thing from making such a racket, but the screen was illuminated, the message on it clearly visible.

> Can't wait to see you! Looking forward to making sweet music together. Wake me if I'm in bed. All my love, Sadie xxx

Ceri had always thought that the phrase 'my blood ran cold' was just a saying, that it had no basis in truth. But when she read those words before the screen went black, she knew it was true. Cold encased her from the inside out, a deep chill that invaded her heart and turned her blood into chilly rivers of dread.

Wake me if I'm in bed… Would he slip into her room and make love to Aiden's sister with the same love and tenderness he had just made love to her? *Sweet music…* his lovemaking was the sweetest, and agony ripped through her heart, tearing it to shreds.

The image of Sadie flinging herself into Damon's embrace, her face buried in his neck, flashed into her mind. Ceri remembered how well-suited she'd thought the pair of them were, how good they had looked together, how Sadie was so much a part of his world, and how Ceri was so very removed from it.

Slowly, her heart crumbling into ash, her body cold, she knew she had to leave. She couldn't return to his bed, to lie next to him in stunned and crippling silence for the rest of the night. How could she face him in the morning, knowing what she had read? Knowing that he was travelling to London where Sadie was waiting for him, and he would be waking her from slumber...

The French door was still open, a breeze stirring the fine voile curtains, and she was about to close it when something occurred to her.

She couldn't run away without explanation, but she could hardly leave him a note, and she didn't want to send him a message. Neither did she want to wake him – she couldn't face speaking to him, because she didn't know what to say.

His garden called to her, and she ventured outside for a moment, seeking a peace amongst the growing things that she suspected she would fail to find. As she drifted bleakly along the path, her feet took her to an old rose bush. It was a hybrid tea rose of such deep red that it appeared black, and she knew what she had to do.

She chose a bud that was half-unfurled and broke off a length of stem. A faint scent emanated from it that would grow stronger when the flower was fully open, and she held it to her nose as the first of many tears filled her eyes and spilt over.

Her heart broken, she went back inside and with a slow, heavy tread she climbed the stairs.

It was time to say goodbye.

Ceri stood in the doorway, taking a final long look at the man she loved.

Then she placed the black rose on the snowy white pillow where her head had rested a short while earlier, and wondered whether the symbolism of its colour would mean anything to him – black for sorrow, deep red for undying love.

When she kissed her fingers and touched them briefly to his lips, tears falling like rain on his bare chest, Damon didn't stir. Neither did he hear her whisper, 'Goodbye, my love, goodbye.'

Chapter 20

It was already light when Damon woke, which at this time of year could be as early as four-thirty a.m. The dawn chorus was in full voice, and he groaned. It was loud, even though the window was closed.

Did he have time to make love to Ceri, he wondered as he turned onto his back. But when he saw that her side of the bed was empty, his spirits sank. A deep red, almost black rose lay where he had expected her to be, and he smiled ruefully. It was so typical of her to leave him a flower instead of a note. He wished he'd had a chance to say goodbye, but he could understand why she hadn't hung around this morning. He, too, had been dreading this parting, even though he would only be gone a few days. She had been so upset last night and had tried her best not to show it, but he'd been able to tell. He hoped Frank would give him the green light to share the news that the band was dissolving, so he could tell her he would be staying in Foxmore forever. He hadn't even left yet, and already he couldn't wait to get back.

He might be gone a little longer than a few days though, because he wanted to sort out his flat. He was undecided whether to rent it out or put it on the market, so he wanted to have a chat with his accountant. And there would also be the legal aspects of dissolving the band and its contract with the record company which would have to be ironed out.

He wasn't looking forward to any of it, apart from seeing Luke, and it would be great to spend some time with him, although it would never be like old times. How could it be, without Aiden?

With Ceri already having left, he guessed he should probably make a move. He was supposed to be at the studio by eleven and he wanted to swing by his flat beforehand to drop the car off. He'd collect Sadie at the same time (he'd told her she could stay at his place for the duration) and they'd grab a taxi to the studio together.

When he eventually found his phone – he'd plonked it down in the parlour last night and had forgotten to take it upstairs – Damon saw he'd had a message from her. Wake her up indeed! He'd phone her and wake her up now! Or maybe not. It was only five in the morning – a little early. But it was time he was on the road. The four-hour drive wasn't something he relished, but he had refused Frank's offer of a car. He liked his independence, and if, for whatever reason he decided he'd had enough of London and the whole damn caboodle, he could easily hop in his car and hightail it back to Foxmore.

Hastily he leapt into the shower and was out and dressed in less than ten minutes. Grabbing his case, he slung it in the back of the car, checked the house was secure, and set off. Although he was excited to chat with Frank about his new career as a songwriter and it would be great to catch up with Luke and Sadie, he wished he didn't have to leave Ceri and his new life. And he had two pieces of exciting news to tell her when he returned – that Black Hyacinth had disbanded so he would be staying in

Foxmore permanently, and that he was gifting her the allotment.

–

Ceri briefly closed her eyes and valiantly tried not to let her heartbreak show. What she really wanted was to curl up in a ball and howl her anguish, but she was at work and she didn't want to scare the kids, although she suspected it would take more than a teary teacher to drag them away from their mobile phones.

'Put your phones away,' she instructed. 'We've got a lot to get through this morning.'

The class was slow to settle, and she had to ask them again. They kept shooting her looks as though they expected her to demand to know what had got them so het up, but frankly she didn't care. What went on outside college was none of her business. The closer it came to the end of the academic year, the more restless the class had become. And not just this one. The other classes she taught were the same, and when she'd mentioned it to Mark he'd said he didn't blame them and he felt like that too. He couldn't wait for the last day of term and the freedom of the summer holidays. Ceri couldn't wait either, but it wasn't freedom she craved – it was solitude and the privacy to grieve in peace.

Seeing Portia and her sidekick with their heads still bent over their phones, she almost yelled at them, but she managed to hold herself in check. It would be unprofessional to take her heartache out on them, even if they were being royal pains in the backside.

That said, she didn't know how she was going to get through today without breaking down, and when she noticed an email in her college inbox asking her to call into the principal's office this morning, it felt like the last straw. It probably wasn't anything to worry about – she knew Mrs Nash had been catching up with the staff for an end-of-year chat – but she could do without it.

Nevertheless, she plastered a smile on her face when the principal's secretary showed her into the office, and hoped it looked more natural than it felt.

'Ceri, take a seat.' Mrs Nash was a tall, painfully thin woman, who wore designer dresses with matching jackets and tortoiseshell spectacles. Today she was in a red and white dress, with the accompanying jacket hanging on the back of her chair.

After she'd waited for Ceri to sit down, she rested her elbows on the desk and folded her hands under her chin before she spoke. 'A matter has come to my attention that I need to discuss with you.' Her glance dropped to a sheet of paper in front of her, before returning to Ceri.

Ceri swallowed nervously. Whatever this was, it appeared to be serious.

Mrs Nash unfolded her fingers and picked up the sheet of paper. 'The college has received a letter of complaint.' She paused and took a breath. 'About you.'

Blast! Portia *had* filmed her and Damon kissing after all, and now the girl's mother had written to the principal.

'That's not fair,' Ceri protested. 'What I do in my own time is my own business. Yes, I invited the students to come to the allotment opening ceremony, but it was on the weekend, and it was only a peck.'

'Pardon?'

'The kiss, it was only a quick peck.' She pressed her lips together and ignored the sting in her eyes, determined not to cry.

'I'm sorry, I think we might be at cross purposes. What do you think this is about?' Mrs Nash shook the letter.

'A couple of the students on my first year BTEC course came to the opening ceremony of an allotment they've been working on. They saw my... someone kiss me. But as I said, it was a peck, nothing more.'

'This isn't about a kiss, but it is about the allotment. The letter claims that your students have been used as – and I quote – "free labour".'

'That's a lie!'

'I have to ask... do you have any commercial interest in this allotment?'

'Absolutely not! It's a community space, owned by the church. I admit to having a plot there, but so do fifteen other people.' Ceri gulped and her eyes filled with tears. 'I took those students there as part of their assignment.'

Mrs Nash reached behind her, took a box of tissues off a shelf and slid it towards Ceri, who took one and dabbed at her wet cheeks.

'I guessed it was something like that, but please understand, I had to check. I'm sorry you're upset; that wasn't my intention.'

'Is that all?' Ceri asked, trying not to bawl.

'Yes, and please accept my apologies,' the principal repeated.

Ceri fled the room before Mrs Nash had finished speaking. She had to get away.

Blindly she headed for the ladies' loos, not wanting anyone to see her like this, least of all her students.

Letting out a sob, she hurried along the corridor, wondering how people could be so nasty. What had she ever done to Mrs Drake?

'Ceri, what on earth is wrong?' Mark was coming the other way and Ceri's heart sank.

'Nothing. I'm fine.'

'You're not fine.' He glanced up and down the corridor, then took hold of her elbow and guided her into an empty classroom. 'Can I do anything to help?' he asked, closing the door behind them.

'There's been another complaint. I've just come from Mrs Nash's office.'

'A complaint about what?'

'Me taking my BTEC group to the allotment.'

'Why would anyone complain about that?'

'I don't know,' she sobbed. 'I thought it was a good idea.'

'It was. I wouldn't have signed off on it if I thought it wasn't. What did Mrs Nash say, exactly?'

'Someone accused me of using the kids as free labour.'

'That's ridiculous. Mrs Nash should have checked with me first. I would have put her straight. In fact, I'll go do that now.'

'Thank you, but I already explained. It's all sorted.'

'She still should have come to me first. I'm your line manager. If she had, this nonsense could have been avoided.'

'Please don't say anything. It's fine, honestly.'

'It's not fine. Look at you, you're upset. Why don't you go home, take the rest of the day off?'

'What about my classes?'

'Don't worry about those. Just get off home. You can't teach in this state.'

Ceri had to admit he was right. She couldn't seem to stop crying. It was as though being summoned to the principal's office had poked a hole in the dam she had constructed on her way to work this morning, and now that it had been breached the flood of her emotions threatened to overwhelm her.

With tears streaming down her face, Ceri cried all the way home.

–

Someone was knocking on the door, but Ceri ignored it. She didn't want to speak to anyone. She didn't want to see anyone. She just wanted to be left alone.

She was tempted to go to bed and hide under the duvet for the rest of the day, but all the crying she'd done had made her thirsty, so she heaved herself off the sofa, catching sight of herself in the mirror above the fireplace as she did so, and winced.

It wasn't pretty. Her face was alarmingly pale, her eyes were red and the dark circles underneath them reminded her of bruises, which was apt, because she felt as though she'd been punched. Her chest hurt, her heart ached, and she felt sick.

Damon would be in London by now. He would have seen the rose she had left him. What had he made of it?

Nothing, probably.

Had he woken Sadie with a kiss? Had they made languid love? Or had it been hot and frantic?

Ceri let out a low moan of anguish.

Unable to stop herself, she checked her phone and saw a message from him.

Missing you already. Love you XXX

The stab to her heart as she read it made her gasp, and she didn't know what to think. Why was he continuing to string her along? Or did he mean what he said? If so, what was all that about with Sadie? *What the hell was he playing at?*

Fresh tears fell and she brushed them away. Maybe he did intend to return to Foxmore after all, else why would he have sent her such a message?

Ceri had never felt so confused, or so alone. She desperately wanted to talk it over with someone, but who? Could she betray Damon's confidence and let her brother in on the secret? Huw wouldn't tell anyone. Except for Rowena… she was his wife, after all.

And that, Ceri thought, is how secrets get out.

Thinking about her sister-in-law must have conjured her up, because the knock came again, and although Ceri didn't answer it, a few moments later two faces appeared at the window, hands cupped around their eyes as they peered inside.

Ceri let out a sigh of resignation and opened the door.

'We were on our way to the allotment and we saw your car,' Rowena said. She nudged her daughter. 'Say hello to Aunty Ceri.'

'Hello, Aunty Ceri,' Nia chorused.

Rowena said, 'Mrs Moxley was telling me how her great-grandchildren have been helping on the allotment, so Nia now wants to help, too. I told her that we haven't got a plot, but she threw a wobbly. Can we spend some time on yours this morning, do you think? The school's got a teacher training day, and I'm trying to keep this little munchkin occupied. I thought a bit of gardening might burn off some of her excess energy.'

'I'm not going to the allotment today.' Ceri's voice was flat. She couldn't face it – it was too close to Damon's empty house. 'You can go if you want.'

'OK, if you don't mind. Is there anything in particular you'd like us to do? Mulching, or something? Or if you've got anything that needs sowing or planting, that would be even better.'

'There are some packets of peas in the shed, if you feel like sowing them. Come in and I'll give you the key.'

'Hang on, why aren't you at work? Are you coming down with something?' her sister-in-law asked, as she stepped inside. 'You don't look the best.'

Nia's eyes were round. 'When I had chicken pox Mammy said I had a temperature because I felt hot and was itchy all over. Are you hot and itchy, Aunty Ceri?'

'No, sweetie, I'm not itchy.' She crouched down to give the little girl a cuddle.

'Can you show me how to grow sunflowers, please?'

Rowena said, 'Not today, Nia. Aunty Ceri said we can sow some peas.'

'Here's the key.' Ceri handed it over. 'Be careful, because there's a rake just inside the door. You can drop the key through the letterbox when you're done.'

'Come with us. It might do you good to get some fresh air.' Rowena was examining her closely and Ceri squirmed under her scrutiny. 'Are you sure you've not picked up a bug?'

Without warning, Ceri's chin began to wobble and her eyes filled with tears.

Alarmed, Rowena cried, 'What is it? Can I do anything to help?'

'Not unless you can mend a broken heart,' Ceri sobbed.

'Can it be mended, Mammy?' Nia asked, gazing at Ceri with fascination. 'Skye broke her arm and she had to have a plaster on it. It was pink and she let me draw on it.'

'Not that kind of broken,' Rowena told her daughter over the top of Ceri's head, her eyes warning Ceri not to say anything further.

'Can Huw fix it?' the little girl asked.

'We'll see. Why don't you show Terror the garden while Mammy dries Aunty Ceri's tears, then we'll go to the allotment, yeah?'

Ceri was vaguely aware of Nia taking a cuddly toy cat out of her little rucksack, and she made a valiant effort to pull herself together. Nia did not need to see her Aunty Ceri bawling her eyes out.

'What's wrong?' Rowena asked, as soon as Nia was out of earshot.

'Damon, work... *everything*. I wish I'd never left Cardiff.' She sniffed and dabbed her cheeks.

'Put the kettle on and start at the beginning.'

Ceri led her sister-in-law into the kitchen and ran the tap. 'He's gone to London.'

Rowena frowned. 'So...?'

'I don't think he's coming back.'

'Did he tell you that?'

'No... he said he *is* coming back.'

'Well, then.' Rowena stroked her arm. 'If he says he is, then he is. Why would he lie?'

'It's complicated.'

Her sister-in-law pulled a face. 'In what way?'

'I can't say. It's... delicate.'

Rowena's eyes widened. 'You make it sound as though he's up to no good. He's not into anything shady, is he?'

273

Ceri snuffled out a wet laugh. 'Nothing like that, but it's not my secret to tell.'

'*Secret?* Curiouser and curiouser. It all sounds very intriguing.' Rowena gave her a hug. 'I'm here for you if you want to talk about it, OK?'

'I think he's got someone else,' Ceri blurted.

Rowena blinked. 'What makes you think that?'

'She sent him a message asking him to wake her up when he got to London this morning. It was all kissy-kissy. Her name is Sadie and she's the sister of one of his best friends.'

'Have you asked him about her?'

'Not really.'

'Don't you think you should, before you go jumping to conclusions?'

Ceri hung her head. 'I suppose.' She still couldn't shake the feeling that he wasn't coming back, but Rowena was right – he hadn't told her that he *wasn't*. Maybe she had been a bit hasty and had overreacted? And he *had* assured her that he and Sadie weren't an item…

After Rowena and Nia left, Ceri sent him a message.

> Hope the recording goes OK. Missing you too xxx

Hopefully he'd read it soon and reply.

But even if he did, Ceri knew she wouldn't rest easy until he was back in Foxmore and she was in his arms once more.

–

The first thing Damon did when he eased his car into the underground car park was tell Ceri he was missing her. He'd debated whether to phone, but she might be teaching, so he sent her a message then headed upstairs.

It was strange being back in his flat after all this time, and as he walked into the hall, Damon realised he no longer belonged here, if he ever had. It had never felt much like a home, but now it felt alien and impersonal with its clean lines and minimalist decor, and he realised he'd never actually put his stamp on it. The apartment was almost as pristine and impersonal as the day he'd moved in.

After dumping his bag in the living room and throwing his keys on the marble-topped table, he hesitated outside the door of the guest bedroom. Sadie did say to wake her up…

'Sadie?' He tapped on the wood. 'Sadie, are you awake?'

He uttered a cry of surprise and almost fell into the room when the door was yanked open, and Sadie launched herself at him and smothered his face in kisses. Damon gently extricated himself and held her at arm's length.

'What have I done to deserve a welcome like that?'

'I thought you might have changed your mind.'

'I said I would finish the album and I meant it.' He pulled his hair out of its ponytail and let it fall around his shoulders. Ah, that was better. It had been starting to give him a headache.

'Er, Damon, the word is out that Black Hyacinth is going to release the new album.'

He rolled his eyes. 'It's to be expected, I suppose. You can't blame Frank for drumming up interest. It could be a big earner for him and the record label.'

'It'll be an even bigger earner when Black Hyacinth fans find out it'll be the last album you ever release. That story will even top this latest one, although I bet there are girls all over the world who are bawling their eyes out right now.'

'What are you talking about?'

Sadie bit her lip, looking worried. 'Don't you know?'

'Know what?'

'There are photos of you and Ceri all over the internet.' She fetched her phone and tapped the screen.

Damon's voice was grim. 'Let me see.'

When she passed her mobile to him, what he saw made his blood run cold and his heart turn to ice.

There wasn't just one photo, there were several, and although the one where he was kissing Ceri had been taken from some distance away and wasn't as sharp as it could be, in the others his face was clearly visible. So was hers.

He clicked on one of them, dread making him clumsy, and he almost dropped the phone when he read that the whole world now knew he lived in Foxmore and that he was dating a local teacher.

That was bad enough, but there was worse to come. According to the article, Ceri herself had apparently admitted to her students that she was dating him. Two girls were quoted as having asked their teacher outright, because they had spotted him in Foxmore, where he had been 'hiding out after the death of band member Aiden Thomas'. And speculation was rife that Black Hyacinth had found someone to replace Aiden on vocals and guitar, in the form of Aiden's sister, Sadie. The band had yet to comment.

He'd give them a comment, all right! One that wasn't fit to be printed.

'When did all this kick off?' he demanded.

'Um, this morning, I think. I only noticed it when I woke up. I'm pretty sure there was nothing about it last night.'

Suddenly Damon had to get out of there. He had to leave. Going to the studio now, after Ceri's gross betrayal of his privacy, was unthinkable. With no idea where he was headed or what he would do when he got there, he grabbed his keys and darted into the hall. He just needed to get out of there. Now!

'What are you doing?' Sadie demanded. 'I thought we were going to grab a taxi to the studio?'

'I'm not going to the studio,' he growled.

'*What?* You've got to!'

'No, I haven't.'

'But what about the album?'

'Stuff the album.' Damon softened when he saw her face. 'It will get done,' he promised her. 'Just not today...' He shouldn't take it out on her; this awful situation wasn't Sadie's fault. He was guilty of shooting the messenger when the only person he should be furious with was Ceri.

He'd thought she loved him. He had bared his soul to her, had let her into his heart, his home and his life, and *this* is how she repaid him.

Did she honestly think he would forgive her? She knew how he felt, and the reason he was keeping a low profile, yet she had discussed him with her bloody *students*. It might have been done inadvertently, but how could he trust her again? Perhaps she'd thought nothing would come of it, but for God's sake, she knew the score with Aiden. She should have guessed what this would do to him.

How could their relationship ever recover from this? She was responsible for details of his private life now being splashed all over social media.

Distraught, Damon stormed out of the flat and headed to the basement and his car.

As he slid into the driver's seat, his phone began to vibrate and he switched it off before starting the engine and roaring up the ramp and onto the street, not caring which direction he went.

It was only when he saw he was on the M40, did he realise that he was heading back to Foxmore.

Chapter 21

Ceri stared at her phone's screen, willing a message from Damon to appear. She'd only sent it an hour ago, and she assumed he must be busy. He might be in the middle of recording, or whatever it was they did in the studio.

She was about to take a sip of the tea she'd just made, when there was a knock on the door. Guessing it was probably Rowena returning the shed key, she hesitated about answering it. She had embarrassed herself in front of her sister-in-law once today, and although she wasn't feeling quite as despondent, she didn't want to risk a repeat performance. What must poor little Nia think of her Aunty Ceri!

But then she felt guilty as the knock came again, so she put her mug down and went to the door.

A man and a woman were standing in her step. 'Ceri Morgan?' the man asked.

'Er… yes. Can I help—?'

Before Ceri had a chance to finish the sentence, the woman lifted a camera to her face and began snapping away.

It took Ceri a moment to understand that it was she who was being photographed, and as soon as she did, she put out her hand to block the lens. 'What's going on?' she demanded. 'Who are you, and why are you taking my photo?'

'Can you tell me about your relationship with Damon Rogers? Is he your boyfriend? How long have the two of you been dating?' The man rattled off a flurry of questions, one after the other without waiting for a reply.

Ceri gasped. '*What?* No! It's none of your business. Who *are* you?'

'*Stone Alley.*'

'*Who?* Look, please can you get that thing out of my face.' She was tempted to grab the camera and fling it into the road. How dare these people—

Realisation struck. Oh, God! They knew her *name*. They had asked her about *Damon*.

'*Stone Alley,*' the man repeated. 'The heavy rock zine?' He sounded sarcastic, as though he couldn't believe that she'd made him repeat it.

Ceri was frozen. She didn't know what to do, or what to say. Her mind was numb, her limbs leaden, and it was only when the guy demanded, 'Is he here? Damon? *Damon!*' and tried to peer past her into the cottage, that Ceri was able to move.

'Get lost!' she yelled and quickly backed away, slamming the door in their faces. She was trembling violently, and her heart was racing so fast she thought she might faint. A pounding on the door made her jump and was quickly followed by knuckles rapping on glass, as the horrid pair outside began knocking on her window.

With a strangled cry, she dashed to the living room window and yanked the curtains closed, and did the same to the one in the dining area. Then she hurried to lock the door, because she wouldn't put it past them to try the handle and walk straight in.

Only when she felt marginally safer, did she turn around to rest her back against the door. Then she slid down it until she was sitting in a heap on the floor, and started to cry.

She had no idea how long she sat there weeping, but the sound of her phone ringing broke into her misery. Clambering ungainly to her feet, she went to answer it, praying it was Damon. He'd know what to do—

Shit! *Damon!* She had to warn him.

Ceri grabbed her mobile, but when she saw that the caller was her sister-in-law, she felt like wailing again.

'Can I call you back?' she said, before Rowena was able to say anything.

'No, Ceri, *don't hang up,*' Rowena hissed. 'There's something going on I think you should know about. Can you hear me? I've got to keep my voice down.' Rowena was speaking in a whisper. 'I'm in Pen's Pantry, and a man came in here a few minutes ago asking if anyone knew you, or where you live. And another chap is here now, asking the same. What's going on, Ceri? Are you in some kind of trouble?'

Ceri let out a sob. There was no point in keeping Damon's secret any longer, not if the likes of *Stone Alley* knew, so she swiftly told Rowena everything.

'Bloody parasites,' Rowena snarled, after she had got over the shock of learning who Damon was.

'What are bloody parasites, Mammy?' Ceri heard Nia ask.

'Mosquitoes,' Rowena said without a pause. 'Finish your milkshake. Sorry Ceri, little pitchers have big ears. Are they outside now?'

Ceri tweaked the curtain aside. 'Yes.'

'You can't stay there, you're a prisoner in your own home. Can you get out the back?'

'I think so.' Behind Rosehip Cottage was a stand of trees, and beyond that was a meadow leading down to the river.

'OK, go now, before they stake the back out, too. Make your way to my house and we'll figure out what to do when you get here.'

This is ridiculous, Ceri thought, as she opened her back door and stepped warily into the courtyard garden. Close to tears, she peered over the fence, but there was no one in sight, so she pulled one of the patio chairs over to it and stood on the seat. When she'd clambered over the fence and dropped to the other side, she tried calling Damon again.

She listened to the phone ring and ring, muttering, 'Pick up, please pick up,' but eventually gave up and sent him a message.

> Reporters??!! At my door asking about you! Gone to Huw's house to hide. Call me when you can. Love you xxx

All she could do now was wait, and pray she made it to her brother's house without being accosted.

–

Three hours later, with his hair tied back, a baseball cap on his head, and sunglasses hiding his eyes, Damon drove past Foxmore's old church and along Ceri's road, hoping no one would realise it was him who was driving the nondescript black VW estate.

Eyes peeled, he scanned the road for strangers, and was dismayed to see a couple of what he assumed to be reporters, hanging around outside her cottage.

He was even more dismayed when he turned into Willow Tree Lane and saw more of the buggers loitering outside his house. Two vehicles were blocking the lane, so he came to a halt outside the entrance to the allotments and considered his options.

Leaving the car here and walking across the allotment to the little wooden gate would be one of them, but what would he do when he got to his house? Hide in it like a rabbit trapped in a burrow with a fox prowling around outside?

No bloody thanks!

Angry that his sanctuary had become a prison, he uttered a low growl, then let out a snort of rage when he saw a couple of teenagers at the far end of the allotment open the little gate and go inside. They were on his property! In his garden! And to add insult to injury, he thought he recognised them as being some of Ceri's students. He was sure he had seen them at the allotment's opening ceremony.

That damn allotment had a lot to answer for, and in a fit of temper he climbed out of his car, strode over to the entrance and yanked the sign off the gate. His lawyer would soon order this lot off his property. Damon mightn't be able to come back to Willow Tree House for a while, but when he did, he would do so safe in the knowledge that there wouldn't be a bunch of strangers peering through the hedge and trying to get into his garden. He was so mad he could cry. Having his heart broken into a thousand pieces by the woman he loved made him want to bawl too, and he blinked back tears.

Quickly returning to his car and relieved he hadn't been spotted, he eased his phone out of his pocket. He'd call his lawyer now – no time like the present – but as soon as he switched his mobile on, it began to ring. Luke, Sadie and Frank had all called him – several times – but he didn't want to speak to anyone. It was Frank who was phoning him now, and he dropped the call.

He'd also had a couple of missed calls from Ceri, and he narrowed his eyes, mainly to stop the tears from falling. Seeing her name made him want to weep. He'd also had a couple of messages from her, and the most recent one caught his eye.

Ceri was at her brother's house.

He knew where that was, Cowslip Lane, in the house with the lilac bush in the garden and honeysuckle around the door.

Executing a swift three-point turn, he drove out of the lane muttering, 'Bad idea, very bad idea,' under his breath. But he couldn't help himself. He had to see her one last time, even if it was to let her know how badly she had hurt him.

Careful to drive slowly and not draw any attention to the car, Damon circumnavigated the green and trundled up the high street until he came to Cowslip Road.

He could feel her drawing him towards her an irres- istible siren call, and although he knew he should drive away and forget her, the urge to see Ceri one final time overrode rational thought.

A curtain twitched as he pulled up alongside Huw's house and got out.

Taking his sunglasses off, he was dismayed to see that his hand was shaking, and he grasped the car door to stop the tremble.

He should walk away. This wasn't going to solve anything; if anything, it would make things worse. But just as he was about to turn on his heel and let his head rule his treacherous heart, the door opened.

Ceri, pale, drawn, and tearful emerged, and the thousand pieces that his heart had already shattered into became a million.

'Why?' he croaked, shaking his head. He still couldn't believe she had done this to him, to *them*. She had ruined everything and had broken his heart in the process. 'How *could* you?' His voice caught.

'Damon I'm—'

'I *loved* you. I thought you loved *me*!' he cried. 'Do you know what you've *done*?' He didn't need an answer; her stricken expression told him she knew, and he said, 'I never want to see you again.' Tears trickled down his face but he made no attempt to brush them away. Let her see the damage she had caused.

She was crying too, and with all his heart he wanted to scoop her into his arms and kiss her tears away, but it was too late. He would never hold her again, never kiss her again. Never see her again.

They were over and he didn't know how he'd ever recover.

With grief and despair threatening to overwhelm him, he got in the car.

'Damon, please… I love you!'

Her cry seared his soul and he almost gave in, but an image of teenage girls walking through his gate flashed into his mind, and for one brief, blessed second, anger rose up, swamping the terrible sadness.

He pressed a button and as the window glided down, he called, 'By the way, the land the allotment is on belongs to *me*. I want you and everyone else off it today.' And with that, he slammed the car into first gear and gunned the accelerator.

He could see her saying something as she hurried towards him, her hands outstretched, but the noise of the engine drowned her out.

His final view of the only woman he would ever love was of her anguished face in his rear-view mirror as he drove away.

–

It was Huw who picked Ceri up off the pavement. She lay in a heap on the ground, sobbing bitterly, the sight of Damon's devastated face seared indelibly on her mind.

'Who was that?' Huw asked, staring after the disappearing car as he put his arm around her and helped her to her feet. 'Was it a reporter? Rowena told me what happened. I got home as fast as I could.'

'It was Damon.' Her voice was dead and flat.

'Damon? I thought he was in London?'

'So did I. He never wants to see me again,' she keened, and once again her knees gave away.

Huw held her up. 'Let's get you inside,' he said, glancing worriedly up and down the road.

Ceri allowed her brother to lead her into the house, where he relinquished her into Rowena's tender care.

'Take Nia to my mother's,' Rowena instructed him, 'and stay there for a bit. I reckon Ceri needs a bit of space.' Rowena waited until Huw and Nia had left before she said, 'I hope no one spotted Damon – I don't want those bloody parasites knocking on *my* door. What did he say?'

Ceri's tears had finally dried, replaced by a terrifying emptiness. She felt hollowed out, as though her very soul had been sucked out of her. 'He never wants to see me again.'

'Why?'

'He said "how could you?".'

'I don't understand.'

'He thinks *I* told them. Or told someone, who told them. He thinks I betrayed him.'

'You wouldn't do that! You didn't even tell Huw, your own brother.'

'I know.'

'What's his phone number? I'll put him straight.'

Ceri wordlessly handed her the phone. She doubted whether Damon would answer, but the fact that Rowena was prepared to try made her want to cry again.

'It's dead,' Rowena said. 'Did you bring your charger?'

Ceri shook her head. She had only thought to bring herself.

'I haven't got one to fit this,' her sister-in-law said, examining the charging jack.

'It doesn't matter. I won't be calling him, and he certainly won't be calling me.' The only way she would hear Damon's voice again would be when she heard his music on the radio. She swallowed hard, remembering last night and the hauntingly beautiful songs he had played for her.

Blowing out her cheeks and holding herself together by the thinnest of threads, Ceri said, 'There is something you could do for me though, if you wouldn't mind…?'

'Anything. What is it?'

'Call Terry. He needs to know that the church doesn't own the allotment on Willow Tree Lane – Damon does. And he wants everyone off his property today.'

And with that, Ceri collapsed into floods of tears again. Not only had she lost the man she loved, she'd let everyone who had a plot in the allotment on Willow Tree Lane down.

–

The car ate the miles as Damon blindly headed as far away from Foxmore as he could. He had no particular destination in mind – he simply wanted to put enough distance between him and Ceri so that he would stop thinking about her.

In reality, he knew it was impossible. No matter how far he travelled, his heart would still be in Foxmore. It belonged to Ceri, all seven million pieces of it.

But he couldn't stop driving and it was only the threat of running out of petrol that forced him to slow down and pull into a garage.

As he filled up the tank, he wondered where he was and was surprised to discover that he had driven almost as far as Anglesey. The coastal town of Conwy was only a short distance away.

He paid for his fuel and purchased a couple of bottles of water. His throat was dry and his eyes burned, but the water did little to help, despite drinking a whole bottle.

Blindly, he got back behind the wheel and carried on driving.

–

Morfa Beach was a stretch of golden sand, and although it was high summer, it was mostly deserted.

Damon got out of the car, staring at the sea. He had no idea how he had ended up here, but it was as good a place as any.

A ridge of grassy dunes led down onto the beach and he stumbled through them until he found a spot to sit. Sinking onto the warm sand, he lay back, one arm above his head, and listened to the silence. The only sounds were the waves, the wind sighing gently through the grass and the distant cry of gulls.

Ceri would have loved this.

Fresh tears leaked out of the corners of his eyes, dampening his hair as they trickled down his temples. He couldn't rid himself of the sight of her face, the anguish on it and the desperation, and he had an awful feeling her heart had been breaking as much as his.

Had he been too hasty?

He hadn't allowed her to explain, to tell her side of the story, and although it was logical to assume she had been the one to divulge that he was living in Foxmore, he clearly hadn't thought it through. After all, Ceri hadn't taken that photo of the pair of them kissing the day of the opening ceremony. Someone else had, and he had an image of the teenagers sneaking into his garden.

He needed to speak to Sadie. She was the one person who he could trust to give it to him straight.

'Thank God! I've been worried sick. We all have. Where are you?' she cried.

'North Wales somewhere. On a beach.' He rubbed a weary hand across his face. He had been driving for hours and was exhausted. 'I think I've been an idiot.'

'What have you done?'

'I accused Ceri of selling me out.'

'You did *what?* Oh, Damon, you prat.'

289

'I know. It was a knee-jerk reaction. I wasn't thinking.'
He gazed out to sea, his eyes resting on the sparkling water.

'No shit. You need to apologise big time. Of course she didn't sell you out. Why would she do that? Anyone with half a brain can see she's head over heels in love with you. You plonker.'

'You only met her once, and that was for less than five minutes.'

'So? I have highly tuned female intuition. Stop messing about on that beach, go tell her you got it wrong and beg her to forgive you.'

'What if she doesn't?'

'Damon, you daft sod, haven't you listened to a word I've been saying? She. Loves. You. There, I've spelt it out for you.'

Scrambling to his feet, he dusted the sand off his jeans and straightened his shoulders. She was right – he had to at least try. 'Wish me luck?'

Sadie's laughter followed him back to the car as she said, 'You're not going to need it.'

He hoped she was right. Because he didn't know how he could face the future without Ceri by his side.

–

Huw's couch was the most uncomfortable thing Ceri had ever slept on in her life, she decided, as she turned over yet again. It didn't help that it wasn't only her weary limbs that were aching. Her heart was, too. It hurt so badly that she didn't think she would recover. It was in pieces. Little itty-bitty ones that would take a miracle to put back together.

All she could think about was the look on Damon's face as he got in his car and drove out of her life forever.

Disgust, pain, disbelief, betrayal…

Huw had wordlessly shown her what was being splashed over the internet, and when she'd read it for herself, she had been horrified. No wonder Damon thought she was responsible.

Portia and Eleanor had a lot to answer for. They should be ashamed of themselves. It wasn't just *her* privacy they had invaded – they had also invaded Damon's. And their actions had destroyed her life. The only man she would ever love had walked out of it, and she didn't know how she was going to live without him.

Tossing and turning, Ceri thumped the pillow and stuffed it under her head at a different angle, before giving up. It was no good – she wasn't going to get to sleep. How could she when there were daggers in her chest, stabbing her in the heart?

Rowena had loaned her a pair of pyjamas, and Ceri took them off, got dressed in her own clothes, then silently unlocked the door and slipped out into the night.

The village was quiet, the streets deserted. There was no one hanging around the green, and she guessed it was unlikely anyone would still be outside her house. Reporters might be back in the morning, but for now, she was safe.

However, she didn't head to her little cottage. Instead, she opened the lychgate and stole into the graveyard.

There was someone she wanted to talk to.

The rumble of a car on the lane made her freeze and she held her breath, but it drove on past, and she heard it stop briefly at the junction before pulling out onto the high street, the sound of the engine fading.

Breathing again, she walked softly towards Hyacinth's final resting place and sank to her knees in the grass. The hyacinths Damon had planted were still there, but their leaves were almost dead and soon they would be gone completely.

Ceri stroked one of them absently.

Now that she was here, she didn't know what to say and she felt self-conscious. Leaning against the cool marble, she wished she could speak to Hyacinth in person – although she didn't have the faintest idea what good that would do. But there was no one else who knew him the way his grandmother had, and she was desperate for some comfort.

Ever since she had discovered the truth about him, Ceri had known this day would come. Hadn't she already said goodbye to him? Last night she had placed a dark red rose on the pillow next to his head and had walked out of his life.

But she had stupidly allowed herself to hope. She had let the belief that he loved her and that he had meant it when he'd told her he was coming back, seep into her heart.

He *had* come back – but only to tell her they were over. Through no fault of her own, she had killed his love for her. He thought she had betrayed him, and nothing she could say would make him change his mind.

But even if she could make him believe her, it would be fruitless. He would never belong to her. His life was music, bright lights, and screaming fans. Hers was the sound of wind in the branches, seedlings poking through the soil, and the gentle turn of the seasons.

No matter how hard she prayed and how much she wished, her world wasn't his.

Tears fell again, trickling down her face, soft like summer rain.

She had cried so much, that it was a wonder she had any left, but they kept coming, and she suspected they always would. Although she might one day find laughter again, Damon would remain forever in her heart. And in the depths of the night, when the world slumbered, she would lie awake with her memories and cry silent tears.

Tracing Hyacinth's name with her finger, Ceri wept, 'Oh, God, I've lost him, Hyacinth.'

'Ceri…'

Damon's voice, coming out of the darkness at the side of the church, made her jump and she scrambled to her feet, her heart threatening to leap out of her chest in shock.

'Damon?' She couldn't believe he was here. She began to tremble, and put her hand on Hyacinth's headstone to steady herself as she peered into the shadows.

A figure emerged, walking slowly towards her, and when the streetlights illuminated his face, she thought how weary he looked. He halted a few paces away.

She wanted to run to him, to fling her arms around him and hold him close; but she was too scared. She couldn't face rejection a second time.

Drinking in the sight of him, knowing this would definitely be the last time she would be alone with him, she had to force herself to move. She'd better leave. Hyacinth was *his* grandmother, not hers, and she had no right to be there.

'Don't go.' His voice was little more than a whisper.

Ceri hesitated. She wanted to stay, but she didn't think she could take it. Misery coiled inside her, tightening its grip on her heart, squeezing it mercilessly, the pain unbearable.

'I love you, Ceri, please don't go.'

Swallowing hard, she drew in a shaky breath. She was frozen, her limbs a dead weight, her mind numb. Had she really heard him say he loved her? Or had she imagined it, desperation making her mind play tricks on her. But even if she had heard him say that, it didn't change anything.

'Ceri, please...' His voice caught. 'Don't tell me you don't love me.' He sounded anguished, broken. It made her heart bleed.

He stepped towards her. He was so close that if she put out her hand she would be able to touch him, and it took all her willpower not to.

Blinking away fresh tears, she said, 'I do love you. I'll never stop loving you, but...'

'I'm so, so sorry, you must believe me. I was stupid – I wasn't thinking clearly and I jumped to the wrong conclusion. I know you didn't betray me.'

'It's not that.'

'Then what is it?'

'I don't fit into your life.'

He frowned. 'I don't understand.'

Was he being deliberately obtuse? Did she have to spell it out for him? She shook her head. 'You are the lead singer of Black Hyacinth, I'm—' She held up a hand as he opened his mouth to interrupt. 'Please... let me finish.' When he subsided, she said, 'I'm a horticulturist. Your home is on a stage; mine is in a garden. You perform in front of hundreds of fans; I plant things and dig up weeds. Is that enough to be going on with?' Her last words ended on a sob.

Damon was silent for several seconds, then he said quietly, 'I should have told you sooner... and I wanted to, but Frank asked me not to say anything for a while.' He took a deep breath. 'I'm no longer in Black Hyacinth.'

Ceri's eyes widened. She couldn't believe it. 'You've *left the band*?'

'Luke and I decided we didn't want to carry on without Aiden.'

'But what will you do?'

'Stay here.'

'Stay in Foxmore for good?' No, he couldn't do that. Music was his life. If he gave it up he would regret it. 'You can't. You *mustn't*.'

'I'm not leaving, Ceri, not unless you want me to go. I'm done with being on stage and I'm done with touring.'

'You'll regret it. Music is in your blood – like gardening is in mine.'

'I'm not going to give it up.' He gazed into her eyes. The emotion in them took her breath away. 'I always did prefer the composition side of things more than performing. I'm going to write songs. So you see, I won't be giving up music at all.'

A small, tender flame of hope, easily extinguished, ignited in her heart. 'Do you mean it?'

He nodded earnestly. 'I do, and even if I don't stay, I'm not going to perform again.'

The flame stuttered and dimmed. 'I thought you said you weren't leaving, that you were going to stay in Foxmore?'

'I want to, but that depends on you. I couldn't bear to live in Willow Tree House and for us not to be together. It would break me, Ceri. I love you. I think I've loved you from the first time I saw you dancing in the field under the stars.'

Oh, God, he meant it, he really did. Gulping back happy tears, she whispered, 'I love you, too.'

His sigh was ragged, and he closed his eyes. When he opened them again, they were filled with so much love it made her heart ache with joy.

When he held out his hand, she took it gladly. And as they began to walk away from Hyacinth's grave, Ceri trailed her fingers across the top of the smooth marble once more, and made a silent promise to his grandmother that she would love and cherish Damon with all her heart, forever.

Chapter 22

Ceri was peering out of Damon's sitting room window. 'Are you sure you want to do this?'

He pulled a face. He didn't *want* to do it, but he *had* to, so he nodded. 'If I give the... what did your sister-in-law call them? "Bloody parasites"? If I give them an interview now, they might bugger off and leave me alone. It's the hounding I can't take, so if I throw them a bone, they might go away.' That was the plan he had hatched with Frank last night, and he hoped it would work. Even if it didn't, he anticipated that they would soon be gone, hunting down the next story.

'A car is parked across the drive, effectively blocking us in, and a couple of people are standing around in the lane,' she reported.

'I suppose the sooner we get this over with, the sooner they'll leave. Ready?'

She nodded. He put an arm around her waist and opened the front door. There was an immediate flurry of interest as the news hounds lived up to their name, going on point like so many dogs.

He beckoned them closer, and as they hurried onto his drive, he saw them exchange glances as though they couldn't believe their luck. There were five of them altogether and they began talking at once. Damon heard the snap and whir of cameras, and tried to maintain a pleasant expression.

'Can I have your attention?' he said, only speaking again when the journalists quietened down. 'I'm going to make a statement and answer questions, but if you all shout at once, I'm going back inside.' He glared at the nearest guy.

Ceri gave him a warning squeeze and for a moment Damon couldn't work out why, until he looked beyond the journalists to see several villagers walking towards the house.

'What are they doing here?' he whispered out of the corner of his mouth.

'No clue.'

'You're no help, are you?' He raised his voice, directing his attention to the press. 'I want to put some rumours to bed,' he began. 'Yes, I live in Foxmore and yes, this is my home. You're on my property, so I expect you to respect it,' he added in a stern voice, when a woman dropped an empty coffee cup on the ground.

She gave him a contrite look and bent down to pick it up.

He continued, 'I'm no longer a member of Black Hyacinth, although there are several unfinished tracks which may or may not be released. You'll have to talk to the production company or my agent if you want further details.' He held up a hand as two of them started talking at once. 'I will not be forming another band, nor will I be joining an existing one. I may, however, write songs in the future. For details, again you'll need to speak to my agent. You've already worked out that this lovely lady is my girlfriend, so thank you for scaring her out of her wits yesterday.' A couple of them looked sheepish, and it was his turn to give Ceri a squeeze as he felt her tense. 'She doesn't have anything to do with the music business, so I would be grateful if you left her alone.'

'You're a teacher, aren't you?' a bloke called out.

'She is,' Damon acknowledged. They already knew this, but they were hoping for a snippet more.

'And a damned good one,' Mrs Moxley's strident voice from the back called. 'She teaches horticulture – that's to do with plants, if you're wondering.' She was standing with her arms folded and a stern expression on her face. 'If you lot have finished sticking your noses in where they're not wanted, you can bugger off. We've got allotment business to discuss.'

There was a bit of shuffling and some muttering from the five journalists, but they must have guessed they weren't going to get more today, and they began to move off. Damon knew one or two might come back, but the others would have got what they came for.

Mrs Moxley glared at them until they returned to their vehicles and drove off, then she rounded on Damon. 'Right, young fella-me-lad, what's this rubbish I hear about you kicking us off our allotment?'

Damon had already guessed that was the reason the villagers were here. Mrs Moxley was accompanied by the vicar and his wife, plus Pen from Pen's Pantry, Bernie Williams, and several others. Among them, he saw a woman with the same hair as his, and his stomach lurched as he recognised Rachel. She hadn't changed a bit since they were kids.

'Well?' Mrs Moxley demanded.

'Actually, I—' he began.

But before he could say another word, Mrs Moxley interjected, 'Your grandmother must be turning in her grave. She would be so disappointed in you. Anyway, that's a moot point, because the allotment doesn't belong to you.'

'Er, it does,' Damon said. 'That field doesn't belong to the church; it's mine.'

'It isn't!'

'I'm afraid it is.'

'No, it *isn't*,' Mrs Moxley insisted. 'It actually belongs to *me*.'

'Excuse me?' Damon's mouth dropped open. There was a swell of noise as everyone gasped, then the villagers all started talking at once.

Mrs Moxley held up her hand for silence, not taking her eyes off him. 'You heard. Your grandmother left the allotment to *me*.'

'Pardon?' Damon was confused. Why on earth did Mrs Moxley believe she owned the field?

Mrs Moxley tutted and said to Ceri, 'He might be pretty to look at, but he's not very quick on the uptake, is he?'

Ceri leant closer and whispered in his ear, 'Could she be telling the truth?'

'I don't think so.'

'Have you seen a copy of your grandmother's will?'

'No, Dad was the executor.'

Ceri frowned. 'Then how could—?'

Mrs Moxley clapped her hands. 'Stop whispering amongst yourselves, it's rude.' She drew herself up. 'I've got proof.'

'What sort of proof?' Damon wanted to know.

'Before your gran passed away, she said that when she died – assuming she went before me – there would be something in the garage for me. I always thought she meant that old car of hers. The one Victor bought her.'

Damon gaped at her, and he heard Ceri's sharp intake of breath as he tried to regain his composure.

Mrs Moxley tittered. 'You think I didn't know about your gran and Victor? Of course I did! Victor told me everything. I don't know why Hyacinth didn't want anyone to know that she and him were half-brother and sister, but I think it had something to do with not wanting to besmirch her father's memory. I can't think why – Lloyd had done enough besmirching of his own. Of course, Hyacinth's mother, your great-grandmother, would have been mortified if she knew, so there was that. Anyway...' Mrs Moxley cleared her throat. 'Hyacinth probably expected me to fetch that stupid motor as soon as she was in the ground, but she knew I couldn't drive, so why she left it to me, I simply don't know. I'd forgotten all about that car until you came back. But when I remembered, I thought I'd take a gander yesterday, being as you were off making a spectacle of yourself all over the interweb, and see if it was worth anything. Guess what I found?' She waved a piece of paper in the air. 'The deeds to the allotment!' she cried. 'She signed it over to me, and the bloody car. So, that allotment is mine and you can't do a damn thing about it.'

Mrs Moxley's look of astonishment when Damon began to laugh was a picture to behold.

–

Ceri didn't want to go to work this morning, but this was the last day of term and considering Mark had sent her home yesterday, she felt she should. The impromptu press conference (if it could be called that) had already made her late, but as there weren't any lessons today, she didn't suppose it mattered.

There was another reason why it didn't matter if she was late, and that reason was sitting safely in her bag.

After giving Damon a hurried kiss goodbye, she jumped in her car, laughing when "Dark Dimension" came on the radio. It seemed she couldn't get away from Black Hyacinth; not that she wanted to – the band was a massive part of Damon and she vowed to listen to the new album when it came out. Damon had asked her to go to Rockfield Studios in South Wales with him next week, where he would be recording the rest of the album. They were going to call it *Midnight Mystic,* and Ceri hadn't been in the least bit surprised to be told that this was another variety of black hyacinth. She made a promise that she would plant some bulbs on Hyacinth's grave in the autumn. Damon's grandmother would appreciate that.

Ceri walked into the smallest of the polytunnels, which she mentally referred to as the plant hospital, and took a final look around. In some ways she would be sorry to leave the college; Mark had been brilliant, really supportive, and most of her students had been lovely. It was just a pity that one or two of them had made her life a misery. She still wasn't entirely sure who had filmed the soil-eating incident, or which parent had sent in the complaint, but she had her suspicions. It was fairly evident who had taken the photo of her and Damon at the allotment, so she suspected Portia Selway was probably behind it, although she didn't have any proof.

Feeling a little sad, she stacked a load of seed trays and swept the benches clean. There, it was all set for the next teacher. She was aware she would be leaving the college in the lurch, and they'd have to scramble to find someone to take her classes in September, but after everything that had happened, she couldn't face coming back in the autumn.

She had no idea what she was going to do with herself, apart from tending to her allotment, but she was sure something would come up. She wasn't choosy (not as far as jobs were concerned), so she should be able to find another one soon, even if it didn't involve working with plants.

With a final glance around the polytunnel, Ceri picked up her bag and removed a letter. She would find Mark and tell him that she was going to resign, and then she would pop along to Mrs Nash's office. It was only right and proper that Ceri gave her the letter in person.

'Um, Ceri…?'

She turned and was surprised to see several of her students standing at the entrance to the polytunnel. 'Hi.' She looked at them curiously, wondering what they wanted.

One of them, Kyle, stepped inside. The rest of them shuffled in after him.

'We, um, wanted to say sorry, like, for, you know… stuff. We told Portia and Eleanor not to do it. Here.' He held a package in both hands, and thrust it towards her. It was wrapped in pretty pink paper with white flowers. 'We got you this. To say sorry. And because we think you're an ace teacher. We love your lessons – they're fun. I want to be a gardener when I leave college.'

Ceri was taken aback. She popped her bag and the letter on the table, and took the gift from him, absently noting that it was heavier than she'd expected. Her gaze travelled over the faces, and she saw that tentative smiles were mixed in with wary expressions.

'Thank you.' She was more than a little touched.

'Go on, open it,' Kyle urged, and the others nodded.

She began to tear the wrapping paper off, wondering what she might find, and as they moved closer and began to crowd around, she started to worry that the students were setting her up for something nasty.

But when she saw what they'd given her, she began to laugh. It was a cake with an allotment made of fondant icing decorating the top.

'Guess what flavour the cake is?' Kyle said. 'Chocolate!'

'That's wonderful. Thank you.' Her eyes were beginning to sting and she hoped she wasn't going to cry. She'd done more than enough of that over the past day or so.

'Well, aren't you going to give us a slice?' the boy asked cheekily.

'Would anyone else like some?' She smiled at them.

A chorus of 'yes, please' and 'I would', was accompanied by nods and smiles.

'I think there might be plastic cutlery in that cupboard over there, and some paper plates,' she said, gazing at the cake and marvelling at the attention to detail. Someone had taken a great deal of time to make this. 'There's a bottle of strawberry cordial, too, and some cups, so if anyone would like a drink to wash it down, help yourselves. Shall we go outside and sit on the grass to eat it?' She picked up her bag, slung it over her shoulder and walked towards the door.

'Ceri, you've forgotten something.'

She glanced over her shoulder, and saw what Kyle was holding. 'It's nothing,' she said. 'Can you rip it up and put it in the bin for me, please?'

Ceri waited just long enough to watch the lad tear her letter of resignation into quarters and drop it in the recycling bin before heading outside to join the rest of her students.

–

'You could have knocked me down with a feather when Mrs Moxley said she knew all about Victor and Hyacinth,' Damon said.

Ceri was snuggled up to him on the sofa in the parlour. The French doors were open, a warm breeze ruffling the curtains and filling the room with perfume from the flowers in the garden. A bottle of wine was open on the coffee table and she was pleasantly full from the supper they'd just eaten. It was hardly what people would expect a rock star to be doing on a Friday evening, but Damon wasn't any old common-or-garden rock star. He was *her* rock star, and he had been the one to suggest they had a quiet evening after the excitement of the past two days.

He was saying, 'As soon as she said it, I thought it was odd that she and Gran were friends if Gran had been having an affair with her husband, but when she said V was Gran's half-brother, it all made sense. According to Mrs Moxley, Lloyd Jones, Hyacinth's dad, had been having an affair with a woman in the village, and Victor was the result.'

'So, who is your dad's father, if it isn't Victor?' *Gosh, this is all very* Lady Chatterley's Lover, Ceri thought.

'No idea. The only thing I'm sure of, is that it's not Charlie Rogers.' He chuckled. 'Go Gran!'

'Are you going to tell your dad?'

'As I said, I don't think there's any point. He's only interested in people who have been dead for a couple of thousand years.'

Ceri's heart went out to Damon. She felt lucky that she had such supportive and interested parents. Which reminded her: she'd better tell them about Damon before someone else did. Her dad would be thrilled. He loved heavy metal.

'Do you know what's ironic?' Damon said. 'I was going to sign the allotment over to you.' He grinned ruefully. 'I'll buy you another field instead.'

Ceri was incredulous. She didn't want him to buy her a field – she would buy one herself when she could afford it. Anyway, seeing her students today had made her appreciate that her job in the college was more than a means to an end: it was a privilege, and if she was able to cultivate a love of gardening in her students, then she would be happy, because as far as she was concerned the world could never have enough gardeners.

'I don't want you to buy me a field,' she said.

'But what about your dream of owning a nursery?'

Scooting around to face him, she said softly, 'I've got another dream – that one day I will be your wife. Will you marry me?'

If she hadn't been so worried that he was going to turn her down, she would have laughed at his shocked expression.

Slowly he reached out a hand to cup her face and said, 'Yes, a thousand times yes.'

His eyes were so full of love, it made her heart sing, and as she brushed her lips against his, she swore she heard a woman's soft laughter and a whisper on the wind... *'Follow your heart...'*

Acknowledgements

My biggest thanks have to go to my husband, for nagging me to take a break from writing now and again, and for the endless cups of tea. My mum deserves a huge thank you too, for her wonderful, unstinting support and love, as does Catherine Mills for listening to me prattle on... endlessly (sorry, my lovely x).

I also need to thank Emily, my editor, and all the wonderful people at Canelo for making this story the best it can be. They have my utmost gratitude.

Lilac x